BOOKS BY JOHN SANFORD

NOVELS AND STORIES

1933: *The Water Wheel*, Dragon (reissued 2020 by Tough Poets)
1935: *The Old Man's Place*, Albert & Charles Boni (reissued 1953 by
Permabooks; 1957 as *The Hard Guys* by Signet)
1939: *Seventy Times Seven*, Knopf (reissued 1954 & 1957 as *Make My
Bed in Hell* by Avon)
1943: *The People from Heaven*, Harcourt, Brace (reissued 1995 by
University of Illinois)
1951: *A Man Without Shoes*, Plantin (reissued 1982 by Black Sparrow)
1953: *The Land that Touches Mine*, Doubleday & Jonathan Cape
1964: *Every Island Fled Away*, Norton
1967: *The $300 Man*, Prentice-Hall
1976: *Adirondack Stories*, Capra

CREATIVE INTERPRETATIONS OF HISTORY

1975: *A More Goodly Country*, Horizon
1977: *View from this Wilderness*, Capra
1980: *To Feed Their Hopes*, University of Illinois (reissued 1995 as
A Book of American Women by University of Illinois)
1984: *The Winters of that Country*, Black Sparrow
1997: *Intruders in Paradise*, University of Illinois

AUTOBIOGRAPHY AND MEMOIR

1984: *William Carlos Williams/John Sanford: A Correspondence*, Oyster
1985: *The Color of the Air*, Black Sparrow
1986: *The Waters of Darkness*, Black Sparrow
1987: *A Very Good Land to Fall With*, Black Sparrow
1989: *A Walk in the Fire*, Black Sparrow
1991: *The Season, It Was Winter*, Black Sparrow
1993: *Maggie: A Love Story*, Barricade
1994: *The View from Mt. Morris*, Barricade
1995: *We Have a Little Sister*, Capra
2003: *A Palace of Silver*, Capra

THE WATER WHEEL

THE WATER WHEEL

Julian L. Shapiro

(John Sanford)

Tough Poets Press
Arlington, Massachusetts

ISBN 978-0-578-64021-1

This edition published with permission from
the Estate of John Sanford in March 2020 by:

Tough Poets Press
49 Churchill Avenue, Floor 2
Arlington, Massachusetts 02476
U.S.A.

www.toughpoets.com

No character in this book is the portrait of any actual person.

J. L. S.

This book is for

O. B.

INTRODUCTION

LITERARY REMAINS OF AN UNAPPRECIATED GENIUS:
A NEW INTRODUCTION FOR *THE WATER WHEEL*

John Sanford published his first book, *The Water Wheel*, under his birth name, Julian L. Shapiro. Two years later, when the author assumed as his pen name the name of his *Water Wheel* protagonist, life imitated art. In the novel, Sanford the character is a young man desperate for transformation. He longs to receive the love of a woman and to become a writer, but he feels incapable of achieving either aim. The book opens with him sourly surveying his law office—a space in which Julian Shapiro, nascent lawyer who would become an author, and John Sanford, lawyer yearning to write, merge. *The Water Wheel* is a window into this twinning.

The Water Wheel both documents Shapiro/Sanford's overwhelming stasis and embodies his means of his escaping it. It both argues for the impossibility of change and is the vessel of its author's transfiguration. For, by writing this highly autobiographical novel Julian Shapiro unshackled himself from his past and set in motion the remainder of his life as John Sanford. Bringing *The Water Wheel* into being opened doors—as a writer and as a person—that he could not have imagined as an apathetic law school graduate in New York.

The Water Wheel's first pages capture Sanford's profound ambivalence about his aspiration to become a writer. The futility of writing is suggested by comparing a covered typewriter to "the ploughed body of a runover dog, and a dirty cloth that someone had flung across the mush to keep the flies away." The hollow vanity of his mahogany-encased library—objects on display in a pretense of erudition—mortifies him:

> Sanford was sorry he had bought books that he had never intended to read; he was ashamed of having thought they would look impressive behind glass. Most of the books were secondhand, chiefly because secondhand books would make visitors think they had been read, perhaps even by their owner.

And, yet, when he finds scraps of paper in his desk that bear his tentative attempts to write, Sanford thinks:

> He wanted to be a creator. The glamor of the word made him save every page he had ever written. He liked to think that some day they would be referred to as the literary remains of an unappreciated genius—by then appreciated.

Could there be a more trenchant portrait of the tenuous hopes of the neophyte writer? And could there be a more apt metaphor for this novel? Sanford's younger self was indeed prophetic.

As for *remains*, there is an aspect to which republication of *The Water Wheel* is akin to unearthing a long-rumored relic—a "fossilized manuscript"—from an archeological dig. The novel's existence has been known, but few people have had the wherewithal to read it. Coming out in 1933, in the depths of the Great Depression, from a tiny publishing house, by an obscure first-time author, the book sold perhaps seven hundred copies. On top of this, it was cheaply made. So few of those copies have survived.

As for *unappreciated*, John Sanford, who died in 2003, has attracted a small but fervent following. But he never achieved a wide readership. Until the end of his life, he struggled to find publishers for his work. This, even though his early books had been issued by premier houses such as Knopf and Harcourt, Brace. As to *genius*, two of Sanford's later works were hailed as "masterpieces" by the *Los Angeles Times*. And before Sanford's death at the age of ninety-eight, the *Times* lionized him as "an authentic hero of American letters."

So it is a joyful event that Tough Poets is republishing Sanford's first novel, making it available to the reading public after over eighty-five years of obscurity. Even though *The Water Wheel* is stylistically distinct from the author's later work, one can see in it the striving for unique expressions and the verbal vigor that characterize Sanford's oeuvre. And, even though Sanford spent the last twenty years of his life devoting himself to writing eight volumes of memoir, in *The Water Wheel* we have a *roman à clef* that reveals autobiographical details that were no longer vivid to the aged Sanford looking back decades later. Chief among them is the unpublished lawyer honing to be an author.

Given Sanford's ultimate skill and productivity, it is fascinating to observe him when he was merely a literary striver in late 1920s New York. Sanford's youthful incarnation, Julian Shapiro, has preserved that place and that stage of his life in this novel, a book that remains as fresh and compelling today as it was then.

Julian L. Shapiro was born in 1904 to an upwardly mobile Jewish family in the newly fashionable neighborhood of Harlem in New York City. His mother was born in America; his father immigrated from Russia as a youth. Sanford's father apprenticed to become a lawyer, serving the flourishing Jewish building trade, as New York City pushed northward and skyward around the turn of the twentieth century. Sanford's first home was a luxurious new brick building, the Gainsboro, at the corner of Fifth Avenue and 120th Street—at the south entrance to Mount Morris Park. His apartment overlooked the park's namesake promontory of Manhattan schist that made an extension of Fifth Avenue impossible.

The boy's early life boasted both material wealth and a mother devoted to her only son. However, the affluence of the Gainsboro was short-lived, as boom-and-bust cycles depleted Sanford's father's legal practice and his mother fell ill. As more and more money went to doctors' bills and rest cures in the country for the ailing mother, the destitute family was reduced to wandering from rooming house to rooming house. In 1914, when Sanford was ten years old, his mother died of an infection of the lining of the heart that would have been easily cured today.

The loss of his mother was the defining event of Sanford's childhood, not only depriving him of his doting maternal bond but also singling him out as different from all other children who had mothers. In fact, the boy was unable to say the word mother for years after her death. The mother's passing also instigated a battle for the child's loyalty, between his mother's family and his father, that resulted in partial estrangement from the father and a deepened sense of alienation and homelessness that would gnaw at Sanford throughout at least the first half of his life.

Sanford's mother had committed herself to his education. But after her death, Sanford's diffidence about life overall made him a listless student. In fact, he never graduated high school, because he was caught with a cheat-sheet during his final exam in English his senior year. Only through a well-connected family member's bribing a state official did Sanford receive a forged diploma out the back door of an Albany office. He attended three colleges in three semesters, until the directionless Sanford finally decided to follow in his father's footsteps. He enrolled in Fordham Law School, which held classes on the twenty-eighth floor of the Woolworth Building in lower Manhattan. However, Sanford dropped out before finishing his first semester. The next year he returned to Fordham, from which he eventually obtained his law degree.

It was a chance meeting, though, on a New Jersey golf course in 1925 that would forever alter the path of Sanford's life. While playing a round by himself, he happened upon another solo golfer, whom he recognized from his Harlem youth. As the two discussed their current lives, Sanford proudly proclaimed that he was studying law. Nathan Weinstein, who was now going by Nathanael West, stunned Sanford by responding, "I'm writing a book." From that day forth, the idea of writing a book—of being a creator—bedeviled the budding lawyer. Sanford spent much time with West, rambling the streets of New York City, as West lectured his new acolyte about literature. They corrected proof together multiple times for West's first novel, *The Dream Life of Balso Snell*. Under West's tutelage, Sanford began to read, striving to make up for the arid years after his mother's death, when knowledge and culture had held no interest for him.

Another important figure in Sanford's transformation into a writer was George Brounoff, whom Sanford had attended kindergarten with in Harlem and was reintroduced to by a college friend. Brounoff was a talented pianist who was barred from a professional career by his inability to memorize scores. Brounoff—known as "the master"—presided over salons in his family's apartment, at which he played piano and held forth on politics and the arts. Only after the master had finished speaking could others chime in. These salons are depicted sarcastically in *The Water Wheel* as "knowing talk about music, sculpture, painting, literature, the evils of Capitalism, and the imminence of the World Revolution . . . so illuminating, so worldly, so progressive . . . intellectual urination."

Brounoff's younger sister, Olga, the novel's dedicatee, is a love interest in the book—rendered as the boarder. A talented singer and dancer, she was a chorus girl in the Ziegfeld Follies. Though Sanford and Olga felt a mutual attraction, they never became lovers. In 1927, as Sanford sailed for England in a failed attempt to study law at Oxford, Olga begged him not to go. However Sanford left anyway; before Sanford returned to New York, Olga was dead of abdominal adhesions.

After Sanford passed the bar, he joined his father's practice in downtown New York. The young Sanford was smart and cocky, and no doubt he could have been a successful lawyer: "I used to talk in long words. Ive always tried to bowl people over with language."

15

But under West's influence, his legal work no longer inspired him: Sanford confides to the boarder, "I want to avoid the profession as long as I can. My excitement about it tapered off to nothing in my last year at law school." "The glamor of the word" had captivated him; he had consecrated himself to becoming an author.

The quick progression in Sanford's growth as a writer can be seen in his first forays into print. In 1929 and 1930, a trio of negligible sketches appeared in Harold Salemson's *Tambour*, a modernist little magazine published in Paris; Salemson's uncle worked in the Shapiro law office. In 1931, Sanford condensed several sections from *The Water Wheel* in *The New Review*. By 1932, an excerpt from *The Water Wheel* appeared in *Contempo*, and Sanford contributed two short stories each to Richard Johns's *Pagany* and the reincarnation of *Contact*, edited by West and William Carlos Williams. These last periodicals were showcases for top literary talents of the day.

During the summer of 1931, Sanford and West rented a hunting cabin in the Adirondacks, where Sanford refined *The Water Wheel* while West worked on *Miss Lonelyhearts*. Through the thin wall between their adjoining rooms, the two could hear each other daily banging away at their typewriters. Sanford later described in his autobiography how West surprised him—after weeks of showing no interest in what Sanford was writing—by asking to see his manuscript. The next day, the expectant Sanford was crestfallen when his mentor's only comment was that the Olga Brounoff character was recognizable: "It simply isn't done," West sniffed.

One important theme of *The Water Wheel* revolves around Sanford's "fear of filth, of contaminated public objects," things that have been soiled by others. His deepest horror was of contracting venereal disease, which was the reason Sanford could not bring himself to have sex with the boarder during a night of passion. A lengthy stream-of-consciousness passage portrays his dread, intermingling other autobiographical elements.

Sanford's mother's brother Dave was the black sheep of the family. In addition to being leftist politically—a supporter of Eugene Debs—he was wayward, skipping from one part of the world to the other and one line of work to the next. When Sanford was thirteen years old, while his uncle was serving in the merchant marines, Dave mailed the youth a government-issued pamphlet for sailors, full of lurid pictorial warnings of the consequences of venereal disease.

In his autobiography, Sanford recalled being forever scarred by this pamphlet:

> The illustrations, most of them photographic, simply pasted themselves in your mind, became part of a fadeless album you'd leaf through with dread for the rest of your life [causing] a fear that never left you, that for some later generation, you yourself might be on display; you might turn up in another pamphlet, you might pose for a snapshot of the clap.

Although Sanford irrationally shies from having sex with the boarder—"She was clean, he [later] thought. Her blood was clean. He realized that he had been a Godamned fool"—he ends up having an affair, a "sudden licentious interval," with a woman he has only just met—whom strangers blatantly sneer at as a tramp. This impulsive tryst leaves him terrified of contamination.

The Water Wheel was originally accepted by Mohawk Press, but the agreement was later rescinded. West introduced Sanford to Angel Flores, a literature professor at Cornell University. Flores was publisher of Dragon Press, which focused on the avant-garde. Dragon had already issued a Williams book of stories, *The Knife of the Times*.

An early working title for Sanford's novel was *Among the Rocks*, but Flores rejected it. Sanford reported that "the water wheel" was suggested by West, although Sanford claimed later to be uncertain of what the title really means. There are many references to water in the text, but Sanford speculated that "the water wheel" may pertain to the protagonist's being swirled by forces beyond his control. In general, Sanford the character feels paralyzed by indecision, unable to dispense with fantasy so that he can act: "He would never do anything. . . . He would never act. He would think all the life out of it, he thought. When would he do something?"

In the book we see the influence of Sanford's legal experience in several ways. First of all, even though there is only a smattering of evidence that the protagonist actually engages in the profession, he has an office at 51 Chambers Street, which was the actual address of the Shapiro family practice. In Part IV, we see Sanford's perspective as a lawyer at work, as he tries himself in front of a one-woman jury of the boarder. Sanford presents testimony of a great many instances of his thoughtless or selfish behavior, as if daring the girl to still care about him after hearing his litany of self-loathing: "You couldn't think me lower than I know I am." Finally, we see legal language in the novel, in particular the triangle of law terms in Part V. This triangle caused a vexing typesetting problem for *The Water Wheel*. Over several rounds of galleys, the printers continued to split the triangle across two pages, ruining the effect. Finally, an exasperated Sanford scrawled on the proof, "God damn it, get this right!" They corrected it.

Stylistically, the novel is heavily influenced by James Joyce's wordplay and idiosyncratic punctuation. Sanford eschewed apostrophes in contractions and quote marks for dialogue. There is no distinction between spoken speech and interior monologues—all set in italics. He also played with combinations of words that contained other words, such as "wiDEWet" eyes, "the Statue of Liberty was a steeple of junk . . . sCRAPiron," and "SpaniSHAMerican" war. One aspect of *The Water Wheel* that would continue throughout his career is Sanford's aggressively pushing the boundaries of language by such strategies as using nouns as verbs: for example, a baby's brown eyes "pennied up."

On the whole, *The Water Wheel* is unlike anything Sanford later wrote. Still, important lifelong themes appear in it, as evidenced by Sanford's preoccupation with history and his idealizing of the land before Europeans destroyed the natural environment. Quotes from Robert Juet's *The Discovery of the Hudson River* would return much later in Sanford's career to form titles of volumes of his autobiography. The lengthy pastiche in Part V portraying Philip Nolan, the

Man without a Country, anticipates the historical interludes that Sanford would sow into his most accomplished novels—*Seventy Times Seven, The People from Heaven, A Man without Shoes* and *The Land that Touches Mine*—and that he would devote himself fully to in the non-fiction books, starting with *A More Goodly Country*, that constitute the highly productive second act of his long career.

The Water Wheel was designed by Sanford's cousin Melvin Friedman, who worked for the Haddon Craftsmen bookbinders, and was dedicated to "O. B."—Olga Brounoff. The jacket, reproduced for the current edition, was created by Sanford's friend Lester Rondell. Its rear panel bore praise from Williams, whom Sanford revered: "I can't say that I've ever seen better work. It is really written, it moves, it has the quality of a novel. . . . It is excellent." Its front flap declared:

> In form, *The Water Wheel* has no counterpart in American letters. It deliberately avoids the traditional, but its objectives are always clarity and simplicity. The many technical and typographical innovations are designed to suit the subject matter, and are *not* fake-modern tricks.

The Water Wheel came out in March 1933, the very darkest period of the Depression, at a cost of $2.50 per copy. Sanford and his friends had solicited subscriptions for the book by mail and forwarded the receipts to Flores. But soon after the novel appeared, Dragon Press went belly up, and Sanford never received a dime from sales.

The number of copies printed is uncertain. Generally, Dragon issued five hundred copies of each book. However, correspondence from Sanford in the run-up to publication suggests the possibility that as many as fifteen hundred copies might have been printed. After Dragon's bankruptcy, Sanford recalled that the Haddon Craftsman came after him for unpaid bills related to the novel. Regardless of how many copies were actually printed, *The Water Wheel* is a very scarce book today.

The few reviews that the book received were not kind. The *Miami Herald* was appalled by the sordidness of the novel. Its review, titled "Sex, Sin, Slime," lamented that "God's trees were massacred to provide paper for printing this stuff." The *New York Times*, while admiring the writer's flair and "originality of language," condemned the protagonist as "an unpleasant egotist." The *Times* review concluded:

> The rest is sensitive, neurotic workings of the Sanford mind, with its defensive egotism and pleasure in self-torment—a study in the immature egotist and his inferiority sense. Mr. Shapiro, with his verbal brilliance, will do better work in a more objective novel.

It seems that Sanford took this message to heart, for his next effort was the polar opposite of *The Water Wheel*.

Sanford's second book was *The Old Man's Place*, an example of the sensationalized realism, in the vein of the *proletarian grotesque*, that had brought Erskine Caldwell fame. Its spare, direct language—with none of *The Water Wheel*'s interiority—followed the violent exploits of a trio of returned World War One veterans. It was based on an actual rampage Sanford had learned of during his summer in the Adirondacks with West. While Sanford worked on this book, his father suffered a series of heart attacks, and Sanford's extended family entreated him to give up his unremunerative writing and rededicate himself to the withered law practice. But Sanford spurned their pleas.

When A. & C. Boni published *The Old Man's Place* in 1935, Sanford chose to use as a pseudonym the name of his *Water Wheel* doppelganger, in hopes that a gentile name would aid sales by obviating an anti-Semitic rejection of a book penned by a Shapiro. In the end, Sanford's willful pursuit of the novel in defiance of his family paid off grandly. Though only about two thousand copies of *The Old Man's Place* sold, on its basis Paramount Studios brought Sanford to Hollywood with a six-month screenwriting contract that enabled him to support his ailing father financially.

It was in the hallways of Paramount that Sanford met his future wife, the top-flight screenwriter Marguerite "Maggie" Roberts. Soon after they met, Sanford gave Maggie copies of his two novels. Later, she told Sanford that it was the flawed and self-flaying protagonist of the autobiographical first book that attracted her to him, much more than the aloof realist narrator of the second. Sanford and Maggie wed in 1939. Thereafter, she supported him (and Sanford's father), as one of the highest-paid screenwriters in Hollywood. Sanford had the luxury of staying home to write stylistically unconventional, politically radical books without needing to worry about sales.

But in 1951, Roberts and Sanford were subpoenaed to appear before the McCarthy-era House Un-American Activities Committee hearings in Los Angeles. Both took the fifth amendment, refusing to name names, and both were blacklisted. Blacklisting had little practical effect on Sanford, who had authored nothing but novels for the past decade. However, his wife's beloved screenwriting career seemed over; she was unemployable in Hollywood. It would be ten heart-rending years until the blacklist ended and Maggie was able to ply her trade once more. She would go on to write the script for 1967's *True Grit*, which won John Wayne his only Oscar.

The Sanfords' marriage lasted fifty years, until Maggie's death in 1989. For the remainder of his life, Sanford set about documenting Maggie to keep her memory alive. His final book, published shortly before his death, is a paean to his beloved wife and their time together. *A Palace of Silver* consists largely of imaginary dialogs between the couple, either in the yard of their Santa Barbara home or during visits to the cemetery where Sanford's ashes would be interred next to Maggie's. The backyard Sanford had once tended to delight his wife is now overgrown and deep in decaying castoff from trees. The landscaping's disarray mirrors the toll the years have taken on Sanford's vitality and the devastation Maggie's loss has wrought. In total, the book is a vivid portrait of the hardship of old age. As such, it fittingly bookends a career that started with *The*

Water Wheel: the same mood of alienation and of loss haunts both books. But, while Sanford's body has paid the price of nearly a century of living, Sanford's talent—the verve and elegance of his language, first evidenced in *The Water Wheel*—remains undimmed.

For years, it was nearly impossible to buy *The Water Wheel* at any price. Currently, two copies are known to be offered for sale—both in the very rare dust jacket. An unsigned copy is listed at three thousand dollars, while the price is over six thousand dollars for an inscribed one. Clearly, this Tough Poets paperback edition fills a gaping niche by bringing the novel within reach of more than a handful wealthy collectors.

To read *The Water Wheel* is to be vividly reminded of the freshness of modernism that pushed the boundaries of fiction in the early twentieth century. The book gives evidence, if rather undisciplined evidence, of the burgeoning talent that John Sanford would master during a career that spanned over seventy years and produced twenty-four books, ranging from novels to memoir and autobiography to creative interpretations of American history.

It is a wonderful occasion to have Tough Poets put *The Water Wheel* in the hands of readers again. It would be fitting if these literary remains, at long last, help the genius of John Sanford be more fully appreciated.

Jack Mearns
October 2019

Jack Mearns is a professor of psychology at California State University, Fullerton. He is the author of *John Sanford: An Annotated Bibliography* (Oak Knoll Press, 2008).

THE WATER WHEEL

PART

I

T_{HE}
Hudson River was a quarter of a mile from his window. He watched a long Cunarder move slowly downstream along a strip of water that showed between two tall buildings.

After the liner had disappeared, Sanford continued to stare at the river, but he let his attention dwindle until the water blurred away to a dull fragment of glass, hardly distinguishable from the dusty windowpane through which he was looking. Then his eyes came wearily back into the room. The first object they saw was an oak table. Near one end of it lay a muffled typewriter. Sanford thought of the ploughed body of a runover dog, and a dirty cloth that someone had flung across the mush to keep the flies away and save the feelings of passersby.

He was annoyed by two books to the left of the typewriter. He read *Meechems Cases In Agency. Starbuck On Bills And Notes.*

Table to typewriter to books to door was the routine. He read *4 mooR - drofnaS .B nhoJ* and again he was annoyed, that time because his name was senseless when spelled backward. He remembered the pleasant shock he had had when he was about to leave the offices of an attorney named Dennis I. Livesey. With his hand on the doorknob, Sanford had read *yeseviL .I sinneD*. There was a name. *Able was I ere I saw elbA*.

The pictures on the wall. Three were watercolors he had cut out of a book. Two were by Winslow Homer, the other by Sargent. All three were marines. The Homers he had liked for the boldness of the strokes, the freedom and roughness of the water. For contrast, he had hung the Sargent between them. It was a tame talented picture of a sloop anchored in a calm bay; the sails of the boat were limply furled and the water was glib and slick. In addition to the watercolors, there were a sketch of a womans head, an architectural drawing of a mans body rotating on the axis of his navel, and a charcoal of a pair of draped hands. These were da Vinci prints. A reproduction of a pencildrawing by Forain hung near one of the corners of the room.

The broad mahogany bookcase where he stored his library. Sanford was sorry he had bought books that he had never intended to read; he was ashamed of having thought they would look impressive behind glass. Most of the books were secondhand, chiefly because secondhand books would make visitors think they had been read, perhaps even by their owner. When he looked at a red cloth set of Shakespeare and thought of the many migrations it had made, he wished he could control his habit of *judicious arrangement*. He remembered when the set had been in the middle of the top shelf, flanked on one side by Marlowe, Jonson and Massinger; and on the other by Dryden, Steele and Wycherley. That was *obvious association*, but its formality had become tiresome after a few months. In consequence, the set had been dropped one shelf and moved a little to the right to start the dynasty of *puristic innovation*. On that shelf, Shakespeare had been permitted to consort only with the poets. This was followed by *heterogeneity and literary humor*. The set was broken up and distributed all over the shelves. *Antony and Cleopatra* was alongside *War and Peace*. *The Rape of Lucrece* stood next to *Crime and Punishment*. *Madame Bovary* was hemmed in by *A Winters Tale* and *Much Ado About Nothing*.

But even *heterogeneity and literary humor* had gone and all the Shakespeare were reunited. Sanford hated his playing around with objects. He hated to feel like the windowdresser of a drugstore.

He thought *I make a description: A phantasy; a wraith of intangibilities; a spectral fog; a vapor lined with loneliness and bewilderment. I think of GHOST. I came near dishonoring the dead. I felt a slight substance in the process of consuming itself. I felt her breasts and they were a hot unfertile plain that rejected my hand with fire. GHOST will not do. Then it seemed that an unnameable force choked her in the doorway of speech. It no longer seems so. Now I know she had nothing to say. I asked questions that nagged remotely at her past. Her answers were disappointing. To whether she had ever been sick, YES, YES, ONCE. She had been in an automobile wreck, a smash into a tree; when she was pitched out on her back, her head had hit a stone. BUSHWA. That crappy cockandbull was part of her romancing. I think now of fainting fits and moans in disembodied passion. I think of the contemptibility of postures. I think of eyes that brimmed over with fright and tears that only irritated me. I think of coarse long hair of a fakely gold soprano gold. I said O DIME NOVEL that I loved to bury my face in it. I lied, but it made no real difference. She wanted the talk, the talk, and I made it for her; nightlong orations, anything, everything, but just talk. My voice was like a waterfall, so persistent that after a while the sound went away. What was she doing while I was flattering myself that my wordfingers were clouting golden chords on her spiritual piano? What was she thinking? Maybe that I was a bloody horses ass. Or that I was just another of those Godamned adolescent fools.*

He felt the intrusion of the small detalia and objectry that the room contained. He thought of the cheap texture of the paper on which he was writing, its sick yellow color, its strawy surface that tripped the nibs of his fountainpen. He thought of the necessity of considering what his penmanship would look like to the man in the street; to one who might be looking down over his shoulder; to a transom peeper equipped with fieldglasses; to posterity as fossilized manuscript. He thought of the margin, spacing and erasures; of the fact that he wrote better with a pencil. He damned the fellow, a lawyer named Barratry, who had left his fingerprints on the creamy wallpaint in the corner near the door. Barratry had not been the only offender. What about Greenstein, the tailor with the claim for thirtythree dollars against the Standard Oil Company? That was his mark under the electriclight switch. And Fink, too, had left his imprint, four fat fingers clutching the wall to the right of the window.

Sanford remembered having been impelled that morning, the morning before, many mornings, to read the names on all the doors as he left the elevator and went down the corridor. He thought of the force of those mute arrangements of letters, mute but almost speaking themselves out of his mouth. He knew the words so well that a recollection of little more than the door was sufficient to start the silent recitation. He thought *Suite 850 - Law Offices of Subornation, Champerty, Bribery & Maintenance - Entrance - Charles P. Subornation, Charles P. Champerty, Charles P. Bribery, Charles P. Maintenance.* As Sanford recalled his approach to the door, he thought of other words painted below a goldleaf bar to indicate that the men there named were not members of the firm *Mr Varian, Mr Lipschitz*, and as much as he had ever seen of the blur that began with *Mr Vul.* The rest of the last name was a smudge in his memory. *Mr Vul.* Sanford was by no means sure there was more to the name. He knew that it might be plain *Vul*, but there were equal possibilities for *Vulgate, Vulpecular, Vulpine, Vulture, Vultern* and *Vulva.*

Two more unspoken points completed the usual recitation, *Fire Exit - Eighth Floor* and *Mens Toilet Room.*

Sanford rarely had enough time to read all the names on his own door before going through it, but sometimes he made the reading of every letter an unusual kind of test, almost an ordeal, before allowing himself to touch the knob. On those occasions, he felt that if he could accomplish the feat of reading all the names before he reached the door in the normal course of his walk down the hall, without slackening his pace in order to perform, a singular event would occur at a near future time; an event that he would not regret, since it was vaguely associated with money crossing his palm, or the romantic seduction of a mysterious beauty in a stormswept logcabin in the Sierra Nevadas. And because he thought it unfair to promise himself gain or pleasure for successful performance without the corollary of loss or pain in the event of failure, there always lay before him the experience of a penalty, grave but nevernamed.

Sanford knew that his ordealizing was no new game with him. It was a variant of an old one that he had played when he was a boy, a practice of trying to walk the pavement for a block without stepping on the cracks between the flagstones. He recalled a nervous discomfort that had followed his carelessness in touching the forbidden line. But the line had been of arbitrary importance only. Often the trial had consisted in walking on the same cracks which, if touched at a different time, would have plunged him to his destruction. Sometimes the cracks had been eliminated entirely and the proscribed objects were empty matchboxes, cigarette butts, scraps of leadfoil, dead leaves, petrified blobs of chewingum, rivulets of dog urine.

He thought *Her vapors and nostalgias confused me. I thought she was spiritual.*

He thought *What does spiritual mean?*

He thought *She told me she loved music, but she never said MUSIC. Always it was THE STRAINS OF SOME SWELLING SYMPHONY or THE DRILLING OF A THOUSAND LUNATIC VIOLINS. I did not play, but I guessed that music could have drugged her into a seduction. I describe the seducer. He would believe that the world undervalued his talents and that women invariably misunderstood him. He would be a quiet simple fellow, reticent of his grief except among those who knew. A large fellow, possibly, saved by his one talent from being a rumbling lout; a fellow with long legs that would seem to be dangling from places high up in his body, from his pectoral muscles. He would have arms that hung, and the great girth of his hips would make him look like a capstan. He would be a broadbeamed clown. Shyly he would stroll over to the piano, shyly, only after much coaxing. There he would sit in a dimlylit corner and improvise. Girls loved improvisation. He would hold his head a little to one side and without appearing to do so—without foaming at the mouth, of course—he would inject his soul into the music; music that the girls would say was throbbing and sweet; music that would be the plaintive cry, properly restrained, of a sorrowful heart with which love and duty had played all Hell. And BANGO, down would come baby, cradle and all.*

Sanford thought *TO DROWN IN MUSIC was what she used to wish. I am sorry that I did not tell her to bathe in it. John B. Sanford, the hard hard guy. TO DROWN IN MUSIC. I thought I was qualified to explain. I composed a letter choked with hysterical observations on the nature of music, the relationship of music and life, the problems of life. I still have the letter. For months it has been in my desk among moldy handkerchiefs that still give off odors of dying perfume; among old theatre programs and ticket stubs; scraps of paper on which are randomed figures and scrawls in the handwriting of this girl; lines of her now forgotten poetry; a bill from a florist for three dozen American Beauties; two dried tearoses.*

He thought *There is no approach to things so vastly dead and irretrievable. I think my way through them like a curious stranger in a cemetery.*

He opened a drawer in the lower part of his desk and rummaged up a miscellany of junk. He dug out his lyric and felt as though he were holding a rattle or a firengine that he had played with when he was a child. He read the opening blast *It is not enough that some remote ecstatic romanticizes a personal hypodermic into an isolate cell of the music, for music must be related to many lives in being.* He tried not to see them, but other wordworms—*experience, humanity, interpretation, technique, Art*—dead worms, stiff and black, bulged out of the paper to trouble him. He was glad he had never shown the paper to anyone. Mystified now by the points he had wished to make, he wondered for a moment, more to console himself than because he believed in the possibility, whether his declarations were of such magnitude that they had become too much even for their creator.

He wanted to be a creator. The glamor of the word made him save every page he had ever written. He liked to think that some day they would be referred to as the literary remains of an unappreciated genius—by then, appreciated—but none of his hopedreams saved him from being dismayed that any effort of his should have worn as poorly as the lyric. He was annoyed because it was still in existence. He knew that its phrases were reverberating only because its ideas were hollow. He knew they were nothing. He knew the words were catchwords, the thoughts faint echoes of opinions bellowed out year after year from Carnegies Olympus, from Fourteenth Street east, from Intervale Avenue in the County of Bronx. He knew the words had never meant anything.

He thought *Franconia Notch—dowds, old maids, meddlers, frumps, minds that fornicated twentyfour hours a day. She fled them and forsook them to live the full existence in the big town, to study art. She went to an art factory. I do not know what they taught her there, but she came out of it caring for nothing but the spirit of the thing (I do not know what thing) and the virtue of austerity. She learned to wear black; no collars or cuffs, no ornamentation of any kind.*

He thought *What thoughts are induced by a recollection of this austerity?*

He thought *I think of nunnery; of white starched cotton bandages; of the fact that I have never seen a nun laughing. I wonder why they all wear goldrimmed spectacles; why their eyes are so palely blue; why none of them is attractive. I think of ravens, crows, ouzels, charcoal, ants, ichthyol, shoebuttons, negroes, cascara sagrada, argyrol, iodine, morticians, licorice, bridegrooms, nightime. Again I think of starched cotton, of black cloth making a sound like a wind among dead leaves.*

Sanford went on a second quest through his mementopile and his hand came out with another neversent letter, a companion to the lyric. He read *From jigging veins of rhyming motherwits and such conceits as clownage keeps in pay, I shall lead you to the stately tent of Life.* He read the lines again to assure himself that they were really there. Then he went out to the receptionroom for a drink of water.

The telephone operator was a pretty Irish girl of about nineteen. She would get fat after a while, Sanford thought, but in the meantime she would make a pleasant piece. Whenever he looked at her, he thought of a bed in a furnished room, doughy breasts and banalities. She would cry, too, but the right would triumph in the end, and the villain would turn out ok in the end, and he would marry her, and then. Sanford took another drink and thought of the stately tent, of jigging veins, of soggy breasts flopping over hired sheets, of Great Bear Spring Water, of Christopher Marlowe, of the stately tent of Life.

He went back to his room and again looked through the window. He thought *I was the fool and the motherwit. I plagued her for nothing. Nothing was there. The jigging vein. The stately tent. LIFE.*

He remembered a story she had told him *My father was a heavy drinker. He made plenty of money, but he spent it all drinking with his friends. Hed go anywhere and do anything for a drink. Once he took four of his cronies down to Boston on a drunk that lasted two weeks and he insisted on paying for everything. We never had enough money to live on and mother was always in debt. For years she tried to reform him, but the more she talked about it, the more he drank. She got tired of living that way and being the joke of the town, so one night she locked the doors and windows and wouldnt let my father come into the house. He stood out there in the snow for a long time, raving that hed kill her if she didnt open the door and let him in. Then he went somewhere and got a pistol and shot it off under the windows a couple of times to show that he meant business, but the neighbors interfered and took him away. Afterward, he left Franconia Notch and went out west. Mother took me to Canada. I think it was Canada. I never saw my father after that night. Mother divorced him and shes much happier now without him.*

He thought *Vapors and bluethin water. Fears like straw.*

Clouds came under the sun. The buildings were dimmed to gray, but Jersey was still bright under sprays of beams that came through the clouds in opening fans.

He thought *Then she got sick in my rooms one night. She fainted. Was it with a moan or a groan? A growl or a grunt? I tried to bring her out of it and I was ridiculous. Faint, syncope, nausea, coma, dream, trance, stroke, epileptic fit. I was ridiculous. When I thought I looked like a fool, her unconsciousness began to annoy me. I doused tons of water on her. I made a Niagara, a Yosemite, a Victoria, and all that happened was that both of us got wet. I sent for a doctor. He came with his shirtails evading his beltarm. He wore house slippers, but no tie. His eyes were the rims of recent wounds. His eyes were sleepcut and complaining. He charged ten dollars for that faint. He gave me a faint goodbye.*

He thought *Then she said she wanted to go home. I said she was foolish. She changed her mind and stayed. We did nothing. Why? I do not know. She was dry, parched, arid. She cried imponderably. She confined herself in umbilical cords. We did nothing. In the morning, she did not like my attitude. I do not know why. She became dramatic. WHY DONT YOU OFFER TO PAY ME? That was what she said. I got angry and said WHAT FOR? At breakfast, she told me she was going back to Franconia Notch. I was glad she said that. I wanted her to go. I gave her no chance to back out.*

He thought *I was relieved when the lamps of her train went out in the dark hole of the tunnel, when her tears and her dryness disappeared. I went back to my rooms and deliberately fell into a long crying drunk. I washed myself out. Afterward, I felt good. Why did I bang my head against the wall? Sometimes now, when I recall the scene, I am ashamed of the headbanging part of it.*

He thought *Later, I had a revisitation mania. Or shall I say that my memory failed me? I wanted to resurrect by place. Again I wanted to see familiar sites and old scenes, famed in my mind as the battleground of cherished events. I went up to Franconia Notch. Three days were enough. I came back to New York. Three days of tears and selftorture. I had found that she was worse than dead. After those three days, she was nonexistent.*

As he looked at the river, Sanford remembered an old resolve of his, to go away some day. He thought of the necessity; the futility; again and finally, the necessity. Then he thought of the summer he had just spent in New Jersey. He thought *Over the Colgate factory, over all the surrounding factories along the waterfront, over Weehawken and the Hackensack meadows, over all those, further. Jersey is more than the engine roundhouses, the ferryslips, the smokestacks, Palisade Amusement Park. Jersey is a hundred miles of sandune; marshes filled with bloodywinged blackbirds; sandpipers blurring their toothpick legs along the tideline; a fishawk hunting Mantoloking Inlet; Mother Careys Chickens flying like scattered paper. Those are just as much Jersey as the citycysts of the north that mound the face of the state. To Hell with the cities.*

PART
II

M<small>ANY</small>
people sat quietly in the room while Sanfords friend played the Seventh Symphony. With his back to the piano, Sanford stood at a window and looked down at Riverside Drive. He did not like to watch people who were hearing music. He was embarrassed by indications of beatitude, by heads nodding in time with the music. He saw the lamps of motorcars making lanes of light through the dark.

The room was sparely furnished. There was no rug on the floor. The gay pianoscarf was *dismal*gay and depressing. On the walls, five Soudekine prints for a Russian ballet failed to brighten the place. The cover for the couch repeated a wearying design of soiled flowers. On the mantel over the gaslog fireplace, a plaster Wagner wore a pale plaster scowl. The bust was almost buried under a lattice of ferns that grew together between two guarding red pots. Elsewhere in the room, pots tried to sprout green into the overheated air, but the tips of all the leaves were curled and brown. Corroded and filled with earth, a broken samovar was now a flowerpot. Thin strings of discolored grass came out of it and flopped down like wet hair over the sides.

Sanford wondered why he had come. He knew that music lost

everything but its thump in that room. The walls were thin. The woodwork was shaky. The windows rattled in the wind. There was nothing to encase the sound. He wondered why he had come. The music thumped.

The music thumped.

The music thumped. In that room, Sanford always felt as if he were listening to occasional notes coming through a wall of wood, to a playerpiano from the next flat.

The halldoor opened and someone scraped in over the worn linoleum. Someone entered the room. No word was spoken at that time; it was against the etiquette of the house to speak during music.

The tension and the symphony ended simultaneously. People stopped straining. Imprisoned in the bathroom, a terrier stopped moaning.

Sanford thought *I am a member of the Soulsniffers Club. I am a Souldetective. With my shirtsleeves rolled up, with sweat streaming over the eager mask I wear, I hunt down the Soul. I am a Soulhound.* He turned away from the window, wondering whether he ought to make some remarks about the music, or say nothing for fear he might be thought affected. He wondered, too, after deciding to remain silent, whether it was worthwhile to join an aftermusic conversation. Recalling his rhapsody *MUSIC MUST BE RELATED TO MANY LIVES IN BEING, PERSONAL HYPODERMIC*, he was glad he had avoided the trap.

As soon as the pianist had taken his hands off the last chord, the room became noisy with talk. There were jokes, greetings, laughter.

Sanford looked for the person who had come in during the playing of the last movement of the symphony. A girl was bracketed in the broad dark hip of the piano. Sanford wondered why she was inspecting him as though he were a stranger. They knew each other. She was a boarder at the house. He had met her a few months before and had talked to her then for a little while. Afterward, he had seen her several times when he came to visit his friend.

The noise in the room began to subside. Sanford heard the girl say *Its my birthday. Isnt anyone going to congratulate me?* The news was loudly received by everyone but Sanford. They got up from the couch and chairs and formed a crowd around the girl.

Sanford did not look at her. He stayed near the window, staring at the ashen putty of Wagners lips. He tried to recall the birthday of the Franconiablue. He thought *I have forgotten it. At last I have really dishonored the dead. A day repeats itself in a cycle year by year forever. Every day is a holiday, a commemoration, an event returning again in periodicity, like a menstruation. In memoriam. This is the day on which the Confederates pounded away at Fort Sumter. The repetition. The repetition.*

The forced excitement was over. The crowd was spreading out again. The chairs retched. The couch sagged once more.

The girl was still looking at Sanford. He went over to where she was standing. He felt her tight handshake. He heard himself talk. He felt as if he were a ventriloquists dummy. His jaws quacked. He looked at the girl for a moment and then asked her to kiss him. Knowing that he was being watched by all the others in the room, he became nervous and continued talking. While his mouth was still making words, he felt the warmsoft dampness of the girls kiss. He put his arms around her, partly because it was routine, partly because the feeling of her mouth made him want to pull her nearer.

He wondered why she did not try to move away. In an attempt to appear casual, he said *Not so bad. How about another?* He was given another. The girl slowly removed her mouth from his. A faint cosmetic made his tongue harden and become smaller. He wanted to remain impassive, to seem unmoved, but he knew that he would fail if he let the others see his face. Without saying anything more, he walked out of the room. He went down the hall to the bathroom. As he opened the door, the terrier leaped against his chest. He picked up the dog and rubbed its nose. It felt like a button of wet rubber. He put the dog down again and entered the bathroom.

After washing his face, Sanford went to the kitchen and helped himself to a glass of seltzer. Under the sink, the terrier was chewing a lambchop bone. Sanford sat down and lit a cigarette. He stared at a row of red teacups. In the sink, a bluenameled basin was filled with soupy gray water and greasy dishes. On top of the water floated a waxy layer of scum.

Again the music had begun to thump through the rooms, but it was dim and toneless when it reached the kitchen. Sanford thought *Music must be related to many pots in dirty water.* The dim sounds mingled with soiled pots and dishes, with blurred linoleum figures, red teacups, a dog scratching its ear, cigarettesmoke growing up fast into a tall blue plant.

Why had he come? Why had he asked the girl to kiss him? Why twice? And finally, why had he walked out of the room?

An exciting thought seemed about to occur to him. He wanted to have the thought. He tried to understand what was happening, but the room was too small and shrinking to contain him. He felt the contraction of the walls, ceiling, floor, teacups, rows of torn grocery boxes. The contents of the room were forming a mass of shapes: pots, boxes, lumps of silverware, a dog.

The impending thought no longer suggested an excitement. Sanford no longer wanted to have the thought. The pressing shapes, their movement toward him. Sanford knew that he would never be able to forget them if he did not leave the room at once. He went down the hall, taking his hat from the stand as he passed by. When he had closed the outside door behind him, he stood still for a moment. The music continued to thump through the panels. The depressing jangle of an electric piano in a carousel. The mechanical hired man playing Mozart in a nickelodeon.

Sanford walked down nine flights of steps to the street.

The girl was standing near the curb, looking across the Drive toward the river. She did not seem to know that Sanford was behind her. He wondered when she had come downstairs. He had not heard her leave the house. Remembering that it was her birthday, he wondered why she had left so soon.

He said *I didnt like it in the house. Lets take a walk in the park. Central Park.* He looked at the dark trees and listened to the rumble of a distant freighttrain.

The girl turned around and looked at him. She said *Im glad you asked me. I came down because I felt like walking. When I was in the street, I realized that I didnt want to be alone.*

They turned east at the first corner and walked across town until they reached Central Park West. They climbed over the ditches in the torn avenue and went along a dark path through the park. They walked past a man and woman, who were sitting on a bench in the round shadow of a tree. The man had his hand on the womans thigh. He did not take the hand away when Sanford and the girl passed the bench.

After they had gone some distance down the path, the girl said *You havent been very friendly to me.*

As the path curved upward toward the Reservoir, it crossed a small wooden bridge built over a bridlepath. In the quiet of the park, Sanford liked the deep hollow sound of footsteps on the planking. After he and the girl had left the bridge, they stopped on the gravel ring to look at the water.

It would run to every kitchen sink in New York, Sanford thought, even to the one where the red teacups were. This was the water he would drink. The girl would bathe in it. The other had said *Drown.* Sanford said *Twentyfour dollars worth of cyanide in this pool and Manhattan Island would go back where it belongs, to the Indians. I can almost see the headlines in a Jersey City newspaper:*

MANHATTAN ISLAND A DESERTED
VILLAGE

Bodies Litter Gutters Like Confetti,
Commuters Say

THE CITY IS DEAD—LONG LIVE
THE CITY

The girl said *Ive heard better jokes.*

Think about it Sanford said. *Those of us lucky enough to have been out of town would return to hear no more autohorns, no elevated trains, no whistletooting, no riveting, no complaints. But best of all, no streetquarrels between husband and wife. During the day, the park would be as quiet as it is now. The park would be the city graveyard. All over the lawns there would be rows of small numbered crosses. Every day would be Sunday, but no one would ever be depressed by the bellow of the manythroated Christian tiger, the churchorgan. No more would the devout tamp down Hellfire with a frugal meal of roast beef and boiled potatoes. Christ, how I hate this country. Im going to leave it some day. Im sick of it, the people, the ways, the noise. I hate it. I mean the cities. Ill blow one of these days. I feel it coming on. Ive felt it for months. My people think they can block me. They tell me Im crazy to quit a profession for an idea, but I cant stick it much longer.* He wondered why he was talking about himself. Long before, he had decided that his affairs were to be private. He said *All my life Ive been reproached for my extravagances. Im wasteful, people say. My people are frugal. Theres a whole civilization in that word. My people are satisfied with secondbests. Learn the value of a dollar. Save. Once I warned them to be careful never to prevent another from rendering unto God the things which are Gods. When they asked me to explain, I refused because my meaning was obvious.*

Sanford and the girl continued walking until they reached the end of the south Reservoir. There they sat on the parapet of the Weather Observatory. Sanford said *But lets forget about money for a while. I think youre a beautiful girl. I want to know why you kissed me. Did you want to kiss me? Or did you do it just to be obliging?* He flipped a butt down to the rocks below the ledge. He wondered if the girl were thinking of something to say, something smart.

She asked him if he would like to hear a song.

He said *Yes.*

She sang a German song. Sanford understood a few words *heart, eyes, love* and he was embarrassed. When the song was finished, he started to laugh. The girl wanted to know why he was laughing.

Because those doublebreasted German songs always make me think of a stein of beer he said.

She said the song was by Wagner.

That doesnt make it any better Sanford said. *In fact, it makes it worse. Fat instead of grace. I hate the ugliness of opera, and I hate all its fat stupid rôles. I hate dirges for muscular love, for love among grotesque trees, love and passion in steel and sweat, love in a beergarden, swooning love in the Schwarzwald.*

You dont understand the song the girl said. *It isnt from an opera. Its a love song, thats all.*

Sanford said *Whats the difference? Those songs embarrass me. When I hear them, I think love is fat and stupid. I didnt know you could sing so well.*

The girl asked him if he had ever been in love.

I didnt know you could sing so well.

Again the girl asked him if he had ever been in love.

He said he did not know.

She said *Have you ever thought so?*

He said *I dont know that either.*

She said *You wouldnt have laughed if youd ever been in love.*

He said *How do you know that? Maybe I think I can do a better job than that clayfaced seducer, Wagner. Maybe nobody would become embarrassed. But what the Hell has love got to do with it? Songs like that make me uncomfortable, even though I think I know what love is as well as you do. Or as well as you pretend to know it. Why do you go around with love in your lips all day long? Like a baby with a milkbottle. Dont you ever hate? How can you love so hard? How can you be so feverish about it? How can you hunt for it with a dog and a shotgun? How can you force it? For me, the milkbottles are only fake nipples, rubber pacifiers. The milk gave out. The bottles are dry. I hate to talk about love, Christ or no Christ.*

She said *Would you rather talk about hate?*

He said *Ill take your arm when we cross the street. Ill take off my hat when youre in the elevator. Ill walk between you and the curb; Ill protect you from runaway horses, but not from the sewage thats dumped from under the eaves. Would you ha the wall o me? And Ill send you flowers, candy, telegrams. Ill get flamy and my nostrils will distend like gates. Ill do all that, but I wont love you. Sometimes when I hear about love, I could puke.*

Did I say that love was anything like that?

He said *You dont have to say it. The magazines say it for you. The cheap novels and the streetcar ads. The faces of telephone operators. No one can escape it. Love is shoved down your maw like jalap down a horses throat. You get periodic injections of love. You have to bathe in it, sleep with it, eat it, rub it in like salve, talk it, think it, hope for it. And then when its all over, you get buried in it. Wherever you go, someone craps you to the eyes and heels with love. You think I talk about love as though it were a joke. At least thats a damned sight better than treating it as if it had three dimensions.*

Sanford looked up at the sky. It was very dark. There was no moon out. Like bits of ground glass, only a few faint stars showed off the black. Sanford felt an itching in the back of his left thigh and realized that his leg was asleep. When he tried to move it, the leg felt as though it contained a sheaf of needles that had been driven all the way down to the toes. He straightened out the leg and sat still for a while. Then he climbed down from the parapet. Not very painfully, the needles quivered again. Then they shot up quickly to concentrate in his throat. He smiled with the pleasurepain and wanted to laugh out loud. Then the needles went away.

Sanford said *To Hell with love. Lets get a cup of coffee somewhere. Childs Fiftyseventh. Its quite a walk, though. A couple of miles.*

The girl said she did not care how far it was. *I promise not to talk about love any more* she said.

Sanford held her arms while she jumped down to the pavement. Then they walked toward Fifth Avenue.

Sanford asked the girl to talk about herself. He said *Leave out the hard luck, the parts where the decent girl cant get a decent job, the advances of bold men with dark beards.*

The girl said *I dont remember my mother. She died when I was a couple of years old. I was brought up by my father. He was a composer. He played the piano pretty well and wrote some good songs, but he made the mistake of trying to mix politics with music. He had a long tongue and soon got himself snarled up with all the critics and conductors by denouncing them everywhere in New York to anyone who cared to listen.* The Metropolitan Museum and the Obelisk were on their left. They turned south toward the Boat Pond. *When the stories got back, those people hauled off and took a few slams in return.*

*They blacklisted my father. No one ever played his compositions. They
even made it hard for him to sell the little Jewish songs that he wrote
in between the piano lessons he had to give in order to make a living.
He gave lessons for twelve hours a day at twentyfive cents an hour.
He was so tired at the end of a day that he had no patience to practice, or to write as he wanted to. It must have been terrible to try to
teach a tenyearold boy how to play. My father always wanted to make
each of them another Liszt, while they were always dying to get back
to the gutter to play crokinole, or threeAcat, or swipe mickies from
the dago who came around every afternoon with his stove on wheels.
My father used to lose his temper with the kids. He sat right at their
elbows and when he couldnt stand the stupidity any more, he gave
the kids a good swat across the knuckles with a ruler. Some of the
boys were squealers. They went home and told their mothers what a
mean old man my father was. Then the mothers came and shouted
at him for hitting their dollings. Hed try to explain and theyd shout
some more and finally hed lose his temper with the mothers, too, and
tell them to get the Hell out of his house and take their Godamned
dumb bastards with them. Theyd go and never pay my father what
they owed him. Next week, little Oiving and little Abie and little Icky
would be taking lessons from Professor Arnfelt around the corner.
Arnfelt charged only twenty cents an hour. The mothers on the block
were usually willing to give my father the extra five cents because
hed been graduated from the Moscow Conservatory and had a big
framed diploma on the wall, with seals and scrolls and a long line of
impressive signatures.*

The girl was silent for a while. Sanford wondered what she was
thinking about. He knew that if he were telling a story similar to
hers, he would be remembering in detail the one important scene.
He imagined an unknown parlor in a coldwater flat, a room in
which the windows faced a whitewashed court where stiff clothes-
lines made a dizzying geometric maze. The room had a few sooty
glassframed paintings sunk into the greengilt mildew of corinthian
leaves. The piano was an old Knabe upright, on top of which were
a pyramidal metronome, a goldheaded walkingstick, a portfolio,
a black hat with a wide oily brim, and a plaster bust of Richard

Wagner.

The girl said *I dont care what anybody else thought. He wasnt a mean man at all. He was always kind to me. If he only could have stopped talking Karl Marx to everyone he met. He had no business fooling around with politics. He was a good composer. No Brahms, of course, but he wrote a fine piano concerto and a dozen sonatas. Theyre still in manuscript. During the last years of my fathers life, we moved in with those people on the Drive. Father had known them a long time, from the old country, I suppose. Nobody had any money, but it was easier for a couple of families to run a home. Anyway, the house was an old one—every year the landlord talks about tearing it down—and the rent was very cheap. When father died, I had no place to go, so I just stayed on. After the funeral, we went through fathers trunk and found the manuscripts of the concerto and the sonatas. Your friend played them for me and we both cried.* They passed the bandstand on the Mall. Then they went down a broad avenue that was fenced with statues of FitzGreene Halleck, Scott, Burns, Columbus and Shakespeare. The girl said *I guess father felt that if hed busted out of his own career, at least he was going to see to it that I had a chance. He saved what he could and borrowed the rest to send me to vocal school. Ive been studying for ten years. My father has been dead three, and Ive had to pay for those years myself. Ive been in several musical comedies to earn the money. Thats where the bold men with dark beards come in.*

Sanford said *What do you mean?*

She said *Well, if I wanted to get next to the casting manager, I could double the pay, but because Ive refused to get next to him, I get next to nothing. Im usually in what they call a special singing chorus.*

Sanford said *How much do you get?*

She said *Fifty dollars, out of which my agent takes a cut. I take twenty, half for school and half for silk stockings. The balance goes to the people Im living with. Your friends mother makes all my street clothes.*

They left the park at the Fiftyninth Street Plaza. When they were near the equestrian statue of General Sherman, they stopped to read the inscription on the plinth. Sanford looked up at the oversize horse.

The old Savoy was being torn down.

They crossed Fiftyseventh Street and went into Childs. They sat at a small table in the rear of the place.

Sanford said *What will you have?*

Ham sandwich and a cup of coffee.

A whitecoated waiter came over with glasses of water and two paper napkins.

Two coffees and a ham sandwich Sanford said.

The waiter went away.

The girl said *Next to roast beef, I like ham best. Beef is one of your hates, though, isnt it? Ive noticed that when you hate a person, you hate everything belonging to him. You hate beef not because its really lousy, but because you think people eat it when they return from church. And you hate love because youve heard a few husbands and wives arguing in the streets, or because you hate the dreams of shopgirls. Whats the matter with you? Why are you so resentful? Why do you try so hard to be bitter? Bitter is a romantic word, you know.*

Maybe I do try Sanford said. *But Ive always thought myself pretty good, a whole lot more intelligent than most of the mugs Ive met. They make fools of themselves. Theyre stupid beyond hope. I can forgive everything but stupidity. If I had the same experiences, Id be a fool, too. They save me a lot of annoyance by getting themselves laughed at first. What are you laughing at?*

At you the girl said. *If youre such a smart boy, why arent your experiences naturally different? Maybe you hate the others because youre afraid to be the same, not because you know youre different.*

The food was on the table. The girl seemed to be enjoying her sandwich.

Sanford said *What show are you in?*

None.

I thought you said. . . .

I got the sack this afternoon the girl said.

Thats tough. On your birthday, too.

The chorus I was in had fourteen girls. The efficiency expert must have told the Jewboy who backs the show that he could get enough

45

volume out of eight girls. I happened to be one of the six.

Sanford said *How long will it be before you get another job?*

Hard to say. That depends on how many shows theyre going to produce this Fall. Not more than a few weeks, I suppose. But I thought you hated hardluck stories. Tell me something about yourself.

Sanford said *Theres really very little to say. And its a hard job to tell a story plainly, the way you did. I used to talk in long words. Ive always tried to bowl people over with language. Ill start in by saying that I just passed my Bar Examination. Ill be admitted to practice in a few months.*

The girl said *I know that.*

Sanford said *Who told you?*

Your friend at the house the girl said.

I want to avoid the profession as long as I can. My excitement about it tapered off to nothing in my last year at law school. The first two years I went along fine. They used to let us argue with the professors in class. The long words worked pretty well there and it was fun to talk before a couple of hundred people. There were a lot of girls among them. One in particular was lovely. I remember she was the first person I saw the first evening I went to school. I remember she wore a blue dress. Her hair was light and very fine and long. Most of the time, her face was serious, but when she smiled, there was a burst right across her mouth and eyes. I tried to be friends with her for two years. He thought back through an emotion that had wavered between humility and anger. He thought of years of injury, of the insulted and injured. He said *But to Hell with her. Do you want anything else to eat?*

The girl said *No. Lets walk some more.*

They left Childs and walked west on Fiftyseventh Street. The girl stopped to look at a dress in Henri Bendels window.

Sanford thought of the money he had just spent. He thought *Ham 20, coffee 20, tip 25, butts 15, hatcheck 10. One dime left. Counting pennies again. What a gesture to drop it furtively in the street;*

furtively, because if obviously thrown, people will think Im trying to be daring. And I DO care about the dime. Its ten cents more than nothing. Its two carfares, a tip, a small pack of Luckies, a busride, a shoeshine, a cheap cigar, a cheese sandwich, five twocent stamps. Its a symbol of trade. Further, its a Federal dimecrime to mutilate currency, deface walls, Post No, Defense d Afficher, Nie Zanieczyszczac, Vietato, and this would be dEFACEMENT. Finally, whom shall I benefit? The chances are that some bum will get it and buy a needlebeer. Why not OH, IT COULD NEVER BE a widowoman with ten children starving in a garret? Her husband ran away from her last year. Six of the kids have tb. One has the croup and the other three are rickety. Oh, the widowoman would never find it. It isnt written. It isnt in the cards. Its never that way. No, never hands that claw and clutch, never motherlove, never motherinstinct. Tb is frightful. You get it because you havent got a dime for an egg or a bottle of A CRUEL STORY:

Sanford thought The poor widows eyes lit with weary joy as she squinted to test her senses evidence. She blinked at a small round shining spot six inches removed from the curb. Could she be fooled again? She was so tired of bending down. She remembered the last time she had thought a small round shining spot was a coin. She remembered having touched it. She remembered a wetness, a stickiness. The sputum had been wet and thick. No, she would not be fooled like that again. This was the same, not yet frozen. The widow started to move away, but intuition gave pause to her feet, gave paws to her, and back she came, crouching like a catanimal. She made her snatch. Lo, it was solid, this shining thing. Lo, it was a coin. IF her gnarled IF and frosted fingers did not deceive her. She popped the coin into her mouth. After all, that was the real test, the only test.

Sanford thought It tasted like money. It tasted of pantspockets and purseleather and oilfingers. It tasted of the sugarymarble of sodafountains; newsprint; the greeness and verdigris of a conductors hands. It tasted of tobacco. It tasted of soupgrease from the mohair coat of a waiter, and it was caked with the taste of stale rye bread and slop. It tasted of cheap booze and the foamy wash of a shorefront saloon. And it tasted of personal flavors. This coin had been stuck into the ear of an Irish kid who lived over on West Fiftyfourth Street. When he saw that tough McGoorty bastard coming up the block, he had known that he was in for a shakedown. Desirous of concealing some of the plunder, he had quickjammed the dime into an ear that his mother had not made him wash for five weeks. She was that busy. And, to the widow, the coin now tasted waxy and flat.

Sanford thought *And on the obverse of the coin, there was a fleck of oxidation where Ginsburg, Section 4-13, second row, had dropped a little acid on it in the Chemistry class at Dee Vitt Clinton High School. The spot had turned green and eaten a smallpock into the metal. The fleck was salty and biting. And the coin tasted of department-mentstores and percale, and it had about it a taste of cheap cotton acquired while lying under a counter in John Wanamakers, for two months lost to the world. And it tasted of the dust and tuberculary stink of a vacuumcleaner.*

Sanford thought *And there were other tastes to convince the widowoman that she was mouthing money. The coin had been through the Great War. The widow tasted iodoform on the dime, and she tasted dried blood, potash, lysol, argyrol, salvatyl, sixOsix, French butter, German sausage, French butter again, cheap wines of the country, prostitutes perfume, engineoil, traindust and brine.*

Sanford thought *There was no question about it. This was real money. The widowoman spat it into her hand and pressed her fist between her gourds. She raised grateful eyes to thank Heaven for the booncoin, the dimeboon, the dineBOOM, and her pious gratitude was rewarded by the opening, for no longer than an instant, of the portals of the saintly, and by a view theyreTHROUGH of the Gods at work and play. Then a luminous something, swathed in golden light and rampant on a field of skunk couchant, was seen to rise steadily from a urineyellow fog. As the vision faded, a look of beatitude came over the widows worn old face. She walked east on Fiftyseventh Street. A man was sweeping off the marquee of Henri Bendels. As the widow passed under it, a shovelful of slush plumped down her back. She made a right turn at Fifth Avenue, the melten snow dripping from her at every step. But she seemed not to mind.*

Sanford thought *A CRUEL STORY.*

Sanford thought *No, Ill not drop the coin. Suppose a bum should get it and pour it away on a beer for his pufFEDOUT belly. He, rather than the widow. No good purpose will then have been served. Ill not plant the coin. Letting it fall into my changepocket, where it makes a tiny muffled clink against a key, I forget.*

The girl said *Ive been looking at you for five minutes. Youve been very far away.*

Wrong Sanford said. *Ive been here in front of Bendels all the time. Ive been busy counting pennies.*

🐚

They passed Carnegie Hall, crossed Fiftyseventh Street, and reentered the park at Columbus Circle. Opposite the Century Theatre and just south of the police buildings, there was an enclosed plot of grass where a small flock of sheep were grazing. Sanford and the girl went over to the railing and strained their eyes through the dark to see the almost motionless gray figures.

Theres one off to the right Sanford said. *I cant make out any others.*

I see a few against the back wall the girl said. *Theyd be easier to see if they werent so dirty. I guess it isnt much of a life for them in a city park.*

Sanford said *Not when every brat has a slingshot and an imagination that makes over his miserable rope and wood and rubber into a bow and arrow, and the sheep into a pack of timberwolves. Once I saw a kid playing that he was Christy Mathewson. The kid was on his way home from the grocery with a loaf of bread. He was so busy imagining that he actually pitched the bread into a mudpuddle. And what did he get for it? A crack in the jaw from his ma. What the Hell do people have to do so much imagining for? Why cant they be satisfied with the natural? Im sick of seeing a man raise a napkin to his mouth to hide the fact that hes picking his teeth.*

The girl said *Do you always do that?*

Do what?

Wander.

Sanford said *I dont think Ive been doing that.*

The girl said he had been doing it all evening. She said *I just made a remark about the sheep. I suppose you remember that youre still standing in front of the sheepfold. You used my remark as a jumpoff for a spiel about brats, slingshots, timberwolves, Christy Mathewson, a loaf of bread, and a man picking his teeth. When you began talking about yourself in Childs, you told me your profession and the fact that you didnt like it. Then you started to pound out a story about a girl in a blue dress, and broke off in the middle by cursing her out. When I ask you to talk about yourself, I dont want you to show me how you look in the clothing of a timberwolf.*

Sanford said the joke about the wolf was putrid. He said he did not care very much for the way the girl in the blue dress had been spoken of; he wanted it understood that the story had not been pounded out.

The girl said *Forget the asides. I asked you to talk about yourself.*

Sanford wanted to know whether she meant that he had to tell her when and where he was born, the names of his parents, the books he had read, the ideas he had stolen.

She said he did not understand. She said *Im interested in you, not facts. In you.*

Sanford said *Thats what Im beginning to think. Why?*

She said *I like you.*

Why?

She said *You asked me whether I wanted to kiss you before. Well, I did want to.*

You kissed all the others Sanford said. *Did you want to do that, too?*

Yes. I like those people. Theyre a nice crowd.

Sanford said *Then wheres the compliment?*

She said *I told you to forget the asides.*

Why should I? What was your idea in wanting to kiss me?

My idea was to get my mouth on your mouth. I thought your lips would be soft. I thought your mouth would have a good taste.

I hope you werent disappointed Sanford said. *Anyone else might have served. Theres nothing remarkable about my face.* He put his fingers on his lips and pressed them against his teeth. He opened his lips and felt his teeth. He knew that they were white and regular. The girl pulled his hand away from his face and touched his mouth with her fingers. Then she held his face with both hands. She looked away from his mouth; she looked at his eyes.

Sanford was unmoved. He said *Why are you looking at me like that?*

Because I like to.

Youve stolen my thunder he said.

She continued to look at him. He thought of the possibility of a seduction.

The girl said *If youre always going to worry about who should go first, youll probably be innocent till the day you die.*

He jerked his head away from her hands. He walked over to a stone bench and sat down in the dark of a tree. He lit a cigarette and admired the grace with which he held it.

The girl sat down next to him. She said *Maybe I shouldnt have said that, but this is the first time anyone has gotten angry with me for liking him.*

Again Sanford thought of seducing her. Everything was ripe. The girl seemed willing. She almost offered herself. In addition, he had her in a position where she felt a need to apologize. He thought that if he held out a little longer, nothing could stop him. He wondered whether it was true that nothing could stop him. *Im not angry* he said.

Then why did you walk away?

Sanford wondered whether he ought to tell her the truth. What was the truth? *For the same reason that I went out of the room after Id kissed you.*

And what was that?

He said *I dont know.*

The girl moved closer to him and made him turn his face toward her. He did not know why he resisted. She said she wanted him to kiss her.

Her mouth tasted of milk and he was puzzled by the taste. He said *I dont want to kiss you any more. Why should I?*

She asked him whether he needed a reason.

He said *Yes. Why should I let you seduce me?* He was astonished that the girl showed no embarrassment. He knew that he had tried to be very hard.

The girl said *Then your objection is due to the fact that you havent done the asking. Suppose Id refused you earlier in the evening. I guess youd have been insulted.*

Sanford did not answer. He thought of the taste of milk. He thought of other girls whom he had kissed. None of them had tasted of milk.

Take me home the girl said. *You act like a schoolboy.*

They got up and walked along a bridlepath. The way was rough, filled with hardened clods and occasional turdmounds. Their feet crackering dead leaves into the stiff mud, they stumbled over little ridges and depressions in the path. Sanford wanted to help the girl, but she refused to let him hold her arm.

The night was warm and damp. Debris usual to a city park—newspapers, peanutshells, applecores, bananapeels, candywrappers—together with leaves and broken branches, gave off a sugary warmwet stink. Sanford took off his coat. His shirt was pasted to his back. Each time he exhaled, his clothes moved slightly away from his body, so that when he took his next breath, the cooled wet material made him shiver as it came against his skin. He was conscious of his wet shirt.

A drop fell on his hand. He thought it was a sweatball coming off his face, but soon he felt several more drops. *We better hurry* he said.

The rain was steady and straight and fell in long thick lines. The corrugated path became a series of parallel runnels. Rain smeared the lights along the motoroads. Sanford asked the girl to use his coat. She said she did not want it. He tried to see her face, but it was hidden in the shadow of her hat. He stepped into a hole and felt the mud flange over the tops of his shoes.

The path cut over toward one of the Eighth Avenue entrances. When they were out of the park, Sanford stopped on the pavement under one of the streetlamps to mop the wet off his face. He looked at the girl. At first, he thought she was naked. Her light dress was no longer a covering for her body; every color and curve showed through the thin material. He saw the two dark spots of her nipples standing up from the shape of her breasts. He saw the column of her thighs, the oblique creases at the apex arrowheading down to meet in a dark mass. As the girl turned to walk away, Sanford watched the swinging of her rump. He was excited for the first time. Following the girl up the street, he slid his arm under one of hers.

I couldnt help staring at you he said. For all the good your dress does you, it might just as well be home in your closet.

She said *I wish we were out in the country somewhere. Id take the dress off.*

Sanford thought of how she undressed backstage every day. He thought of people poking their heads into the dressingroom for a free look. He did not believe the girl would take off her dress in front of him. When he told her that, she asked him why he thought so. She wanted to know whether he believed she would refuse out of modesty.

He said *Something like that.*

Then she laughed and said *Ive lost that kind of modesty.*

He was a little shocked when she asked him whether he would undress in front of her. He did not think he would have the nerve to take off his clothes if a girl were around. He knew he would be ashamed of the softness of his body. There were no muscles, no clusters of hair on his chest. He would be embarrassed because there was some fat on the cheeks of his ass. When he slept with the blue, he had undressed in the bathroom. He was now ashamed that he had been so unnatural.

Sanford went upstairs with the girl when they reached her house.

Youd be foolish to go home now she said. Its late, after four. Ill fix up the couch for you.

These people might say something about it in the morning

Sanford said.

Why should they?

I dont know. Ill stay if youre sure its all right.

The pianoroom was in an angle of the apartment in which there were windows facing both the east and the west. The couch was along a wall opposite the east window. Removing the stencil of smudged flowers, the girl covered the couch with a clean sheet. Then she stuffed a few small cushions into a pillowcase. While she was doing that, Sanford turned the pages of a book that he had found on the piano. He knew he was reading nothing. He threw the book on a table and moved a chair close to the river window. For a long time, he stared through the glass, knowing that he was thinking of nothing. He heard the girl walk out of the room. He heard the movement of her feet on the wood. He heard the sound sequence that belonged to the removal of a pair of shoes. The light went out. Then Sanford heard the creaking of a wooden bed. He continued to stare through the window.

Later, the girl called to him, wanting to know why he did not go to sleep. He did not answer. She called again, asking him to come into her room and talk to her. He went in and sat down on her bed, wishing that the room was lighter.

He said *What do you want?*

She said *Why were you sitting there like that?*

I dont know Sanford said. *I thought Id read, but when I found that I wasnt making sense out of the words, I just sat in the chair and looked out of the window. The roadway is fine from up here, the big soft globes made by lights coming through the trees, cars moving between the blurred lines, the shine coming off the wet pavement. Its beginning to get light. I saw long bright strips of pale green on the river. Water is almost always calm at this hour. The Palisades are still a dark blue cliff, but up on top the windows in some of the buildings are full of sun. They must be higher than we are. I wasnt thinking of anything. I was just watching.*

Then stay here and talk to me the girl said. *Sometimes its nice to hear you talk.*

He said *Ive been talking for hours.*

She said *That wasnt talk. It was noise. You didnt really say any-thing because you talked as if you had a grudge all the time. Youve got a right to talk as you please, but it seems to me that its no good wasting your time. Let it go, though. I want to ask you something.*

What?

Have you ever thought about me since the first time you met me? What do you think now?

Sanford remembered a night about six months before. There had been a concert at Carnegie Hall. When Sanford and his friends had come down from the gallery, they had gone to Childs for some coffee and the usual discussion that everyone always tried hard to believe was intellectual. For half an hour, Sanford had listened to knowing talk about music, sculpture, painting, literature, the evils of Capitalism, and the imminence of the World Revolution. During that time, a middleaged man had removed from a nearby table to one at the opposite side of the restaurant. After a while, one of the fellows in the crowd said that he was going over to the Ziegfeld to bring back the boarder. Sanford had not known what was meant, but when the fellow asked him to go along, he was glad to have an excuse to leave the table. A cup of coffee, five cigarettes stinking in the green coffeemud, plundered ideas—but ideas, Sanford remem-bered, that had been so illuminating, so worldly, so progressive. He was glad to get away from all that intellectual urination. He and the other fellow had left Childs and walked over to Sixth Avenue and Fiftyfourth Street. There they had waited outside the stagedoor. After eleven, the theatre emptied. A few minutes later, the chorus-girls began to come out. Almost all of them had Johnnies on the sidewalk; some had gotten into cars at the curb. Finally, the boarder was spotted by Sanfords friend. He presented Sanford, and then the three of them had walked back to Childs.

Sanford said *I remember the night we called for you at the the-atre. I remember seeing you at the house a few times after that, but thats all. I havent thought about you, Im sorry to say. Ive had a lot of other things on my mind. But if you want to know what I think of you now, first youll have to tell me why.*

She said *Because I care what you think of me.*

Why? Why? What am I to you?
I said before that I like you.

Sanford suddenly leaned down until his face was close to the girls, so close that he could smell the odor of fresh milk. Again he remembered the taste of it. He said *Did I say that your mouth tasted like milk? Did I tell you that? When I saw you standing in the street before, with your dress strapped so tightly around you that it looked like your skin, I wanted to grab you and tear that fake skin away. I wanted to kiss your mouth and then every part of your body. Youve got a fine body. I like your taste. I like your feel. I like your smell. I can taste milk in my mouth right now. And when you walked away, your hips were wet and your dress was stuck to your back. The swinging of your back was an excitement. Your breasts swing, too. All of you is exciting. I want to kiss you.*

She said *Suppose I dont want you to.*

His head came back fast from her face. He said *Ill go. Ive said more to you in a minute than to all the other girls Ive ever known. Ill not make the same mistake with you again.*

He started to get up from the bed. He was greatly astonished when the girl put her arms around his neck and pulled his head down to her face. He thought of *Victory.* He felt the warmth of the girls breath on his mouth. He thought of a long phrase *the fusion of time into a molten stream flowing down the sides of infinity like lava down the hips of hills.* He thought the phrase lyrical, but too much in his old manner. His hands moved down the girls sides *flow down her sides* and then returned to finger breasts that were like pale farm apples tipped with rouge at their calyxes *the fire at the cone of Etna.* When his lips fixed around the russetred, the applepoints became tiny thimbles in his mouth. Then he kissed her mouth as though he would draw her out through her mouth. He wondered what had happened to his metaphor.

He would say something about the color of the girls hair. He would mention the umberbird, squirreltails, falling leaves, an old brick wall. He would compare the girls flesh to materials, and say that when he put his hand on her breast, he thought he had sunk it into a bin of oats. He would remember the feel of a beagles ears, the bellies of kittens, the stems of waterlilies. When he had exhausted his own supply of phrases, he would borrow some from books. He would say that the girls ears were the pink petals of a nosegay. But why not the pink portals of a gaynose? He said *Youre very beautiful. The important about you is your body. Thats a bad word. Thats an immoral word. Do I have to give you words for it? I could tear your nightgown off. It gets in my way. I want to take in all of you. I could tear off your nightgown.*

She said *Why dont you?*

Grabbing the nightgown by the lace at the throat, he ripped it from top to bottom, so that it opened like a coat. When he saw the girls body stretched out before him, he rose to his feet. He was amazed by his act. The girl did not lose her naturalness, but Sanford thought he looked like a romantic dunce. For a moment, the girl did not speak, and there was nothing to lessen his discomfort. He thought it would be better for him if she thumbed her nose, or called him names, even the same names he was thinking for himself. He looked away toward the window. The sky was much lighter now.

The girl said *I want you to do me a favor. You owe it to me for having torn my nightgown. I want you to get the Hell out of my room, and stay out.*

If she had shouted, he could have bluffed it, but he had never been more humiliated without hope of getting even. There was no chance for talk. There was no possibility of explanation. He knew that anything he might say would make him only more ridiculous than he was. As he left the room, he considered going home, but he was afraid the girl would laugh at him.

He took off his clothes and lay down on the couch. He was glad to lie naked on the cool sheet. He could not yet see the sun through the courtyards or over the buildings, but he imagined the morning as though he were on the roof of a house on Central Park West. Across the forest of park that was below him in his mind, across the hatted houses further east, through the *interstices* of humpbacked Hell Gate Bridge, were thrusting *the golden javelins and incandescent spears of morning.* He liked neither the noun nor the two figures; he thought he could do better with a little care. Westfacing, the houses across the park spread a block of mauve before them, its upper plane resting on the trees and punctured by the green-gold shrubs of their top branches. He thought *the maintrucks of buried trees below, trees like ships entombed in redblue water, only ragged bits of bunting afloat from the topmost yards, pinnacled feathers shaking above the gloom and shadow.* What was a maintruck? What was a yard? Were pennants ever flown from the yards? One of the worst descriptions he had ever made, Sanford thought. He wondered why he was bothering to describe something imagined. He remembered what he had said to the girl about people imagining too much. If the most important occupation for him at the moment were the making of phrases, why did he not get up on his elbow and take a look at Riverside Drive and the Hudson? No imagining would be necessary. The river was probably beautiful now. He thought *Well, let it be beautiful.*

The curtains were parted swiftly. The sun was now up over the houses, but the girl blotted it out, absorbed its light in her transparent nightgown of torn white silk. Surrounded by checkers of creased silk, her body was slightly turned. Under her breasts, there was a bundle of lights, and with her breasts, it swayed heavily and slowly *like the leaves of sunflowers in a soft wind.* Coming down in fine waves, the girls hair stood out like filaments of copper wire. Sanford thought *A shawl of live copper silk drapes her head and shoulders.* What about the two descriptions? He thought the penultimate was fair enough, but he regretted the word *soft.* He lay still and looked at the tear in the silk. He thought it symbolic of his failure.

The girl stood there for several seconds, but Sanford did not move or speak. He no longer cared how the affair turned out. He knew that, lying down, he did not look as fat as he really was. Lastly, he did not know what to say.

He said nothing when the girl lay down with him. He put his arm under her body and kissed her many times, on her mouth, on her breasts, all over her face, throat and body. He could not understand why he was not greatly moved, but he knew that if he liked, he could have the girl without words to make it certain, without protestations, without promises. He wondered why he made no move other than passing his hands over her body. He wondered where he would ever find anyone more desirable should he be fool enough to pass up his opportunity.

The proportion was nine to nine, as nine minutes bore to nine months. There would be rosy vituperative scenes. He would be reviled, condemned and bewildered for his crime. He thought *I ask myself this question: What crime?* And even if there were no crime, what for? He hated scenes. He would hear loud noises, and he did not like loud noises. The whole town would be whispering in a week. In a month, it would be shouting. In two months, it would be turning heads as he walked down the street. In three months, there would be threats. But who would make them? And in four months, there would be a public investigation. But always there would be tears and regrets and unforgetable injury. He thought *I ask myself this question: Do I care what anyone thinks?*

He remembered a pamphlet that his uncle had sent him from Panama during the War. His uncle had been in the Navy. Sanford was thirteen at the time. When he received the pamphlet, he had wondered what it was all about. His father had been there and asked him what was in the envelope. Sanford had said *A circular or something,* and stuck it in his pocket until his father had left the house.

Sanford thought *I read it under the library table and got a thrill more in aversion and disgust than anything else. Disgust and horror. Fear for the future. Fear for the past. And the fear remains as strong now as it ever was. Under the library table, in secret, hidden, ashamed and afraid—under the library table. Thats where I read the pamphlet.*

He had thought *I wonder why he sent this to me. Its for sailors. For Men Of The United States Navy. How To Know And Check The Spread Of. I bet thats what Jassie meant when he said red and green. Thats what he meant, all right. Green. What a dirty word. It sounds dirty and filthy. I hate to touch anything dirty. I hate dirt. I wear white stockings, but only a sissy wears white stockings. Im going to tell Dad that the boys at school laugh at me and scrape their fingers making fun of me because I wear white stockings. I hate dirt. You can*

see when white are dirty, though. Green is dirty. Thats what Jassie
meant. He said red, too. I wonder if theyre the same, red and green.
I bet Jassie doesnt know either. He gets all that dirty stuff from those
fellows live over on Eighth Avenue, Conny Nolan, Jewboy Feinberg,
and that Nooney with the pimples on his face. All of them older than
Jassie and he hates it when they call him Jassie. He likes Jack. Well,
his name is Jassie because his real name is Jasper: Theyre older than
Jassie and hes older than me and he thinks that I think hes a great big
fellow because he says all that dirty stuff about girls. About Minnie.
He likes Minnie. About that French girl, that pretty one lives across
the alleyway. He can see her when she gets undressed at night. He
looks all the time because she never pulls down the shade. He nearly
got caught that night his mother came home early from the movies.
When she came in, he was sitting with his face in his hands, staring
across the alley right at that litup window. And Frenchy nearly all
undressed. His mother said, What are you doing, Jackie? She calls
him Jackie. He said, Why, nothing, Ma, just sitting and thinking. And
there Frenchy was, just putting on her nightgown. Jassie said I was
ascared to look. Maybe I am, but its dirty to look. I told him and
all he did was laugh right out loud and tell me some more of those
things Conny told him. I said it was a sin to talk that way about girls
because Mother told me all little girls were angels and they were clean
and pure and good and we ought to treat them with respect and be a
gentleman and not talk about them that way. And all Jassie did was
laugh right out loud at me and what Mother told me, but she never
said a word about those things Jassie said, red and green. This thing
here says its a disease. I wonder if its like scarlet fever. Minnie had
scarlet fever last year and she was awfully funny the day she came
back to school with all her hair shaved off. They shave your hair off
when you get scarlet fever. She looked so funny we all started to laugh
and she got red in the face and cried for a long time. Maybe its like
scarlet fever. This book is about dirty things. Maybe you get green
touching a dirty book. How do you get green, I wonder, and is green
like red? But green is green and red is red, so they must be different.
Green is a dirty rotten color and red makes me afraid. AVOID PUB-
LIC DRINKINGCUPS, TOILETSEATS, PROSTITUTES. It says red

is worse because grandchildren get it and then their children get it. I wonder if I got it. Im a grandchild. And Jassie is a grandchild, too. Red, green, red, green. VISITING THE INIQUITY OF THE FATHERS UPON THE CHILDREN UNTO THE THIRD AND FOURTH GEN-ERATION OF THEM THAT HATE ME. So thats what that means. Unto the third and fourth, it says. Those boys were talking about it in the toilet at school, but I didnt know what they meant. They said you get mighty sick if you get green. They said you cant get married or your children go blind. Why your children? Why dont YOU go blind? And then when you get married, you havent got any children right away. There must be a mistake some place. I dont understand it. What have children got to do with green? IT IS WELL ESTAB-LISHED THAT EITHER SYPHILIS OR GONORRHŒA, OR BOTH, MAY BE CONTRACTED THROUGH SEXUAL INTIMACY WITH A PROSTITUTE, AND IT WOULD BE WISE TO REMEMBER THAT ALMOST EVERY PROSTITUTE HAS BEEN INFECTED AT SOME TIME OR OTHER you can fool some of the people some of the time and you can fool the dictionary says a prostitute is a woman selling herself for money WOMAN WHO OFFERS HER BODY TO INDISCRIMINATE SEXUAL INTERCOURSE, ESPECIALLY FOR HIRE. Sells herself for money? Sells herself for keeps, I wonder. Then she doesnt own herself any more, like when you sell marbles. And you can get green when you buy a prostitute when she sells herself to you for money. And then your grandchildren go blind when you get married. But who has children when he gets married? Why dont they say what sells herself means? Its terrible to go blind, I guess. And if your skin or arms drop off, thats terrible, too. Its terrible to have your arms drop right off because you got red. Why, both arms might drop off and a man would look mighty funny without arms just because he got red. And you have to be pretty careful if you get red after you get married because your wife can get it if you kiss her. Youve got to be careful after the act unless you want to catch red. What act? Youve got to use argyrol. You cant do it without argyrol. Thats what they put in your eyes and this says it will prevent red if you use it in time. How much time? And then if you dont catch it in time, youve got to wait a long time to get married. Six years, those fellows said. And you *cant tell who has it. Thats the bad part of it. So anyone might have it and not know a thing about it and someone comes along and gets it from him and then make believe he isnt mighty sore because nobody told him, but how could anybody tell him when they didnt know? The maid. I better put this away. She might squeal.*

Sanford knew that he was still frightened. He thought of penalties no longer vague, of a punishment cruel and unusual. He thought of a man being condemned to death for picking cherries. He thought *She may have it. I dont say she has, but theres always a chance. She looks clean, but you never can tell by that.* He remembered a Pine Street bum from his college days in Easton, Pennsylvania. He remembered that she had looked clean *That night Eddie and I had nothing to do and thought about going down there to fool around.* He remembered that neither of them had intended to do anything, that both of them had been scared almost wet in the pants. He thought *We just went down there to have a look, to get a free show. We didnt want to do anything but look. Honest to God, we were scared.* She had not been such a badlooking little Polack. She had exhibited doctors certificates, dozens of them all the same, except for the dates *THIS IS TO CERTIFY THAT I HAVE THIS DAY EXAMINED who the Hell would remember the name AND FOUND HER FREE FROM VENEREAL DISEASE OF WHAT KIND SOEVER. All lies. You could have bet your last dollar on that. Why, she was probably needled to the eyes with mercury, or sixOsix, or whatever it is they use. She was yards wide. You could have crawled in on your hands and knees. The Mammoth Cave. The California redwoods and the giant sequoias. You could have driven in with a coach and four. But this is the point: She looked clean; she didn't look sick.*

He thought *But this one is not a prostitute.* He tried his best to stop thinking, but when he found that he could not, he wondered what the girl would say if he told her of his comparison and conclusion. Then he wondered why she had been so quiet. What was on her mind? Was it something about becoming pregnant? He thought *I dont think so. I dont know what shes thinking. How can you ever tell what anyone is thinking? All I know is what Im thinking. No matter how hot a man is, he can think a little, just a little. How much? Why think at all? He asks himself what will happen to the woman, or hes ignoble. He has in the back of his skull an instilled fear of contamination, or hes unintelligent. The greatest insult.* He thought of authors who had written of the *defilement*, and wondered why so few of them had tried to tell what was going on in the mans head. Why was there always a lot of talk about the *æsthetic, da beeyoodeeful?* Why was the beautiful so darling? When a man had accretions staring him dead in the pan, there were other things than the beautiful. What the Hell did he care about the beautiful? There was always the ugly. But most writers never bothered with the natural. Where was the watercloset in a novel? Were all the characters suffering from strangury and chronic constipation? Or was it assumed that it was unnecessary to mention what everyone must be well aware of? Or was it merely unbeautiful? There was nothing wrong with the word *watercloset*. Sanford thought it a fine word. He thought FOR WATER IS A MOVABLE WANDERING THING. But it was a little late for argument. Speech had limitations, despite what anyone might say. One had to believe that all the people in fiction were turned insideout by Beauty *the Father, Beauty the Son, and Beauty the Holy Ghost—by the towering Trinity, the insurmountable 3in1. Three times round went our gallant ship, and she sank to the bottom of the sea. Three shots for a nickel. Three strikes. Triplets. Crap. El Sombrero de Tres Picos. Beauty the mask. Beauty the falseface. Aye, theyre so extroverted by beauty that theyve never had physical occasion to break wind or pass water. FOR WATER IS A MOVABLE WANDERING THING.*

Sanford remembered samples of the cruel and unusual punishment. He remembered men jerking along the streets with legs like those on mechanical toys. Those were the men who had done no thinking.

What would happen to the girl? After the discovery, she would be called a nogood bum and kicked the Hell out of the house. The pointed finger. STRAYED FROM THE STRAIGHT AND NARROW, all the straight and narrow ones would intone. She would have to droop her head in awfuLAWFUL shame, an outcast. A sinnahhhh, ladies and gentlemen, a sinnahhhh. Sanford thought *Why, theyd ride you to your grave on the shovels of their tongues. Theyd dig the hole with their lips and teeth. Theyd talk you six feet under. With their faces, theyd pack down the loose earth. Theyd walk across your body and in their hearts theyd be glad that the wages of sin is a word, and then mANYMANy words.*

Sanford thought of his duty to the state. The state was a party to every contRact. It was a compassionate, loving, motherly state. It was a bowelcurling state. But how about personal honor? He wondered whether an impartial arbiter would condemn him on the agreed statement of facts. No. But would he contemn? Yes. He would laugh at Sanford for being a damned fool. Sanford thought *Shes very lovely, more lovely than any girl Ive ever seen.* Suppose he acted like a truckdriver. Suppose he dripped words through the cracks in his brain and let through the thickness of his lips a mumbling *She wont tell. She wont tell.*

He thought *Why dont I do that? Why dont I do ANYTHING? Because Im worried about the consequences. Thats why. Nine months is so short a time. I hate the pallor and irritation of pregnancy. I hate its ugliness. I hate the bulby overhanging belly. I hate the womans carelessness and I hate her smell. And at the finish, the screams of a disfiguring and cheapening pain.*

He thought *And how about me? Maybe permanently disabled. Permanently. A long word. A long time. Red or green. Take your pick, Mr Sanford.* And he knew that even if he were able to convince himself that he was not a coward, there was a lie to be acted. He thought *Can I lie? I? I.N.R.I. Iesus Nazarene King of the Iews. Can I? A lie for a lie and a truth for a truth. If yuh lie, yuh wont go tuh Hebben when yuh die.* He thought of right, God and wrong. He thought of morality. He thought *The old ones were nuts way back there when they brought moralities into vogue. They made a f ashion out of them, like velvet britches. The Iews with their exclusive Big Ten. ONE STORE ONLY: BUY FROM NO OTHER: NONE GENUINE WITHOUT THE MT SINAI WATERMARK OF CROSSED MAZUZEHS BLATANT ON A FIELD OF MATZOTH. The Big Ten. The beginning of the decimal system. The beginning of divisions. Thou shalt not, and*

Thou shalt not, and Thou shalt not. Refrain from the evile and then youre good. Theres nothing to it. You can learn it at home in ten easy lessons. Be the life and death of the party. Live a life in tentime negation—twotime, five times over—and youve got the promise of felicity, here and forevermore. Its a cinch.

He thought *Thou shalt have no other gods before me.*

He thought *Thou shalt not make unto thee any graven image.*

He thought *Thou shalt not take the name of the Lord thy God in vain.*

He thought *Remember the sabbath day, to keep it holy.*

He thought *Honour thy father and thy mother.*

He thought *Thou shalt not kill.*

He thought *Thou shalt not commit adultery.*

He thought *Thou shalt not steal.*

He thought *Thou shalt not bear false witness.*

He thought *Thou shalt not covet.*

He thought *Mr Sanford, let me introduce you to the Rt Rev Dexter Ramrod, wellknown evangelist and gospelvendor, first husband of the late Mrs Gertrude Henline, she also known as Sister Smothers. And Rev sir, allow me to present Mr John B. Sanford, one Hell of a hard guy. Mr Sanford, the Rev can explain anything in Christs world.*

He thought *I ask: Rev sir, are we not fully furnished by divine infiuence? That is to say, is not God the Great Interior Decorator? Is it not true that man obtains nothing for himself, that God is the Neverfailing Source of all things, the Omnipotent Horn of Plenty, the Infinite Cornucopia?*

He thought *With a long pan, with caution, with mucus jungling down his throat like tropical creepers, he says: Certainly, my child, my lamb, my kid, my woolen one. You must look to Him on high, lo Him the Giver, for all things.*

He thought *I ask: All things both of the good and of the evile?*

He thought *And he says: Aye, all things whatsoever good and all things whatsoever evile.*

He thought *I ask: Then, Rev sir, wherefore the Thou shalt nots? Wherefore giveth God only to take away? Wherefore giveth He the evile if He meaneth us not to be in some things evile?*

He thought *The Rt Rev Dexter Ramrod says: That is simple to explain, my son. There are explanations for all things. God gaveth the evile that man might recognize and do the good, that he might resist the evile, that he might cast it out, that he might exorcise it. For the evile is the Deviles, and not Gods. Not directly Gods, that is. But Ill tell you about Satan another time. Its a Godamned long story. Aye, at any rate, God gaveth us the evile that upon this earth we might know a trial, an ordeal, a test, a quiz, an examination; that we might say of life that it is but a query, and that query—ARE WE FIT TO PRESENT OURSELVES IN PETITION FOR ETERNITY?*

He thought *From the distance, a faint voice says: But some of us cant lay out the money for courtdress. Now if you know a place where a guy can get some good secondhand. . . .*

He thought *The Rt Rev continues: ARE WE DESIRABLE? HAVE WE MADE OURSELVES READY AND ACCEPTABLE? And, my meek one, I say to you that those who list unto the starboard dictates of the fiesh are but hearkening unto the precepts of the brigadier-general of the horrid whordes of Hell. Aye, thou shalt not commit adultery in any of its ramifornications. The Lord is my shepherd. He maketh me to die down in green ordures.*

Sanford thought *VERILY, O LORD, THOU HAST CAUSED ME TO BE ANOINTED WITH AN INFERIOR BRAND OF COLD CREAM.*

Sanford thought *BUT I REMAIN INCORRUPTIBLE.*

He said *Whats the good of lying here like this any longer? It must be after seven. Im going to dress and go for a walk. I want to get out of the house as fast as I can. Not because its your house, but I feel as if the roof were growing right out of the top of my head. Anyhow, someone might get up and find us here. Its a stupid question, but what would Madame the Landlady say if she walked in now?*

That it was time for breakfast the girl said.

Im not joking Sanford said.

Neither am I. My fat landlady knows more than she tells about.

Sanford asked the girl to tell him what she meant. She wanted him to kiss her first. He found the same fresh milky taste. He kissed her several times.

She knows more than she tells about the girl said.

Sanford said *Do you mean about you and me?*

Yes.

Who told her? Who could have? Whats there for her to know?

The girl said *No one told her.*

Then what can she know?

The girl said *Maybe it really is time to get up.*

He wanted to ask more questions, but she kissed him quickly and got out of his arms. As she went back through the curtains, she gave him a fast smile. For a moment, Sanford lay quietly on the couch and thought of his failure. He knew that before long he would begin a monotonous self justification in phrases. He would think, this time, in hendecasyllabic Alexandrines. He admitted to himself that he did not know what an Alexandrine was, but even the blank name suggested that it could bear cadences of heroic proportions. Before the coming of the first phrase, Sanford got off the couch and went down the long hall to the bathroom. On the way, he passed the open door of his friends room. It was darkened by a green shade pulled far down toward the sill. The shade was flapping in a faint breeze that came in through the open window.

Sanford kept on down the hall to the bath. He took a long shower, first as hot as he could stand it, and then with the cold all out until he had to do a crazy dance to stop himself from hollering, until his scalp began to tourniquet his forehead and eat into his skull like a bar of cold metal.

By the time he had finished dressing, the hall was filled with the smell of coffee. Sanford went into the kitchen. The girl was taking some rolls out of a paper bag. She put the bag on the table and stood still, looking at Sanford. He did not know what to do, or what was expected of him. He left the room and went to the front of the apartment again. There he sat down at a window. He looked at the river and then at its near border of park. The lawns were as yet unpapered, the bending paths still clear of babycarriages and constipated dogs.

After a while, above the street and river sounds, Sanford heard the subdued thunder of the shower.

Strings of cars were beginning to move south along the Drive. A breeze churned up eddies of odor, of trees, shrubs and grass; mostly grass and earth. The air was still fresh and damp from the rain of the night before, the greenery washed off and the dust laid down. The morning was so still that Sanford could hear the rising chatter of riveting from a construction job far up the avenue.

He felt a hand on his head and then a face pressing into his hair. There was a good smell from the girls body. Sanford got up and stood against her. She was wearing only a dressingown. He opened it and moved his hands on her breasts. Then he bent a little and kissed them and they were cool and soft in his lips. The smell of her body came into his head mingled with the grassandearth smell of the park. He kissed the girl again and then they went back to the kitchen for breakfast.

After a second cup of coffee, Sanford lit a cigarette. The girl waited for him to finish it. When he had clinched it in his coffeecup and thought of *coffeemud*, the girl got up and went into the front room of the apartment again. Sanford followed her. At the window overlooking the park, they stood each with an arm about the others waist.

The day was warming, the traffic on the Drive threading south in fattening lines. A haze that was not mist, but a combination of rising dust and sunlight, blurred the buildings on the Palisades until they seemed to be only a high gray wall.

Sanford said *I want to see you again tonight.*

Will you come back to the house for me?

Im going to be downtown most of the day Sanford said. *How about eight oclock in front of Carnegie?*

The girl said she would be there. Sanford took his hat off the rack and opened the halldoor. The girl went into the corridor with him. They kissed each other.

The hall was cool, the red and brown tiles giving off a clean smell of drying soap. Everything had been washed, Sanford thought. The streets. The park. The trees. The grass. The halls. The girl. Everything was clean. He remembered the freshness of the girls body when she had bent over him to kiss his head, the slight persistent agreeable taste of milk on her mouth. He remembered the whiteness of her body and face, no mark, no darkening anywhere, except on the points of her breasts. She was clean, he thought. Her blood was clean. He realized that he had been a Godamned fool.

PART
III

SANFORD

left the damp darkness of the hall and went out into the warm morning. After crossing the Drive, he looked up at the front of the apartment building from the shade of trees lining the park wall. The girl had been watching through her window. She waved to him and then went back.

Despite the heat, he decided to walk downtown as far as Columbus Circle before taking the subway. The smell of the subway suddenly came into his memory. As he walked, he thought of his ability to memorize and recall odors without actually sensing them again. The subway odor persisted, not the direct stench of people, smouldering about them as if it were the heat of their bodies, but the odor engendered by their numberless contacts with the metal, wicker and cement—the smell of use.

The cement platforms reminded him of cellardamp, the almost impalpable wetness of a cellarwall in some remote unused corner, a dampness more for the sense of smell than for the finger or the eye. He remembered the smell of bituminous coalsmoke as it came from the stacks of locomotives; the smell of undetonated gasoline. He still liked both. Then he tried to remember others that had been pleasant, and a rush of odors—some long before experienced—returned with original intensity: His fathers hair; his own felt hat just after he had taken it off; unburned tobacco; tea leaves; brine; a dirt road in the country after a summer shower; washed linen drying in the sun; cigar box and pencil wood; fresh coffee; stables; tar; the inside of a new shoe; haylofts; hot asphalt.

He thought it curious that the smell of no flower had come back.

He thought of sounds that he had liked. He thought of a wind through trees, a drifting wind, like a slowmoving puff of smoke; the leaves made an approaching pageant of satin skirts; the wind came through, and then the tangence of the leaves was like the *sand* of garments being marched up the street. He thought of rain on a tin roof. He thought of the *ing* of a telegraph wire, its long sagging glassthread gleam; the wire fattened with vibration until the gleam of glass was a blur of gray; then the hum went down and the glass returned. He thought of the barbershop symphony; the faraway scissorasp; the light crunch of hairs; the faint scrape of razorblades; the halfswinging song of five electricfans. He thought of pacers on a dirt track, of a pond grinning ripples against the belly of a rowboat. He thought of a girl brushing her hair.

He heard the sound of breaking glass. He smelled fresh milk. He stopped and looked down at a perambulator. The red face of a baby rounded fatly from a pink knitted hat; and great wide brown eyes pennied up, asking questions. Then they went down to observe the foaming of white rivers around concave islands of crystal. The pennies came up again, but suddenly drowned in rising tears. The babys face screwed toward its mouth and long creases sank into its cheeks. Not a sound came from its mouth. Then there was a quick loosening and the creases and shrivelings went away. Wet rings framed further questions in the babys eyes. It smiled incomprehensibly. A scowling nursemaid came running up from a nearby bench.

Sanford said *Im sorry, miss. I wasnt looking and I bumped into the carriage. The bottle fell out of the babys hands.*

The nursemaid said *Well, you oughta look where you goyn, you.*

Sanford laughed and walked away. A little distance off, he stopped and turned around. The nursemaid was still looking at him.

Expertly, quickly, deliberately, he blurted a bulb of spit into the gutter. Then he continued walking. All he remembered were wiDEWet eyes and the smell of fresh milk. At Seventysecond Street, where the Drive ended in an east bend, he thought of Philip Nolan.

He walked across town to Central Park West and telephoned to the Cunard offices from the Hotel Majestic. He said *Whats the next boat for London?*

A voice said *The Caronia, sir. Sailing September thirtieth.*

Sanford heard his nickel drop into the phonebox. He left the hotel and walked down Central Park West. The Portuguese Temple; the School of Ethical Culture; the Century Theatre; a long row of shops in a low triangular building; Columbus Circle; the Maine Monument; Cristoforo Colombo. *In 14a92, Colombo, he didna know whatsa do. So he sat on a grassa, and he scratcha his assa. In 14a92.* This was Columbus Circle, Sanford thought, a place devoted to the memory of the discoverer of America. What thoughts were appropriate? *In 14a92, Colombo, he didna know whatsa do. So he sat on a rocka. In 14a92.* Then he had discovered America, five hundred years after the discovery of America.

Sanford crossed to the island between the cartracks in the middle of Broadway and went down the steps to the subway. Turnstiles lurched irregularly. An uptown express exploded out of the tunnel. An express going by a local station was an experience Sanford always dreaded. He heard the noise coming nearer and knew that nothing could stop it except its own passing. He waited for the apex of sound, watched the lighted windows snap past in a long streamer, shivered because the sound was so overwhelming. Then he heard it less and less, and finally it diminished to a steady dull rumble. But then the same increasing sound began to come back with another train. The shuttle of sound was perpetual.

A fivecar South Ferry local came in. Four conductors used handlevers to open the oldfashioned doors. Sanford noticed that the car he entered bore the number 3296 in numerals of stained cream. He took a seat against a platform partition. He thought why he did so. The remembrance was formulized. It came back in words. He thought *I take this seat because I wont rock over when the brakes are put on.* Although accustomed to the repetition, he wished each time that he could conquer it and sit down for once without thinking about it. *I take this seat because I wont rock over when the brakes are put on.*

He thought of another unspoken explanation for habit *Whenever I break bread, I never put down the smaller piece.* BREAD ONCE BROKEN MUST NEVER AGAIN TOUCH THE TABLE. *Ten years ago I read that somewhere and Ive never for gotten it.*

He thought of his inability to remember the number of days in any month unless he actually thought the organized words *THIRTY DAYS HATH SEPTEMBER, APRIL, JUNE AND NOVEMBER.*

He remembered old Doc Birch, and his formula for memorizing the colors of the spectrum *V-I-B-G-Y-O-R.* Birch had said *Vibgyor. VioletIndigoBlueGreenYellowOrangeRed.* White could be produced by revolving a card striped with those seven colors, but for Birch, with his smeared and dirty card, the result had always been gray. Sanford thought *Birch, old Doc Birch. You old manwitch, you. You uncomprehending Birchwitch, you and your fuming baby temper. I remember the day we got as far as attractivity. You went to your closet and came out with a little wand and a pithball hanging from the end of it on a string. I remember how you said BOYS, IM ABOUT TO DEMONSTRATE THE PROPERTIES OF THE PITHBALL. I SAID PITH, AND THE FIRST ONE OF YOU RUFFIANS THAT LETS OUT A BLEAT ABOUT LISPING, HE FLUNKS PHYSICS COLD. YOU, THERE, IN THE FRONT ROW, WHATS YOUR NAME IN ENGLISH?* Sanford remembered that the boy had been Runkel, Dopey Runkel.

The ads in the ceiling of the car; the people opposite him. Neither were of interest. The heat and the swaying of the car suddenly made Sanford tired. When the doors opened at Fiftieth Street, a wave of warm air rolled in from the platform. Two chorusgirls came in. They were carrying large handcases. Sanford thought of nightgowns and testimonials, dancing shoes and toothbrushes. The girls sat down across the aisle and carefully arranged their legs to show white lengths of thigh. Sanford felt vaguely embarrassed and looked away. When girls wanted to pull their dresses down, why did they always pull them up first? The girls paid no attention to him.

At Times Square, he considered changing for an express just long enough to hear the slamming of the doors as he rose from his seat. Someone slid into it before he could move back, but he felt relieved and was glad he no longer had to sit facing the chorusgirls. Now he could move away without hurting their feelings. As he went around the platform partition and stood in its shadow, he wondered why he had been so concerned with their feelings. He was certain that the girls did not even know he was alive.

For ten minutes, he thought of nothing at all. He heard *Chambers Street* called out by a conductor. Again Sanford could not determine whether it would be better to leave the train or stay on it. He made up his mind to get off at Park Place only after he had stood inert while the doors banged alongside him. When the train was pulling out of Chambers Street, he recalled, in a panic of temporary dismay, that he was on a South Ferry local and that it did not go to Park Place. Now he would have to walk twice as far.

At Cortlandt Street, he got out and went upstairs. An elevated train obliterated parallelograms of sunlight that lay in the gutter. Sanford waited until they were restored. Then he walked east to Broadway.

When he reached the corner, he stopped and looked south. The Custom House was down that way, he thought. Right down there at Bowling Green. The Custom House. A gateway? Bowling Green. A good name, now inapplicable. He wondered how many people thought of its significance when they used it. Few, probably. It no more made a person think of a real bowling green than the plot of banked grass in Central Park near the sheepfold. It was a toy, a weathervane on a skyscraper.

He thought of New York names. Featherbed Lane. Sawmillriveroad. There were only a few descriptive names. Mostly there were numbers, and the names of people and places. Twentyseventh Street, Madison Avenue. Handles. James Monroe, fifth President of the United States, had placards advertising his doctrine all along the length of an alley of tenements. Lafayette Street was noted chiefly for The Tombs. Why not a Birdcage Walk? Why not a Threadneedle

Street? Tooting Bee? Unter den Linden? Via XX Settembre? Paseo de Gracia? Why call a thing something that it was not? Where the Hell were the pines of Pine Street? Where were the cedars of Cedar Street? *In Rome and Lebanon* he thought.

But did Spuyten Duyvil have anything to do with Hell Gate?

The Custom House and beyond. Over the Battery, Ellis Island. Gateways. The Statue of Liberty was a steeple of junk. Bartholdi & Company: sCRAPiron and old bottles—CHEAP.

The upper bay. The bay, supported by the Atlantic on the south and the Hudson on the north. The Hudson, worming deeply into the body of the continent, the long intestine of the Adirondacks. Sanford thought *In 1524, Verrazano proceeded a short distance by boat up the Hudson, but the first European to demonstrate its extent and importance was Henry Hudson, in 1609. The Hudson River, tidal from its mouth to the United States Dam at Troy, is situated entirely within the state of New York. Its source is fourteen small lakes in the Adirondacks, near Newcomb, in Essex County, two thousand feet above tidewater. Its chief tributary is the Mohawk River. The mean tide range of the Hudson at New York is 4.4 feet. The West Shore Railroad runs along the west bank. The New York Central and Hudson River Railroad runs along the east bank. The Hudson River is 315 miles long.* The bay, filling, unfilling, refilling, all changing every moment, yet the same. A human body, the bay, Sanford thought. The inexhaustible container, invisibly fed, endlessly emptying *out of the cradle endlessly rocking.*

He remembered his resolve to leave America some day, and wondered why he had telephoned to the Cunard offices that morning. He wondered when he would do more than think about action.

He walked up Broadway to Park Place, cut over past the Post Office into City Hall Park, and then stopped across the street from the Emigrant Industrial Savings Bank. His offices were upstairs. This was his bank. Would it be wise to go in and have his book balanced? It would be another step, the second. It would not be wise, he thought, but it was wise to compete against wisdom.

He crossed Chambers Street and went into the bank.

Balance this book, please he said.

Yes, sir.

Next to him stood a woman waiting to make a fivedollar deposit. Sanford saw the bill and the end of a blue slip sticking out of her bankbook. No doubt she visited the bank once a week, he thought. She was saving up against a rainy day. She was wise. All thrifty people were wise. Week after week, her crumpled bills passed over the counter. She would have a great deal of money some day. She was wise. She was thinking about the future. The wisdom, the foresight, the rainy day. Five dollars a week. Two hundred and sixty dollars a year. Two thousand six hundred in ten years. Twentysix thousand in a century. The wisdom. The rainy day. How long did you live? What did that have to do with it? Sanford thought *Your children, your grandchildren; think of them, you wastrel.* The rainy day.

Your book, sir the teller said.

Thanks.

As Sanford walked away from the counter, he looked at the figures in his book. He had three thousand eight hundred and five dollars. No pennies.

He went upstairs and remembered *Bribery Champerty Toilet Room.* Someone said *Good morning.* The clock over the switchboard *Naval Observatory Time* read tenfour. The minutehand jumped. Tenfive. Sanford looked at the switchboard operator *banalities and fat breasts and hired sheets and tears and snappy stories.* Tensix. He took a drink of Great Bear Spring Water and went to his room.

For once, his books did not annoy him. The pictures were unattracting smears. He thought again of the taste of fresh milk. He was still puzzled by it. If he had kissed the lips of the baby who had thrown away its bottle, would there have been the same taste? Why had he lied to the nursemaid about bumping into the carriage?

Sanford still had the bankbook in his hand. What was the good of it? He would never do anything with it. He might as well throw it out of the window. He would never act. He would think all the life out of it, he thought. When would he do something?

He looked at the river. He thought *Ive caught tomcod off the Ninetysixth Street garbage docks. Ive caught riverbass among the rocks under the Thurman bridge. The docks and the rocks.*

NOW.

RIGHT NOW.

RIGHT THIS MINUTE.

He put on his hat and went out to the receptionroom. Tensixteen. The halldoor opened and a man came in. The man was wearing a visored cap and a chauffeurs mohair suit. The man was Pincus Fink, the taxidriver.

Sanford said *What do you want, Fink? Im in a hurry.*

Fink said *I got to talk to you about a case, Mr Sanford.*

I cant handle it. Im not a lawyer yet.

Maybe the office it will handle it.

I said I was in a hurry. Cant you come back some other time?

No. Its important. I got a swell idea for a case.

Sanford said *Come inside and make it fast.*

Sanford went back to Room 4. Fink followed him. Sanford shut the door and sat down at his desk.

Talk, Fink.

Last night I was going over the idea with Funk, Moe Funk. Thats my cousin. Hes out of work and he figures why shouldnt he throw himself in front of my cab. Not so he gets hurt, but easylike. Then he can sue me. So when the time comes, I forget to show up in court and so I lose the case. Then the insurance company it has to pay Funk off and he splits with me even. Aint it an idea?

Sanford said *What do you know about the repeating designs of the wallpaper in hallbedrooms?*

Fink said *Hes asking me about wallpaper.*

And what do you know about snappy stories and banalities, Fink? What do you know about romantic dreams?

Fink said *Dreams. Snappy stories. I want you should tell me about the case.*

Sanford looked in from the window and laughed. *Where were you born, Fink?*

Kovno Guberne.

Sanford said *Ill tell you a story about my grandfather. He came here from Suwalke Guberne the same year Lincoln was shot. They were both named Abraham, but there the resemblance ended. When my grandfather landed at New York, he had a hundred and ten roubles in his kick. He looked around and decided to go into the match business, so he bought a few thousand boxes, wrapped them up in oilcloth and hit the pike. He was back in a week. Hed cleaned up. A net profit of four dollars. The next trip was even more successful, and when hed piled up the fortune of a hundred and fifty bucks, he went into the thing for real. He bought a horse and buggy and traveled all over the south in it. Different horse, though. The first one keeled over stone dead going up the main drag of Richmond, Virginia, on the eighteenth trip, but that didnt stop my grandfather. He made a stunning profit on the carcass over and above what hed given for the beast alive. He bought another nag in Richmond, probably for a dozen boxes of matches. And he probably got a Meddler mare in exchange. He could drive a bargain. He drove bargains even further than he drove horses. With the new mare, he kept on going. Six months later, he hit New Orleans with eight hundred dollars. After buying some more stock, he drove up the Mississippi Valley. By the time he got to Memphis, the eight hundred had become twelve. He put up at a tavern there and pulled the first skull of his career when he flashed a part of his roll. If I knew my grandfather, that must have been an accident, but anyhow a few awfully nice fellows, real swells, asked him to make a fifth in a little sociable game of poker that night. After an hours play, the twelve hundred was some place else. They took the horse and wagon. They took the matches. They even took the oats. All they left my grandfather was a celluloid collar, size seventeen. What a rooking they must have given him. In the morning, he damn near got thrown in jail for not being able to meet his bill at the inn. He had to swab down toilets and shine pots and pans for a month in order to make good. But a year later, he got back to New York with two whole grand, a shiny wagon and a horse that looked like Darleys Arabian. And the celluloid collar. I now skip over nearly sixty years. Ive still got thirtyeight hundred and five dollars out of the money he left me in his will. Do you know what Im going to do with that money? Im going to England, Fink. The mother country. The hollowed ground.*

Whatll you going to do there, Mr Sanford?

Nothing Sanford said.

England with nothing to do. Aint that elegant?

Im in for the lousiest time of my life. I dont want to go. I want to stay here. Do you know why, Fink?

He asks me if I know why. All the lawyers is crazy, so why not the clerks, too? If youll going to have a lousy time, maybe you shouldnt go.

I want to stay, but I cant stay, Fink. I hate hired sheets and fat breasts and Great Bear Spring Water and enormous blue billows of sadness. I hate the designs on the wallpaper of hallbedrooms. Ive got to go away. Be a good fellow, Fink. Drive me down to the Cunard offices.

They went out to the receptionroom. The telephone operator was taking a glass of Great Bear Spring Water. Tenthirtytwo.

Sanford said *Dont do that. You oughtnt to be drinking that water. Youre ruining yourself. Its a symbol, that water. I dont know what its a symbol of. I dont even know what a symbol is. Id only speak of banalities and fat breasts and hired sheets and the hideous repeating designs on hallbedroom wallpaper, but mostly about fat breasts flopping over hired sheets, about a tin commode in a table bottom near the head of the bed. You oughtnt to drink that water. You ought to get married. What are you waiting for? Better opportunities? Do you want to flop over hired sheets? Do you want to have that waist ripped off in a strange bedroom? And then your lace brassiere? And then do you want to cascade your fat hot flesh into strange temporary hands? What fun do you get out of dialing numbers all day? Why dont you get married? Thats no fun either. What book are you reading? Do you think I care what book it is? Theyre all the same. Stick to your telephone directory. Its full of indisputable facts. What do you get out of reading? Nothing. Less than you get out of dialing numbers. You might just as well be in a hallbedroom. Youre ruining yourself drinking that water. Its tenforty. Thats not too late. Too late for what? For what is tenforty not too late? How would you know? I was a fool to ask you. Do you know where Im going now? Do you know I didnt go home last night? I slept in the park, Central Park. On a bench. Sitting up. With my eyes wide open. Did you ever do that? Dont answer. I know you couldnt. I know you wouldnt. Youve got a home. Ive got no home. Ive got no place to go. I dont want a place to go. I dont want a home. Why should I? Whats a home? A place to sleep and stow your dirty underwear. But a park bench. A good idea. There oughtnt to be any homes. Only park benches. You ought to sleep sitting up in a park some night. With wideopen eyes. But you cant keep your eyes open. You better stay home. It might rain. You better stay home. Thats what its called, isnt it? HOME. Dirty linen. Blankets. Quarrels. A convenient toilet. You better stay home. A deep couch in the livingroom where you can sink down into the velour and submerge your whole body, nothing showing except your soul. You and the boy friend. Wait. Whats that word? SOUL. That was it. Listen to the fancy language Im using for you. Soul. Isnt that great? Only your soul showing. Youre in for a fine life if you get married. Think it over. A microscopic diamond ring. Good books, but few. Furniture to play on and pay for. Slugs as snug as bugs in rugs. Long conversations, important conversations, on the couch in front of the fireplace. About what? About Fannys new dress. With whom? Da poy frient. Uninterrupted. A home. A HOME. Soiled linen. Marriage, the Lincoln Highway to Heaven. Tenfortysix. Still not too late. Do you know its not too late yet? Why do you sit there with your lower jaw hanging down on your fat lap? Why the damn dumb look on your pan? Why the Hell dont you give Room Five a wire? Why dont you shake the lead out of your. . . . Come on, Fink.*

The cabdriver and Sanford went into the corridor. While waiting for the elevator, Sanford thought of *Mr Vul*. He studied the entrance to Room 850 and learned that *Mr Vul* was *Mr Vulgar*. Sanford wondered why he had not thought of that possibility. Downstairs, Fink pointed out his cab and asked where the ticketoffices were. Sanford told him to drive down Broadway to Number Twentyfive.

Sanford went to the counter at which the cabin tickets were sold. He said to a clerk *Give me a cabin at the minimum rate.*

Where to, sir?

London, on the Caronia.

Thank you, sir. Leaving on the thirtieth of September and reaching London ten days later. The clerk went away. In a few moments, he came back with a ticket. *One hundred and sixtyfive dollars, sir.*

I have no cash with me. Send the ticket to my office this afternoon. No, make it tomorrow. The name is John B. Sanford and the address is Fiftyone Chambers Street.

Sanford Fiftyone. Very good, sir.

Thanks.

The act was done, Sanford thought. That was the end of it. Nothing could stop him now. Nothing. Nothing that he knew of, at any rate. Of course, he could always cancel the reservation.

On his way out, he noticed a clock on the wall. Elevenfourteen. It was too early for lunch. Castle Garden was not far away. The Aquarium. It was years since he had been there; his mother had taken him the last time. Castle Garden. People said that Jenny Lind had sung there sixty years before. They said she was a beautiful woman. America had named a cigar after her. The final reverence, Sanford thought. The last claque. But Jenny Lind was not the only one; America had always bowed before the great. How about *Romeo and Juliet?* How about *Antonio y Cleopatra? Daniel Webster? Henry Clay?* How about *Bering?* Every cigarstore in New York sold a cigar called the *Bering Straight.* Why not an *Apollo Belvedere?* Why not a *Lincoln Blunt?* Why not a *Jesus Christ Perfecto?*

After leaving the Cunard offices, Sanford walked down to Battery Park. Thinking again of Jenny Lind, he went toward the Aquarium. The heat of the softening sidewalk waved up in glassy veils. Men lay on the grass. Tobaccosmoke neither rose nor fell, but hung slowly billowing. For a while, there were no elevated trains on the Battery Park loop. Sanford went into the Aquarium. He thought of the *Swedenborgian Farthingale.*

The Aquarium was cool and, for a moment, dark. Sanford heard the distant subdued fall of water into many tanks, the occasional tearing bark of a seal. In the lifting gloom, he saw a ring of light green windowpanes. Walking over to one of them, he sought into the shadows. The tank received its light through a transom. At the back, there was a wall of rock punched with caves, deepsea rock smoothworn and smoothbored with holes, like a side of Swiss cheese.

Sanford looked up when he heard a faint splash, and saw that an attendant had thrown in a small sunfish. After regaining its balance, it sank slowly and easily to a level about a foot from the bottom of the tank. There it hung almost motionless, only fin or tail now and then slowly waving. The regular pursing of its round small mouth caused many bright colors to ripple along its sides. Then gently it drifted toward a speck of food a yard away. It did not live to reach it. A large fish burst out of the shadows and sucked it whole through a pair of gaping jaws. Sanford looked up at a plaque over the tank and read *Lake Erie Muskalonge.*

He tried to use the scene as the core of an idea, but no thought came to him, no thought either original or banal. He realized that he could watch the same thing happen a dozen times in succession and that even after the last time, he would still be conscious of having had no thought except that the performance was becoming dull. Trying hard to think, he went from tank to tank in search of an idea. Why had he come downtown? Why had he asked the girl to see him again that night? Why was it impossible for him to think? He wondered whether other people had similar dead spots. If they did, they never said anything about them. The almost verbal eagerness in the bulging eyes was supposed to indicate that the brain was boiling with ideas.

He regretted his inability to think that morning. He wished he could thumbandforefinger his temples and press his mind into a form. If that were possible without embarrassment, he would start off with a fine figure of speech *My fingers are pronging my brain like the roots of trees in earth.* He wondered *Like the roots of trees in earth?* Roots drew life out of dirt. With his fingers, then, he would suck ideas out of his head; he would suck it as dry as a cowflop on the burnedout grass of an old pasture. He would run the vacuumcleaner of his hands over the dusty carpet of his brain. Then he would be able to express those ideas with his hands. He would have all knowledge at his fingertips. His mouth would become rudimentary. If people wanted to talk to him, he would turn his head away and exhibit his hands to them. Slowly and gracefully he would show them his fingers. He heard a little boy asking his mother to take him to the toilet for Number One.

Sanford looked into a tile tank in the floor of the Aquarium and watched a bunch of ducks drilling holes in themselves with their bills. He saw the parallel. The pronging root. The pressing finger. The drilling bill. As he went away, he saw a duck flirting its tailfeathers.

He left the Aquarium and walked up Broadway to the Trinity Church graveyard. Above him, the bells made twelve long strokes. He went in and sat down on a bench in the shade of a wall. A bum sitting next to him salvaged a flattened butt from the slatewalk, but searched his pockets vainly for a match. Sanford handed him a mechanical lighter. The bum flipped the wheel expertly and ate a long drag of blue smoke. After that, he passed the lighter back to Sanford, who noticed that the bum had a stack of pamphlets on the seat beside him. When the bum saw that Sanford was looking at the pamphlets, he asked him if he would like to read one.

Sanford said *Yes.*

The bum handed over a pamphlet.

Sanford looked at the title *Russia: Before and After.* He opened the pamphlet and read the first few lines. Then his eyes came up off the page and stared at an old tombstone that was shaling at the edges like a piece of mildewed French pastry. The inscription was worn and indistinct, but Sanford could still discern the name *Sarah Sincerbaugh* and the date of birth *7 March 1753.* Up at the top of the stone were the blurred outlines of a lamb.

His mind began to stiffen when he tried to read more of the pamphlet. He thought *How old was Sarah Sincerbaugh when she died? Russia: Before and After what? Christ? Pushkin? The French invasion? Nick the Prick?* He wondered what the pamphlet was about, but it was impossible for him to read it. He thought *The doors of my brain are closing.* His thinking took the form of pictures and he saw the torn checkers of a white silk nightgown, a scowling bust of plaster, the shaking of curtains, the flapping of shades, the shaking of breasts.

Then he stopped thinking of the night before and recalled the pamphlet his uncle had sent him. *Russia: Before and After. The United States Navy. The Panama Pamphlet: Fore and Aft.* He remembered having been thirteen years old. He remembered a set of de Maupassant. He remembered an old advertising placard for Hudnut perfumes that had hung over the sodafountain of Reids drugstore; there had been a naked woman in the ad, a beautiful woman with long blonde hair and fine full breasts. He remembered having gone to Reids many times. He had liked it there. He had even gone in to ask for the time. He remembered his old home in Harlem, the lock on the door of the bathroom, the comfortable shape of the toiletseat, the mirror opposite—a room for thinking. He had done much thinking there, solved many problems. There had never been another bathroom like that one. Of course, he had done a lot of thinking in dozens of other bathrooms, but they had lacked the emptyhouse Sundayafternoon security, the comfortable seat, the convenient mirror in which to watch himself during his thinking. That Harlem bathroom was the place where he had started thinking. He had thought for many years, with perfect regularity.

The bum said he was selling the pamphlets for a dime apiece.

Sanford put the pamphlet down on the bench and said he had no dimes to throw away.

He walked out of the graveyard, crossed Broadway and went down a flight of steps to the Wall Street subway station. The face of a train shoved up through the tunnel, bearing on its forehead a red and a white light. He thought *Thou shalt bind me for a sign upon thy. As frontlets between thine eyes.* He stood on the platform of car number 4781. A subwayguard looked at a thick nickel watch and informed him that it was twelveforty.

Sanford said *I didnt ask you.*

Im telling you. You cant kid me. I know you want to know the time.

Sanford listened dully and heard at intervals.

The subwayguard said *Dont get me wrong. Im no smarty. Im no wise guy. Im no bum sitting in a church graveyard sniping other peoples halFUSED butts. Ive been a subwayguard since nineteenOnine. Ill always be a subway guard. The years will bring me many little chevrons to symbolize my loyalty. Gray hair. A cracked voice. But Ill know that I gave my best. So dont get me wrong, I say. Im a plain ordinary guy. No frills, no pretense, no show about me. Im just yours truly, Charley Conkling, good old FULLON STREET. FULLN STREE. STEP LIVELY. STAND BACK FROM A DOORS Charley. I tell you straight from the shoulder, Im a plain guy. Now heres my tip to you, young fellow. Play safe. Dont bark up the wrong tree. Dont try to swim upstream. Dont run your head against stone walls. Dont tilt against windmills. Dont think you can beat the old game. The odds are all against BROOKEN BRICH. BROOKN BRIIICH. CHANGE HERE FOR A LOCAL. FOURTEEN STREE A NEEEEXT AND WATCH A DOORS. After all, son, whats life? I often ask myself that question. Whats life? Its a hard nut to crack, but once youve got it open, all the trouble clears up like magic. I got it open one night in the moonlight. I was walking down Intervale Avenue one summers eve and I said to myself: Charley Conkling, whats life? And then it came to me. Just a laugh, just a tear: thats life. Simple, isnt it? Just a laugh, just a tear. You laugh today. You cry tomorrow. You laugh the day after tomorrow. You cry the day after the day after tomorrow. You laugh again the day after the day after the day after tomorrow, but you cry....*

World without end Sanford said.

Till the end. Till there arent any more days. Just crying and laughing, laughing and crying FOURTEEN STREE AND LET EM OUT FIRST. DONT BLOCK A DOORS. Life is like a string of subway stations. Some crowded and gay, like Times Square; others deserted and sad, like Cathedral Parkway. The day and the night. Here today, gone tomorrow. Just a laugh, just a tear. You cant be getting happiness all the time. Youve got to take the good with the bad. But play it safe. Work hard. Mind your own business. Above all, mind your own business. Stay in your own backyard. Be careful the person youre talking to. Keep a close mouth. Dont trust your best friend. Remember your friend has a friend. And your friends friend has a friend. And your friends friends friend has a friend, too. Speech may be silver, but silence is golden. Why, even the walls have ears. Not literally, of course, but you never can tell. Take me, for instance.

Sanford said *Take you?*

I mean when a man tells me the company he keeps, I can usually tell him GRAN CENRAL. GRANNN CENRAL. CHANGE HERE FOR A SHUTTLE. STEP AWAY FROM A DOORS, LADY. EIGHTYSICK A NEXT. Now, take me.

Sanford said *Ill take you to Mobile, where theyve taught the cows to fly.*

I was just saying you should look before you leap. Watch your step. Always stand back from a doors. Be prudent. Be thrifty. Be wise, practical, economical, conservative. Be . . .

Damned.

Frugal. Dont cut across lots. Dont look for the shortest way. Save up for a rainy day. My wife puts away five dollars a week out of my salary. Save the pennies and the dollars will take care of themselves. Dont be a wastrel. Dont be a spendthrift. Learn the value of a dollar. Save.

Only God can save Sanford said.

EIGHTYSICK. EIGHTYSICK.

Sanford left the train there.

He went up to the street and headed west toward Fifth Avenue, remembering an old reluctance to face either the north or the east. The points repelled him. North was unpopulated; east was dark. He stopped at the Fifth Avenue corner to wonder why he had come uptown. What was he doing in that part of the city? As the unanswered query tumbled away again into his brain, he merely stood still and waited for a first impulse to move him anywhere, in any direction. Despite his prejudices, it really made no difference.

The Metropolitan Museum stank of age, dust, mold and preservatives. The sound of shoes dragging over wood and stone came to Sanfords ears in varying intensities. On his way to the Spanish rooms, he passed a Herakles in green slime and wondered why some sculptors saw fit to invade the province of the druggist.

When he reached the Spanish section, the rooms of which were unoccupied by visitors, he stood in front of a painting by Goya. He thought of nothing except the way the frame embraced a window of semidarkness, mysterious and vaguely evile. He did not examine the picture closely, but imagined that under dark trees in the distance, there would be figures moving with scarcely any sound, dancing carefully and not touching each other, but all related in a mild and disinterested cruelty. There would be a little meaningless laughter and the evening would become darker and soon nothing would be seen or heard.

Sanford sat down on a chair in a shadowed corner.

Feet knocked unevenly on the panels of the floor. A man and woman came into the room. The woman was holding an open book in her hand. When they were in front of the Goya, the woman read a passage from the book. The piece was about Goya and his painting. Then there was a clattering of pages and Sanford heard a reference to the particular Goya before which the visitors were standing. As the woman read, the man stared at a small brass tag that was nailed to the base of the frame *Francisco de Goya y Lucientes*. He did not raise his eyes even when the woman closed the book and began to make a description for him. She stated the size of the picture, the number and position of the figures, the different colors. It was only then that Sanford began to wonder how long the man had been blind.

After that, Sanford was unable to remain in the Museum. He left through a rear exit and came out near the Obelisk. He walked toward the gray column and was about to look at the hieroglyphics when he felt that he would like to know the time. A policeman told him that it was twothirtynine.

Without thinking again of the Obelisk, Sanford walked south along a twisting path until he reached the Boat Pond. He stopped on the boardwalk to watch the activity, and remembered experiences of years before when his grandfather had been coaxed into buying him a tin sailboat. The boat was called the *Reliance*. When the Sundays were fine, the old man had taken him down to the Pond, where Sanford sailed his piece of tin all afternoon, until the parklamps were lit and the trees were great purple stains on the sky.

He remembered how he had pretended that the *Reliance* was the America Cup defender, but it was no use pretending, he had found. The *Reliance* was always tin. A look at some of the other boats had convinced him of the futility of dreams, and made him dissatisfied with the modest proportions of his own ordinary toy. One fellow had a beauty, a real yacht model, so large that he was almost able to sit in it. The fellow always had a man with him who sailed the boat and guided it with a long pole when it came cutting for the side of the Pond, leaning over like a quartermoon. The man carefully shoved the pole under the bowsprit of the yacht and fended it off the boardwalk; he adjusted the rudder to a different tack, and the little boy, who had always tried to be very hard, sent the boat away with nautical phrases, the words of which came back to Sanford through the years: *Looks like a blow, sir; stormcloud coming up fast across the port bow, sir; reef in that topsl and look lively about it, sir; so the folksl is complaining about the grub, sir; tell em its mutiny, sir; next man to open his hatch gets a gut full of lead, sir.*

One afternoon, the *Reliance* sat dead upright on the middle of the Pond. For an hour there had been very little wind, and it had begun to rain. The drops beat straight down, making millions of glassy sprouts come up off the surface of the Pond, but the *Reliance* had remained where she was, looking cheaper and more battered than ever now that her heavy cotton sails were further stiffened with water. The sordidness of the secondbest had oppressed Sanford as he watched, in a moment of complete fascination, the course of a steeple of canvas moving across the Pond. So lovely a sight was it that he had not realized where it was bound until, clearly over the water, he heard the dull thump of wood on tin. Then he had heard the other boy hollering with rage and stamping his feet on the boards, so excited that he could not talk. After that, Sanford had been treated to the humiliation of seeing his tin hull on its way toward him, impaled on the sharp bowsprit of the yacht. When the yacht reached the walk, the man had disengaged the two and flung Sanford what was left of the *Reliance*. A long straight gash, from which poured a stream of brown pondwater, dove into the red and white tin. The America Cup defender. Sanford had stared down at the tangle of torn sails and bent tin. He had wanted to cry. The others had been so hard about it. They had chucked him the wreck. He remembered that he had left it on the boarding and walked away.

From the Boat Pond, Sanford walked south inside the Fifth Avenue wall until he came to the Zoo. He stopped at an openair tank to watch a sealion move through the water in scallops, like a dolphin. Sometimes, at the end of a series of curves, the seal threw itself up on a stone ledge and sat swaying like a Hebrew mourner.

Sanford turned away from the seal tank and went toward the house where the lions and leopards were kept. In the open doorway hung an acid curtain of evaporated urine that Sanford could not force himself to penetrate. He thought *The final distillation of raw meat. A lion may be noble, but it stinks.*

He sought the waterbirds, the ducks and geese, and those he watched for a long time. The wings beating on the water. The smooth clean feathers. The exact and ridiculous bills.

Further on, he came to a cage where a large buffalo was sitting in the dirt. Stuck to its dusty hair were shreds of straw and dried bits of turd.

Sanford continued down the path a little way. In the shade of a tree off the walk, there was an unoccupied bench. He went over to it and sat down. A sparrow hopped to within a yard of the bench and waited for something to happen.

Sanford fell asleep.

In his sleep, he had his old waterdream. He was alone in a large body of water and swimming toward the only visible piece of land on the horizon, a high cliff many miles away. For hours he tried to reach the land. The monotony of his strokes so overcame him that he was forced to count their number, sometimes losing himself in the counting. He forgot his primary wish. Then, when the numbers had mounted into the thousands, he suddenly noticed that he had come to within a short distance of the cliff. Still swimming toward it, he saw at its base a broad belt of sloping sand that ended in a grove of trees. At the same time that he saw those details, he found he was making no more headway with his swimming. Despite the length of time he had been in the water, his strokes were still as powerful as ever, but they failed now to decrease the distance between himself and the shore. The condition of the water was just the same; he felt no undertow, nor was he in any crossrip running parallel to the beach. When he realized that nothing would bring him closer to the land, the dream changed from a struggle to a panic. He stopped swimming and began to beat on the water with his hands, but the more excited he became, the further from the beach he found himself. After a while, the dream ended.

When Sanford awoke, the sun was going down over the Fiftyninth Street buildingwall. The irregular notches and spikes of the houses stuck up into the sky like the stalagmites of a torchlit cavern.

A man came along with a burlap bag slung over his shoulder. In one hand he carried a sawedoff broomstick that had a sharpened nail driven into the ferrule. With this, he was spearing scraps of paper and cardboard out of the grass. Sanford asked the man for the time. The man hauled a dollar Ingersoll out of his pocket and said that it was fivefortyfour.

PART
IV

Aᴛ
seven oclock, Sanford started walking on Fiftyseventh Street. He covered the distance between Sixth and Seventh Avenues many times. Near seventhirty, when he was in front of Carnegie Hall, he heard his name called. The girl was standing on the steps leading to the lobby. He was glad she had saved him half an hour of waiting, but he tried not to show it.

You werent supposed to be here till eight he said.

The girl said *I know that, but I finished early at home and came down on the chance of finding you ahead of time.*

I was on my way to get something to eat he said. *I havent eaten since breakfast.*

Ill go with you. Ill talk to you while you eat. A little later. Right now, Id rather walk. Down Broadway.

He took the girls arm and walked close to her. They went around the corner and started down Seventh Avenue. In the distance, he saw where Broadway crossed over and the streets were bright.

The girl said *What did you do today?*

Sanford said *Wandered, thats all, from the time I left you till a little while ago. I was down to the Aquarium and Trinity Church. I was at my office. I was at the Metropolitan Museum, the Boat Pond and the Zoo. After I left the Zoo, I sat down on a bench and fell asleep for a few hours. I had an old dream of mine, the waterdream. When I was a kid, I used to have the dream regularly, but this was the first time in years.*

The girl said *What is the waterdream?*

Im swimming toward land, but I never quite reach it. The swimming turns out to be futile when I get close to the shore. I dont believe the dream means much, but if its anything at all, its more than its very obvious meaning. If the dream were new to me, Id bother thinking it out, but its so dull now and Ive thought about it so much in the past that its only meaning is the meaning of a water fascination. I probably induced it by a great many water associations today. The Aquarium, the Hudson, the bay, the Boat Pond, the waterbirds in the Zoo. Another thing. While I was downtown this morning, I booked passage to England.

When the girl talked again, she said *Why?*

He said *Last night we walked in the quiet. The park was fine, even with the rain. In a couple of minutes, it will be Broadway. In a few days, there will be all that goodbye stuff: The excitement was intense; he proved himself immense; he jumped inside the redhot stove, and pushed out all the dents. Shouting. The waving of hand and handkerchief. The giving and taking of addresses. Drop in and see so&so. I can forgive anything but stupidity.*

The girl said *Why do you talk like that? I dont like to listen to you when youre angry. I thought last night was the end of it.*

Last night was the end of a lot of things he said *but youll listen to me, no matter how I talk.*

From Fortythird Street, a wedge opened north into many lights and a place where there was crossing movement. The sky was pink with glare. They stopped at a curb to wait for a hole in ribbons of traffic.

Youll listen to this he said. *I want to talk about myself. I want to tell you. Last night wasnt enough. Without words, you might find excuses for me. I dont want to be excused. I want you to hear about me from my own mouth. Ive dug these things out of my memory.*

Theyre true. I figured in them all. I dont care what you think of me when I finish. You couldnt think me lower than I know I am.

The girl said *You just want to hurt yourself. Its some kind of self-punishment, but I cant see for what.*

Sanford said *About three years ago, there was a girl I knew pretty well. One day she phoned me and said her father had died the day before. She wanted to know if Id come over to the house. When I got there, a lot of people were in the parlor, crying and moaning around the casket. Someone told me the father had gotten a stroke. The girl came over to me and began to cry. I didnt know what to do or say, so it was lucky she got over the spell pretty soon. Then she took me into the diningroom, where her mother was sitting. When it got kind of awkward for me in there, the girl made me take a cup of coffee. I tasted it and it had that rotten kind of warmness that makes you think youre drinking the water the dirty clothes were boiled in. I put the cup down after one taste. The girl was trying to comfort her mother, but when she saw I hadnt gone far with the coffee, she sat next to me and asked me what was the matter. I told her the coffee was lousy.*

A man wanted to be directed to the place that sold outoftown papers; he said he was from Spokane, Washington. Sanford pointed to the reef on which the Times Tower stood. The man thanked him, touched his hat, and went across the street with many people when northandsouth traffic was stopped.

Sanford said *My grandfather had cancer and died very slowly. The doctors wouldnt tell him what sickness he had. For a long time they fooled him with talk about thyroid trouble, but after a while, he saw they werent making any cure. The dull pains hed had at the beginning were getting sharper and more frequent and finally he had to stay in bed all the time. Then he guessed the truth and nearly went insane. Sometimes at night hed scream out his fear of pain and hed beg and beg, saying he didnt mind about the dying, but he didnt want the pain. All the doctors could do was coke him up as often as they dared and he spent weeks in dopedreams that bubbled over with terrible fears and pain coming through the diminishing morphine. Whenever they made me go in to see him, I sat as far away from him as I could; all I wanted was to get out of the room. I couldnt make*

95

myself touch him. I couldnt feel any affection or pity. When he was near the finish, the family gathered at his house. The nurse came out of the bedroom and said my grandfather wanted to see me. I was so scared that I thought of telling the nurse to say I wasnt there, but I was too ashamed, so I went into the bedroom. The nurse left me alone with my grandfather. He looked pretty calm when he asked me to sit on his bed and talk to him, but I told him I could see him better from where I was, anything, any kind of lie, only to stay far away. Then he had a curious fit. He screamed out he was well and that the doctors were trying to kill him. He raved that he wanted his clothes. He said hed feel fine if theyd let him take a walk. Then he actually tossed the covers off and got both feet out of bed. He called for me to help him, but I only backed up and tried to push my way out through the wall. Even though I believed he couldnt have walked a yard without falling on his face, I was so scared of his touching me that my head stopped working and my body froze up in my throat, but when I saw him staggering toward me, I hollered something at him that Ive never been able to remember. Then I ran out of the room. I didnt stop for anything. I just ran out of the house. I went into the street and looked at everybody in the street and I wanted to touch them and feel the heat of their bodies and the movement and soundness of their arms and legs, the beating of their hearts. I wanted to hear noise, and hear and feel motion, but mostly I wanted to feel heat.

Sanford finished the story standing at the Fortysecond Street corner. He and the girl were bumped around by hurrying people. He looked about him and was depressed by the cheapness he saw. He looked up at buildings that were oldfashioned in their novelty. Nothing was ever new, he thought; the instant it was created, it started to go out of style. He considered his trip to England and wondered whether even that could change his thoughts; they, too, depressed him by their cheapness and their age. He tried to deny that his life was mediocre and that his death would be the same, but he was disturbed by the story he had told about his grandfather. Like his grandfather, he would be buried quietly. Was there a different way to be buried? Did anyone go down with cheers? How about guns popping off over the newturned earth? How about salutes and lowered flags? To Hell with them. He thought again of leaving the country. He and the girl crossed Fortysecond Street and continued down Broadway until the noise of Times Square grew distant.

Sanford said *One winter I ran away from home. I traveled south and got as far as Fort Lauderdale, Florida, after a week of bumming and begging. It was nightime and I was dead broke and had no place to sleep, so I wandered around the outside part of the town till I came across an old negro, a nightwatchman, sitting in a rocker outside an icehouse. I got to talking with him and told him I was tired and wanted to sleep. He said I could have the rocker if I felt like it. It was pretty nice of him, so I said thanks and sat down and was fast asleep right off. I dont know how long I slept, but it was still dark when someone woke me up by kicking my ankle. I got my eyes open and then the man who woke me up told me I was under arrest. I asked him what for. He said because I was a vagrant. He said the negro had reported me after I fell asleep. I wanted to pick up a rock and brain the lousy squealer, but the sheriff grabbed my arm and told me to come along. I begged him to let me go, saying Id quit the town and never come back, but the sheriff gave me some kind of spiel about duty and wouldnt let me go. I got frightened and pleaded with him and promised him all sorts of things, but it wasnt any use. He took me away and stuck me in a big cell in the county lockup. There were four others in the same cell. They asked me what I was in for and when I told them, they all let out a laugh. They made fun of a cheesy crime like vagrancy and started to boast about their own. Two of them were kids of fifteen; theyd been nailed for assault and highway robbery. I wasnt in the cell five minutes before theyd let me in on every detail. They said theyd gotten a ride from a motorist and hit him over the head with a section of lead pipe. Theyd chucked the guy into a ditch and stolen the car as well as all the money the fellow had on him. They said they still thought it was a pretty good crime. A third guy said he was in for bigamy and put on a play about how he was going to kill that bitch of a first wife of his as soon as he got out. The fourth fellow was just a pickpocket and he kept pretty quiet. But even with the rough talk, it took me a little while to realize that I was in jail. When I did, I jumped off the buggy cot Id been lying on and let out an awful holler. I did everything a new prisoner always does. I pounded on the doors and bars and walls. I walked from one end of the cell to the other, back and forth, back and forth, for at least two hours. I shouted and screamed to be let out. All I got for my walking and hollering was a loud jeering from the others, and finally a good beating for keeping them awake. For three days I was in a panic. I didnt eat. I couldnt. Sowbelly and grits all the time. Sowbelly and grits. Christ, how it stank. The stuff was brought up by a trusty who had the run of the jail, but he didnt know when I was going to be tried. Maybe not for a couple of months, he told me. I begged him to tell the sheriff that I wanted to talk to him. He promised, but the sheriff didnt come till the fifth day. In the meantime, I had to try the food. They never changed it. Sowbelly and grits. Sowbelly and grits. I got one load of it down. I dont know how. When I remembered its stink, up came the whole business into the washbasin. The fifth night, after the others were asleep, all of a sudden I remembered God. Full of love, belief and supplication, I got down on my knees. I humbled myself and didnt think of my humility. I accepted everything and declared my faith. I made promises. I said if I were freed, Id devote myself to God and put all my trust in Him and work in His interests. I wound up with one of the few formal prayers I knew and went to sleep. In the morning, the sheriff came and told me that I was going to be tried in an hour. The court found me guilty, but suspended sentence on condition that I got out of Fort Lauderdale at once. The minute I left the jail and got out into the air and sun, I completely forgot about what Id done and said the night before, but I remember having been too ashamed to remember.*

There was no nightlife in Herald Square. That had ended years before with Jim Jeffries and Lillian Russell. Activity in the daytime centered around the departmentstore junkshops, Sanford thought. Crammed with useless trash, the great warehouses were dark now; no crowds stormed the doors to swap their money for crockery or cheapsmart jewelry. Only the McAlpin corner was busy. Further east on Thirtyfourth Street, the marquee of the Waldorf illuminated the sidewalk. Sanford and the girl walked in that direction.

Sanford said *When I was a boy, there was a fellow who used to make fun of me. He worked in a butchershop and he was twice my size. With one hand, he could easily have beaten me into a hamburger, but he never lifted a finger to me. Always he wanted to make me feel he was just about tired of me and that any minute he was going to grab me and kick me to ribbons, but he never touched me. I dont know what stopped him. He bullied me so regularly that I quit using the streets where I knew he hung out. I never got over hating him. While I think about him now, I hate him. In the old days, I used to forget myself sometimes and not care a damn what happened to me. I hated him right to his face. I told him if he ever laid a hand on me, Id get a gun and kill him. I said speeches of hate to him that Id made up all the nights before. I blurted out all the cursewords I knew and screamed them into his ears till my stomach started to turn with anger and I had to run away before I puked in the street. His fat face came up in front of me when I was in bed and I rolled around and beat the covers trying to get rid of the hatefulness of the face. When I found out that nothing saved me from its vulgarity, I lay awake all night making up abusive things to say to him. Sometimes I used to think of how I might triumph over him, even if for only one time. I dreamed of brawn and bravery. I dreamed of the one big time. That was all I wanted. Once. Once only. It never came. The bully tortured me merely by staying alive. Even if hed died, Id not have been satisfied unless I knew hed been beaten to death by a man double his size who had first frightened him the way he did me. I still dream of the one big time. I hate him today just as much as I hated him then. Its ten years since Ive seen him.*

The Waldorf was rose and gold, marble and brocade. Sanford and the girl crossed Fifth Avenue and went as far as the Vanderbilt Hotel. There they turned north up Murray Hill toward Grand Central Station.

Sanford said *At public school, there was a boy named Runkel. Dopey Runkel, we called him. He was the dumbest kid that ever lived. He was thick in every subject we had, but in Elementary Physics he was hopeless. Our instructor was a badtempered old man called Doc Birch. With boys who hadnt done their homework, or with those who had forgotten their lessons overnight, he always went pretty hard, but with those who couldnt understand, he was like a lunatic. He talked to them as if they were little scoundrels or thieves, and predicted all sorts of distressing fates for them if they kept on in their ways. I wasnt exactly one of those who couldnt understand, but Birch used to say Id wind up my career at the controller of a trolleycar. Poor fathead Runkel. He was to be a streetcleaner, or at best, with great good fortune, the man who came around the block buying old bottles and scrapiron. From the showing he made when Birch called on him to recite, there seemed to be something in the prediction. To save his life, Runkel couldnt remember the colors of the spectrum. Red white and blue, he used to say. Birch would jump off his highchair and almost foam at the mouth. Hed shout aimlessly and pound on the table with a ruler till he seemed about to get sick and spoil the fun. Vibgyor, vibgyor, vibgyor, hed scream. It was fun. I cant remember any part of school that I enjoyed more than that class. I think of the spectrum, the splintered ruler, the vacant look on Runkels pan, the red white and blue. Ill never forget how I used to laugh right in Runkels face, how I wanted Birch to let him go on and make a dope out of himself. Whenever I thought about Runkel, no matter where I was, I started to laugh. It made no difference that Birch was unfair to Runkel and never bothered to take him aside and explain things. I didnt want him to talk to Runkel. I didnt want Runkel ever to know. I just wanted him to laugh at. I laughed at him the first time I heard him speak. I laughed at him all year. I laughed when he was flunked, and laughed louder than ever when one of the boys told me that Birch had given Runkel a zero for his years work in Physics. Think of it. No mark at all for dozens of recitations and hundreds of laughs. When I lost track of Runkel, I was sorry. Hed have given me fun all my life.*

Sanford and the girl walked down the hill past the Belmont and entered Grand Central through the Vanderbilt Avenue side. From the balcony, they looked down at the crowds on the floor.

He said *Now I want to read you two pieces that I cut out of newspapers. Theyre not about me, but I think theyre so funny that you can regard them as my own joke.*

The clippings, frayed and soiled, were pasted on a sheet of paper that Sanford took out of his wallet. The girl sat on the marble banister while he read the first article to her:

RATTLER BITES EVANGELIST

UTAH WOMAN, STRUCK WHILE
PREACHING, EXPECTS FAITH CURE

RIFLE, COLORADO, May 15, AP—While Mrs. Gertrude Henline, a middle-aged evangelist from Provo, Utah, was preaching here last night, a member of her congregation handed her a box containing a live rattlesnake.

Mrs. Henline took the snake in her hands, waved it about her head, and challenged it to strike. As she was placing it back in the box, it bit her. She refused to discontinue talking and went on until she fainted on the platform.

Members of her party removed the evangelist to the house of a nearby follower, where all offers of medical attention were rejected.

Upon regaining consciousness, "Sister Smothers", as Mrs. Henline is known to her congregation, said that she would regain her strength through talks with God "in an unknown tongue".

In services here during the past few weeks, "Sister Smothers" declared that because of her faith, no snake would bite her.

Sanford laughed when he finished. He looked at the girl, but she was not even smiling.

A porter came over with a couple of bags and stopped at the head of the broad flight of steps leading to the main level. A woman came in fast through the doors behind him and wanted to know if she still had time to catch *The Owl* for Boston. The porter examined her through a pair of fluttering eyeleaves, round and brown. Then he said very slowly *De Ahl doan leave till twelvethutty, maam.* His face cracked in half when he smiled in the direction of the clock. It was ninefifty.

Sanford said *Heres the second clipping. Listen:*

BIG FUNERAL FOR
EVANGELIST

PROVO, UTAH, May 16, AP—Preparations are being made here this week for one of the most elaborate funerals this town has ever known, in memory of Mrs. Gertrude Henline, who died at Rifle, Colorado, yesterday afternoon as the result of snake-bite.

Mrs. Henline was bitten by a rattlesnake at a revival meeting held at Rifle. The deceased refused medical attention on the ground that she would effect her own cure through faith.

Again Sanford looked at the girls face, but still there was no laughter in it.

Sanford said *Last night I told you about a girl I met in my last year at law school.*

The girl said *Yes. I remember.*

They went out of the station and walked toward Fifth Avenue.

Sanford said *She told me a story once. She said she was going back to her boardinghouse late one night in the wintertime. It was snowing and the street was very dark. She passed a car at the curb and a man got out and tipped his hat. She said shed never seen him before, but when he spoke to her, she answered him. Then he asked her if shed like to go up to his rooms. She wanted to know where he lived and he pointed to a building across the street. She said all right and they went up there. When they got to the apartment, the man took off his overcoat. Then he went behind the girl and she thought he was going to help her get hers off, so she opened it and started to let it slide down her arms, but the man just grabbed her and squeezed her breasts and moved his hands all over her body. She said she tried to stop him, but the man wouldnt let go and she couldnt move her arms*

102

on account of the coat. *The man didnt say anything. He just kept sliding his hands over her. Then he tried to get one of his hands down the
front of her dress.* She said he tore the dress and even scratched her
chest, but finally she got his hand away and bit his finger so hard that
the blood came. *The man let go and she ran out of the apartment. I
dont believe a word she said.*

The girl said *Dont believe what? That she went up to the mans
apartment?*

He said *No. I think she stayed there. I think she did everything
she wanted me to think she hadnt done.*

The girl said *How can you say that? How do you know?*

Sanford said *I dont know. I just think so.*

They passed St. Patricks Cathedral. The girl wanted to go inside.
Knowing that he would not be able to talk as he wished if they were
in the church, he took the girls arm and made her continue walking
up the avenue.

He said *In my second year at law school, a new guy came to class
and sat next to me. Our seats were right up against each other and I
got a whiff of a strange smell coming from the guy. As the hour went
on and the room got warmer, the new guy began to stink like a sewer,
like the buckets of black muck they haul up out of the gutterwells.
He stank worse than that. Like the stockyards on a hot summer day.
Like a crowded subway when its been raining. Like decaying meat.
Like a chemistry lab when theyre making hydrogen sulphide. Like
the inside of a motormans glove. I wish I could make you understand
the stink without experiencing it, because if you really did, youd faint
dead away. The guy stank like the slime that sticks to the inside of
a garbage can. It got me so crazy that I forgot where I was. I forgot
there were two hundred students in the room. I forgot I could easily
have asked the guy to step outside with me while I told him about the
smell. All I could do was stand up alongside him and holler down
so loud that everybody in the room heard what I said: YOU STINK,
YOU DIRTY DOG. YOU STINK. IF YOU COME TO CLASS LIKE
THIS TOMORROW, I SWEAR ILL PASTE YOU ONE ACROSS THE
MOUTH. Then I went out of the room and stuck my head through a
window to get some air.*

When they reached Fiftyninth Street, the girl said she was tired and wanted to sit down. They went over to a granite bench near the fountain.

Sanford said *One of the poorest fellows Ive ever known was also one of the proudest. He made bundles in a departmentstore for twelve dollars a week. His friends tried to help him, but he wouldnt take a thing from them, saying hed rather look like a begger than be one. He did look like one. His clothes were old and ready to fall off his back. I was sure hed have worn them till he was naked, so one day I went through my things and got out a lot of stuff I knew hed never seen me wear. I wrapped them up and mailed the package to his address. The next time I saw him he was decked out in my seconds. I asked him where hed gotten the clothes and he told me about receiving a package without a senders name on it. Then he wanted to know if Id sent it. I said no and that ended the matter. Later, I thought about it and realized that unless I opened my mouth, no one would ever know Id been kind to the fellow. I knew how angry hed be if he found out that I was the one who had sent him the package, but I didnt care about that. All I could see was a good act being forgotten. I thought about the lengths to which people went in order to punish bad acts and wondered why they never went the same distance to reward good ones. They took the good for granted and gave you a swift kick in the ass for the other. I didnt think it was fair. The next time I sent my friend a package, I included a hat hed been seeing on me for a year. Two days later, I got back all the stuff that had been in both packages, and a hot letter telling me where the Hell I got off. The fellow would never speak to me after that.*

The girl asked Sanford for a cigarette. He said he had none, but would go across the street to the Plaza for a pack. He stopped in front of the hotel. After feeling in all his pockets, he turned around and went back to where the girl was sitting. When she held up her hand, he saw that there were a nickel and a dime in her palm.

I was watching you she said.

Sanford said *I havent a penny. I forgot that I spent my last dime in the subway. Downtown this morning and uptown this afternoon.* Then he took the girls money and went away again for the cigarettes.

When he came back, he sat down and said *Before I went to law school, I attended college out of town. I had a very small allowance, just about enough to pay for meals at a cheap eating club and a punk room a mile off the campus. The wealthy fellows lived at frat houses and paraded the place in fur coats. On cold days, I used to see dozens of those coats on the campus. I wanted one, but I didnt have enough to pay for it. During the first vacation, I got a job as a waiter in a summer hotel. It was the lousiest hardest job I ever had in my life, but I was after the money for one of those coats and I earned it. Just before I returned to college, one of my friends came to see me, the fellow Id arranged to room with during the second year. He told me hed not been able to raise his tuition money and couldnt go back to school unless someone made him a loan. Hed come to me because he thought I might be able to let him have the money. I asked him what hed done all summer. He said hed been working, but an illness in the family had used up all his savings. I told him I was awfully sorry, but I couldnt lend him anything. I said I was hardpressed myself. I found out later that the fellow didnt get the money from anyone else and had to quit college.*

Sanford said *I want to tell you one thing more, about my envy. I wish I could tell a story to show you what I mean, but if I tried to do that, youd see I really didnt envy any particular thing; youd see a universal envy. Mine isnt special. I can think of no case of individual or isolated envy, but I envy all those, as if they were one, who have what I have not. I begrudge all men their strength, their intellects, money and positions; I begrudge them their popularity, talents and beauty. I feel that no other man has a right to the things I lack. All men are created. Equals added to equals give mass, but not unity, because no two things are equal. Things equal to the same thing are divided by each other.*

Sanford stopped talking. He looked away from the girl and stared at the bright front of the hotel across the street. When no streetcars were crossing Fiftyninth Street, there was very little noise in the square, nothing but an occasional autohorn or the brokenoff conversation of walking people. Then Sanford heard a whistle and saw the doorman of the Plaza beckoning, to a shabby man who was leaning against the wall of the hotel near the corner. The fellow looked to see what the doorman wanted and then sprang toward a victoria at the curb. He moved so quickly that his old silk hat fell off. It rolled into the gutter and through a squid of horse urine that blotted the stone. It came to a stop cocked against a burst of turds. The fellow got down on his knees and reached through a fence of legs to pick up the hat. With a coatsleeve, he wiped the muck off the silk and then jumped up on the box. When he pulled up in front of the Plaza, a man and woman in eveningdress climbed into the carriage. Then the carriage moved away and Sanford listened to the diminishing plod of hoofs on the pavement.

The girl said *When you started this harangue near Carnegie Hall, you said you didnt care what I thought when you finished.*

And I still dont care Sanford said.

I dont believe you. You wouldnt have told me if you didnt care.

Thats not so Sanford said. *I talked to you for my own sake, because there were things I had to say. What do I care about your opinion? The only one Ive any regard for is my own. I was low before, but Im rehabilitated now. Some people are so graceful when they confess their shortcomings that they seem to change them to virtues. Im one of those people. Does the penitent think of the hidden Father in the filigreed box? Not at all. He confesses for his own troubled conscience, and it makes no difference to him whether the hidden Father listens or goes out to urinate during the confession. Its only the talking that counts. When you say a thing, you understand it.*

The girl said *Do you understand your own stories? I dont mean each one. I mean all together.*

Sanford said *Certainly I do.*

Then tell me what they mean.

Sanford was silent for a little while. He wondered whether the girl knew that he did not understand. She put her hand on his arm. He pushed it off. Then he felt like looking at her. When he saw her face, he jumped up from the bench and started to walk away. For the moment, he was aware of possessing only one sense. He stopped and listened to the falling of water in the fountain. He listened for a long time; he thought it was a long time. When he turned around, with the sound of falling water still in his ears, he saw that the girl was looking at the dark trees of the park.

He went back and sat down again. He took the girls hand and pressed it between both of his. He said *Whats the matter with me? Whats the matter with me?*

The girl put her arms around him and pulled his head down to her chest. When she felt his body shaking, she held his head more tightly against her. He started to cry.

Later, they went back to Fiftyseventh Street and took a bus uptown. Except for one other couple, they were the only passengers on the top deck. Sanford did not have much to say until the bus turned north out of Seventysecond Street into the Drive.

The girl said *Why are you going away, John?*

Without looking away from the river, Sanford put his arm around the back of the seat and held the girl close to him. *Thats the first time youve used my name. I like you to call me that. I like the name John, but I like it even more when you say it.* He watched a ferry coming out of the black at the base of Fort Lee. The moving row of lights bulged out like a string of beads on a fat womans neck.

Why are you going away?

Sanford said *Im going for all the reasons I gave you last night, and for one that I held back.*

Tell me the one you held back?

Sanford said *You asked me about the girl I met in my last year at school. You wanted to know if I loved her. If you were trying to break through a jungle, would you love the vines and creepers that twisted themselves around your neck? If you were in the grip of an octopus, would you love its tentacles? How about the sucking of a swamp, or the yielding of a quicksand? Would you love anything that made you impotent? Would you love a handcuff or a rope?* The bus passed the Soldiers and Sailors Monument. *Ive used bad images; they all relate to something material. This girl Im talking about is almost incorpo-*

real. Shes leaked into me like a mist, like some faint kind of gas, and I cant get rid of her. When I try to escape, I realize that Im fighting against nothing. Her words are humid, her body is damp, her letters are full of fog; but all that moisture of hers is consistent with dryness. I dont know how to explain that, except by saying that her moisture is like the juice you might get out of a cactus leaf, or even out of a stone, if you could squeeze hard enough. But Im sick of straining. Im sick of trying to wring some life out of an arid mummy. Now I just want to go away. Thats all. Just go away.

The girl said *What are you going to do in England?*

Sanford said *Study at Oxford. Im pretty sure I can get in. Its goodbye to this burg for a long time.*

The girl said *How long?*

A couple of years.

The girl said *I dont want you to go. I want you to stay here and be a friend of mine. You asked me to tell you what was the matter with you. I could tell you, but Id rather have you find out for yourself. Youll never find out if you run away.*

The bus went uphill toward Grants Tomb. Lying out in the backyard of the now darkened Claremont, it looked like an enlargement of an aged charlotte russe. Sanford remembered that he had always wanted to have dinner at the Claremont, but he had never looked into the place, never even been on the grounds. He wondered whether he should deny that he was running away.

The bus went slowly over the Viaduct. Sanford looked down through the lace of iron railings and saw a coalyard, a ferryslip and the piers of the Hudson River boatlines. On the right, away from the river, a grayblue gas tank, veined with girders and buttoned with rivets, came up like a phallus through a prepuce of steel.

When the bus stopped at Broadway, Sanford asked the girl if she cared to walk any further. She said she was not tired. They left the bus and went back to the Drive. Halfway across the Viaduct again, they stopped and leaned over the railing.

Sanford said *Ill go away because I want to go away. Ill go even if I lose every reason for going. I want to go. Do I need a better reason than that? I want to go. Ive been thinking of going for such a long time now that if I were to stay, Id always believe Id cheated myself.*

Then without saying anything more to each other, they started walking south again toward the girls house. On the way, they passed the street where Sanford lived. There were very few people on the Drive. The girl held Sanfords arm as they walked.

When they were in front of her house, she put her arms around him and kissed him hard on his mouth, so hard that his lips were jammed back against his teeth. Then she let go and went into the house without turning around even to wave goodnight.

As he went up the avenue again, he remembered some lines of a poem he had read a long time before: *Not till the sun excludes you do I exclude you, Not till the waters refuse to glisten for you and the leaves to rustle for you, do my words refuse to glisten and rustle for you.* He could not remember who had written the poem.

He stopped at a corner and looked across the Drive. The dark trees were still and the river flowed past with the dullness of lead. *Not till the sun excludes you* Sanford thought.

PART
V

Four days before sailing for England, Sanford telephoned the blue at Franconia Notch, and asked her to visit him. Without knowing why, without questioning the truth of the formula, he told her that it would be impossible for him to go away unless he saw her once more.

She came cloaked in her usual power to delude him. Upon an arrival, she never seemed to be the same person; she always looked eager coming off a train, and Sanford would see new possibilities in the way of her walk, in her bearing, in her voice, which a day later would die out of their own death. This time, when he saw her fifty yards away down a platform in Grand Central Terminal, he hurried toward her to say that he loved her. There could be no doubt of it; he was certain it was true. He was unable to think the word love without a belief that he was experiencing it.

Later that evening, after his friends had given him an opportunity to exhaust his vocabulary with her, they made a party for him at the Kav Kaz. It was the first time he had been there. Everyone said it had *something*; when Sanford saw it, he wondered if they meant garbage. The performers worked hard to maintain the reputation of the place—color—but Sanford was sorry that he had let himself be dragged to a retreat for those who achieved immortality only in a setting where lights were glamordim and music a belowthebelt appeal. Quietly he watched shaggy beasts come hopping out of dark corners. The beasts mouthed mocksavagely on pairs of heavy knives and did orgasmic heavy prances of heavy villainy victory, but without drawing blood. Sanford thought *You have to die before you can become deathless.* He could not watch the faces; they were trying too hard. A waiter leaned over his shoulder and squirted a jet of vichy into a glass half full of whisky.

A dozen of Sanfords friends were there, among them both girls. They were meeting for the first time. Sanford thought he deserved a kick in the belly for having been stupid enough to let them see each other. From the distances, the blue had transported all her long unseen dismalia, all her dusty and neverexistent tragedy. Sanford thought *She spreads out around her a tempering drag of sadness while she sits dryfaced and parched among the diluted furies of her thoughts and emotions.* She wore a look spraying out so much sorrow that she aroused a perverse resentment in Sanford, and he hated her for depressing him and for her intangible sadness. He thought *Its a dryeyed sadness, dumb and almost sullen, a sadness like that of a weak animal. Waterdry sadness and tragedy crowd silently on me, making me a factor in their hateful weariness.* He felt imprisoned. He wanted to lean across the table and sock her one in the face, punch her right square in the face as hard as he could, right on her conk. He thought *Id like to wreck her for jailing me in a personal sadness that has no bearing on anything in the world, for herself feeling nothing, doing nothing, thinking nothing, accepting where she ought to do a restful human act, make some human offensive gesture. By God, Id like to hit her over the conk.* The tineedling of the balalaika pierced his inaction. It would be a curious sight, blood dripping from her mouth. It would be curious, the hurt look in her eyes stupidly changing to *what? What can it change to?* Without moving, he gauged the distance between his hand and her face. One fast backhander would do it. He wondered why he could not move. He thought *Shes always to be hurt by this bully of a world.*

Shes unfit even for the brevity of a life. She has a franchise on sad-ness, a monopoly. Its sadness without cause, without object, without purpose, without direction, without meaning. Its a disembodied emo-tion. Its sadness absolute. Christ, come out of it for a minute. Only sadness and despair and burning skin and hard dry cracking eyes.

He looked away from her and saw the other girl talking to the man who played the piano in the orchestra. After a while, she came back and said that he was going to play for her while she sang a song. Sanford looked at the blue and felt like spitting when he found her pressing parallel lines into the tablecloth with a fork. Then the fellow started to play the piano and everyone listened, even people at the other tables.

The girls voice was big and round and the words of the song came out in fine globes of sound that made Sanford think of bub-bles. He forgot about the blue and the railroadtracks she was mak-ing in the tablecloth. It was a good room to sing in. The soundglobes kept floating around under the low ceiling for just an instant after the girls mouth had finished making them. Sanford wondered why he was not embarrassed. When she had sung for him in the park, where he was the only one to hear, he had been concerned with what people might think; now there were many in the room, many strangers, and he did not care what anyone thought. He watched the rising of her breasts as she inhaled. He wanted to hear her sing when she was naked.

After she had finished the song, her friends and many of the strangers clapped their hands and refused to let her sit down until she had sung again. One of the café performers came to a doorway and called for a Russian number that was her own specialty. When the other performers heard about it, they came out of the dressing-rooms and crowded around the doorway to listen. The girl laughed and motioned to the pianist to play the music for her.

Sanford did not think she was making a deliberate effort to do better than anyone else; she did not have a performers look of trying very hard, and seemed pretty cool before a group of strangers who might be quick to find fault with her singing if they thought she was showing off. But when Sanford looked around at the faces of the guests and performers, he knew the girl would not make them think that. All the faces were friendly, even that of the woman who had called for the song. She appeared to know that she was listening to a better voice than her own. When the song was finished, she went over to the girl on the floor and held her hand while she talked to her. Then three or four of the strangers made both of them take a drink at their table.

While the girl was away, there was no one to talk to and Sanford realized how dull the party would have been without her. The blue was not near him, but he could feel her presence on his neck. He knew that if he looked at her, she would give him some kind of sign to mean that she was tired and wanted to leave. The thought of being alone with her again made him reach for his whisky and soda, but the booze was rotten and he could not drink it.

When some of his friends tried to make him talk about his trip to England and what he intended to do there, he could think of nothing to say to them. Then the girl came back to the table and sat down next to Sanford. Because he wanted her to know that he now felt different about her singing, he started to tell her how much he had enjoyed it, but before she could know what he was going to say, the blue spoke to him from across the table. Sanford did not listen; he knew that he was going to hear *Im tired; Ive made a long trip; the excitement is a little too much for me; Im confused by the noise; this place is stuffed with smoke and you know I dont smoke; some of the Scotch has gone to my head; the air will do me good; drowning in music; the drilling of a thousand lunatic violins.*

Among shouts of *See you at the boat,* Sanford left with the blue.

He felt that getting rid of her was imperative, getting rid of her at once. Not wanting to talk, not having a thing he cared to say to her, he took her to Grand Central to get her bag out of the checkroom. After that, he put her up at the McAlpin and left her there. Alone in the street again, he suddenly wanted all his friends to know that he did not love her; they would see that if he went right back to the café without her. He got into a cab and told the driver to *Make it snappy to Fiftythird and Broadway, the Kav Kaz,* but by the time he reached there, the party had gone.

The next day, when he returned to the McAlpin to take the blue to lunch, he carelessly suggested a place where they had hung out during their early lovebungling. Now he found that it had darling memories clinging like parasitic creepers to the tiresome walls. He thought *And I wanted to go back and see the old place. But the old place is never there. Its a slight stale stink you remember far down in the back of your head.* The restaurant was in Greenwich Village; it was on Macdougal Street. Sanford thought *Writers come here. Painters, too. Writers with neverpressed pants, lastmonths socks, lastsummers shirts, lastyears noserags. Painters with greasefilthy blackslime hands that are perpetually in mourning for their crimes, hatchments shrouding the food they intellectually hoist illmanneredly to their intellectual mouths that look like sewers. And bitchwomen, too; bitchwomen fooled into vague gasping dreams of sleeping with greatness and sucking through the mobile lips of their enormous urns all the blear of Washington Square. Soursmelling winebottlewomen. The mean base scum. The hacks of the world.* A few poets came in and crammed the air with loud talk. Sanford believed he could almost touch the odor the talk almost had. The room stank of poets and was polluted by the glib muck of their bellowed excellence. Sanford thought *Id like to fire off a blunderbuss of dung right in their mugs, the subFourteenth Street bums.* In a yellow corner, at a table cluttered roundly with ashtrays and claybrown jugs, sat a horsy knot of rockchested lesbians, flatheeled whores for women, short hair, pat faces.

Sanford thought *Lets leave the ashes for the pretty octoroon to sweep away. You cant resurrect dust. You cant recompose it.*

He said *Lets get out of here before I go nuts.*

The blue had no complaint to make.

She left for home early that evening. Again Sanford had the pleasure of seeing her accompany red dark self dying lamps down a deep tunnel. When they went out, his body felt as mushy and knockedin as a hunk of dough, but that time he did not cry, nor did he bang his head against a wall.

❧

Sanfords predeparture excitement wore through the catalepsy caused by the blue. He told himself that he hoped to be away for years, that perhaps he would never return. To be away for years. To be away from ones own, ones native land. He thought of Edward Everett Hale and his mouth started to twist, but when he thought again of Philip Nolan, he smiled. What was the schoolboy fable? A *who is not?* promising young officer whose career was circumcised by *God damn these United States; may I never see or hear of them again. God damn these United* he said, this Nolan boy. *May I never see or hear* he said.

Sanford knew the story. He knew the *real* story.

They put Nolan aboard an outwardbounder and confined him to his cabin until land had dropped below the curving sky.

Bring Mr Nolan up to the quarterdeck, Mr Detwiler. A crisp salute made the Captain happy. He folded his hands astern and thoughtfully scratched the left cheek of his behind. He paced up and down the deck surveying his universe: Ardent young faces under patent leather hats; grizzled veterans rigidly at attention; a file of officers at a respectful distance; masts, spars, guns, sky and water. The Captain looked at the American flag and felt a thrill of pride crawl slowly up his keel. Again he raked his backside with the broadside of his hand. The thrill continued to barnacle his hull.

Mr Nolan, sir, at your service.

The Captain squinted at the young man who stood before him. He did not like the look in Nolans eyes. He would put a crimp in the upstart before he finished, thought the Captain. *That damned thrill again, but I guess its just seeing the flag.* Captain Bilge took a few folded sheets of paper from the breast of his coat.

Mr Nolan, I greatly regret the sad duty it is mine to GOD DAMN IT, YOU STINKING LANDLUBBER. LUFF A BIT TO STAHBD perform. I greatly regret my split infinitive. Mine is a most oppressive business, sir, but I wish it clearly understood that I express no personal feeling in the matter. I am simply doing my duty. At this, the Captain considerately lowered his eyes, but not so far that he could not observe tokens of approval among his men, nor were his ears too distant for him to hear *Wonderful old chap; forgiving nature; soft as a babe; fat slob; think its fixing for a bit of a blow; grand old man.*

SILENCE the Captain gently roared as he flipped open the pages of the commitment with his right hand and tapped the sheets with the backs of four fingernails on his left.

Mr Nolan remained silent. The expression on his face did not change until the end of the show.

The Captain said *Whereas Civilian Nolan hath, againſt the peace, wellbeing and integrity of the Union, committed divers, ſeveral and ſundry crimes. And whereas ſaid Civilian Nolan hath, by a competent jury of his equals, been tried. And whereas ſaid Civilian Nolan hath, of the crimes aforeſaid, been found, by the jury aforeſaid, guilty. And whereas ſaid Civilian Nolan hath, of the ſaid crimes, been duly, properly, and in the manner preſcribed by law, convicted. And whereas ſaid Civilian Nolan hath, when interrogated whether he had anything to ſay before the paſſing of ſentence upon him, replied in manner following: God damn theſe.* The Captain sucked desperately at the floating syllables. *God damn theſe blankblanks; may I never ſee or hear of them again. And whereas the ſaid declaration of the ſaid Civilian Nolan hath been wholly volitional, unſolicited, unprompted, and obtained without the uſe of force and arms, but on the contrary, gently and with a gentle hand. NOW, THEREFOR, be it decreed that ſuch ſhall be the puniſhment of ſaid Civilian Nolan as he himſelf hath requeſted. So ordered.* The Captain folded the commitment and put it back in his pocket. *Mr Nolan, I feel it is also my duty to add a few words of my own. The journals have been full of your case for a long time. Naturally, I have come to know considerable about it. I may say that I pride myself on my knowledge of public affairs. All citizens ought to have enough interest in . . . but that is hardly to the point. Although certain sheets of the yellower vibgYor kind find extenuating circumstances, in the nature of a plea that you uttered your words in a fit of passion, weariness and disgust, let me say that the law here involved takes no cognizance of the state of mind in which you were at the time of your infamous declaration. But there, Mr Nolan. At the outset, I said that I was going to give no personal opinion. I shall keep my word. Suffice it, if I had my way with you, you would get your bloody belly stove in. That is just between you and me, however. Here, the concern is not with the legal effect of your possible state of mind, but only with the consequences of your words. You cursed our MY country. It is yours no longer, Mr Nolan.* The Captain stopped for a moment *I wish I could scratch my.* He scraped loose a squid of phlegm from the plumbing of his throat and arched it into the ocean. Then he continued. *And you said: God damn these blank-blanks; may I never see or hear of them again. You never shall. It is your fate to sail the bounding.* Captain Bilge omitted the last word of the phrase as too reminiscent. *The bounding blank until the day you die, sir. And you shall die without ever again seeing those blank-blanks which to you were so abhorrent. Never again shall you set eyes on shores that once were your own. Never. Never again, though on clear days you strain westward to cull the flot and jettery—aye, the Flotzenstern and Jetzencrantz—for a faroff churchspire. It shall not be there, Mr Nolan, it shall not be there. Forever shalt thou be outof-sightofland. You have bid goodbye to the earth.* The Captains rudder ran hot with thrills. Flanked forbiddingly by his inferior officers, Deweys and Farraguts all, there he stood ramming the cutwater of his fingers through the groundswell of his rump.

A faint voice whistling through the rigging: *O, Mr Orchardson, please come back and paint this picture.*

Captain Bilge shot a cuff and scanned it for his scribbled figures of knockthemdeadthedogs speech. *Nor shall the name of that which you seek ever again be mentioned in your presence. Those are our orders, Mr Nolan, and that is our duty. But because once in the now dimdistantvagueandforgotten past, you bore the indiciasymbolstrappingsanddevices of an officer under the flag of the blankblanks, you shall continue to receive the respectdeference-courtesyandconsideration that would have been the due of your for-mer exalted station, a station you no longer hold even nominally. For the rest, it shall be as of yore, Mr Nolan, though the telltale insignia shall be stripped from you, and though from your person now goes all the power ordinarily associated with braidbuttonbeltandsword. And, Mr Nolan, if I may be permitted a poetic moment, forever henceforth shall you be as an officer on indefinite leave, on eternal leave. Strip him, my hearties, and then to your quarters. YOU LOUSY BOOBY. I SAID LUFF A BIT TO STAHBD. That will be all, gentlemen.*

For the first time, Nolan changed his expression. He smiled.

Efteemed Mother*

And fo it was. Nolan fmiled when fentence was paffed, but he fmiled on the other fide of his face toward the end. . . . Every time we had to put into port for provifions, fhoreleave, or refitting, we ftuck Nolan onto another frigate outwardbound. . . . I was Nolans perfonal man. . . . You know, I have been failing the feven feas for fixtyfix years, fo they left me with Nolan all the time he was at fea. . . . Always I faw him growing more and more forrowfulike as the years went by and him not feeing his own his native land. Always I faw him growing nearer and nearer repentance, always leaning onto the fame place at the taffrail, always peering far away toward the horizon, as if by fquinting along the great blue comb ftuck in the head of the world, he could raife the Florida palmettoes, or the Virginia Blue Ridges. Never did he raife fo much as a blade of grafs. . . . Never did my maties fpeak of home when he was around, never of the United States. There was a year in the brig for ufing the words aboard fhip. . . . We all got to feeling forrylike for Nolan and did what we could to lighten things a bit for him, fuch as giving him a chew at our plugs, or inviting him down to mefs with us, or to our quarters. You know, fpecial treats. But it was no good at all. Always he had a look on his phiz as if he was fearching for fomething he could not find. . . . Well, that went on for all thofe years and you could fee he was gradually coming

*Extract from a letter found in a bottle in Chesapeake Bay.

to the end. He died from nothing in particular, juſt from continual ſearching. . . . I was with him when he died. I was in his cabin. His face was ſort of whitelike. Suddenlike, he raiſed himself on his elbows, ſtared into the diſtance, as if out there in his imagination he could ſee what he had been looking for all thoſe years, and then he ſaid right out loud to the crew of us that was there, with tears in his eyes, he ſaid: MATIES, I KNOW I DID WRONG AND MAY GOD HAVE MERCY ON MY SOUL. I GOT RELIGION NOW. I GOT RELIGION he ſaid. MATIES, I GOT A LAST REQUEST TO MAKE OF YOU, AND THAT IS YOU BURY ME IN THE AMERICAN FLAG. BURY ME IN THE RED, THE WHITE AND THE BLUE. WRAP THE STARS AND STRIPES ABOUT ME AND GIVE ME TO THE WAVES. I DID WRONG BY OUR COUN-TRY he ſaid. I CUSSED AND SWORE AT HER, BUT NOW I GOT RELIGION AND I AM SORRY. SAY FOR ME THAT I AM SORRY, BOYS, AND PRAY REMEMBER THE FLAG. . . . There were tears in all our eyes. It ſhowed that you cannot cuſs out your country and hope to proſper. We buried Nolan in the flag, though. . . . That is the ſtory of Philip Nolan, reſt his bones.

An American was a man who ran up escalators. Sanford thought his country was detestable. There was nothing in a nation to make him regret leaving it. It was taking the next train. One was as good as another. All wound up at the same place *All roads lead to home.* One reached there a little later. That was the only difference. Sanford wanted to be late, to lose an ambition of his country to get there first. He was sick of mens loyalty to geography, wearied by their *54-40 or FIGHT* attitude and their babyish arguments over invisible boundaries. The result would be the same if the figures were reversed; the big mob would fight just as hard for *40-54*. The fight was the attraction for the animal. How could you owe allegiance to an imaginary line? How could you say *This, this here and here, is America; this you see right here between these two seaboards, this gulf and those splashedout lakes - YOUR OWN, YOUR NATIVE LAND?*

Sanford thought the Rt Rev E. E. Hale had been seeing things *Breathes there a man with soul so dead.*

What the Hell did the soul have to do with it? How could you call your country the stuff, the blob of pink paint, inside the intangible fence? No one had a country. What part did you own? What part was yours? Name it. Point it out.

Aw, crap.

Either you owned it all, or you had no right to crawl over parts of it. Punishing a man for saying *God damn these United States; may I never see or hear of them again* was making a surveyor a national hero. The country was a plumbline and its national anthem was a table of logarithms. It was exclusionary theorizing; it was the old saw about States Rights.

There was no doubt about it any more, Sanford thought: Trespass was the great American tort. The absolute was the agreed. Inside the arbitrary absolute, GET TO HELL OFF. He thought *Put your foot in, let your pipesmoke drift across it, speak through the space over it, and youve committed a crime of which not even God can absolve you. Aye, the space over it to the heavens and beyond the heavens. Cujus est solum ejus est usque ad cælum. And the soil under it to the depths below. I own it. It came down to me from my great-greatgrandfather. How did he get it? Easy. Why, he stole it from the Indians for a dimes worth of calico you wouldnt use even to swab out your toilet with. Thats how the old horsethief got it. But you just try to take it away from me.*

Up.

Here.

Down.

Someone owned it all, Sanford thought. When you talked of a

country, you really talked of a corporeal hereditament; you talked
of distances and courses; of monuments and fences; of

> rubbish thrown on adjoining premises;
> election between jointure and dower;
> water as a movable wandering thing;
> private property : no trespassing;
> lands held in adverse possession;
> bugs as an excuse for surrender;
> private road : no thoroughfare;
> the rule against perpetuities;
> fruit on an overhanging tree;
> usque ad medium filum aquae;
> heirs of patriotic Indians;
> the rule in Shelleys case;
> cujus est solum ejus est;
> the power of alienation;
> estates pour autre vie;
> restrictive covenants;
> the cy pres doctrine;
> death without issue;
> champertous grants;
> lineal warranties;
> metes and bounds;
> borough English;
> treasure trove;
> chattels real;
> Magna Charta;
> coparcenary;
> quitclaims;
> gavelkind;
> mortmain;
> erosion;
> seizin;
> dower;
> uses.

$24 worth of beads.

$24 worth of beads.

$24 worth of beads.

Sanford thought *For water is a movable wandering thing and must of necessity continue common by the law of nature, so that I can have therein only a temporary usufructuary right.*

He remembered the law *No man may erect any building, or the like, to overhang another mans land. Downward, whatever is in a direct line between the surface of any land and the center of the earth, belongs to the owner of the surface, so that the land includes not only the face of the earth, but everything under it or over it.* Pieces of Heaven, Hell, and mundane limbo.

As though the world were too large, Sanford thought. He believed that love of country reduced itself to the opposite of what it purported to stand for:

nation

state

country

city

borough

ward

block

house

flat

room

overcoat

jacket

waistcoat

shirt

bvd

SELF

It was some kind of a joke.

The day of departure.

Get me a cab Sanford said.

A trunk and two valises sat on the sidewalk and a doorman ran up the street. Sanford walked to the corner of Riverside Drive. It was late afternoon; in an hour it would be sunset. The beams were longslanting with the downpress of the sun. The eastern face of the Jersey embankment was almost hidden in its own shadow, and purple back of the stiff sunfronds that came over the top to jab the ripples of the Hudson. A streetcar, transformed by the distance into the luminous larva of an insect, crawled slowly up the Palisades through the shadow. On the Drive, motorcars went north in a long chain. The doorman came to say that the baggage had been put in a cab.

Sanford went back to the machine and said *Go by way of the Drive down the west side to the Cunard piers. The S.S. Caronia.*

The cab went down the hill and turned south. As it passed the Soldiers and Sailors Monument, Sanford thought of bully beef, dysentery, Mausers, smokeless powder and the blockhouse at El Caney. For him, the SpaniSHAMerican war had always been a romantic affair, with just enough killings to avoid a burlesque, but not so many that the war had been real. The soldiers had worn becoming hats. Their KragJorgensens had blown to pieces in their hands. The Press had made a big noise about the glory of the roughriders and the victories at Manila and Santiago, but the Spics were such lousy gunners and the Americans such awfully good fellers that the war had lost all its terrors. Even the name of the war was a giveaway.

The cabdriver nearly ran over an old woman at Seventyfourth Street and the Drive. He swore long and intricately at her while she backed up to the curb and jellied there.

At Sixtysecond Street and Eleventh Avenue, the air sagged out of an aged tire and it went as flat and loose as an empty enema bag. Sanford climbed out over his valises and looked on. The spare tire with which Ilario Putso *If anyone else is driving this cab, call a policeman* was struggling, looked older, than the one that had blown. It was bandaged in black tape and bore several patches where rips in the casing had been vulcanized. Putso took a long time to change the shoe.

Sanford, walked over to a fence and looked at the New York Central freightyards. From where he stood, the tracks fanned out in long fingers to the north. Hauling a halfmile string of opendoored empties, a small switching locomotive puffed by *C., C., C. & St. L.; Rock Island; Western Pacific; Seaboard Air Line; N. Y., N. H. & H.* cars from all over the country. Sanford thought that railroads had attractive names *Nickel Plate, Hocking Valley, Grand Trunk, Central Vermont, Florida East Coast, Denver & Rio Grande, Monon, Pere Marquette, Central of Georgia.* When he was a child, his favorite had been the *Big Four,* but he never found out what they were. On the river side of the yards, a few tracks held files of oldfashioned cars. They had no vestibuling and were humped up in the middle like old people. Sanford thought that cars and locomotives had always reminded him of people and animals *Some are grouchy and snobbish. Those are the engines on the limiteds and the fast mails. You guess they dont want you to look at them and that theyre sore at everybody. The locos on the freights are bulldogs and pant like bull-dogs. The shunters are donkeys, shortlegged and longeared. The ends of passenger cars look like faces perpetually astonished, but some-times the vestibuling makes me think of mouths put up for kissing. The old cars with roofs that bend down at the ends make me think of overhanging brows and buck teeth. The back platforms of the cabooses make scowling faces, but you arent scared of a caboose the way you are of a loco because you know its really a friendly car. It wears a funny little hat on top and in wet weather, theres a man in the hat. The cabooses make me laugh.*

The freighttrain reminded him of something that had happened while he was bumming back east from Oregon many years before *I was riding on top of an empty that was way back in the train, so far back that I couldnt see the white hall of the headlight, or the yellow pyramid breaking out of the opened firebox, not even when we went around a bend. There werent any stars out and the train seemed to be going through a tunnel. That was nearly true, because we were drop-ping fast down a valley and the walls of the valley went straight up and maybe closed over us once in a while. The noise of the rods and wheels* got louder in places and you could hear the rattling coming back at you as soon as it hit the walls. In other places, the noise didnt hit the walls, but spread out and got smaller before it came back. I didnt know where we were bound for. Id gotten on at a waystop a lot of miles back when the train pulled up to let off half a car of cases. I asked the shack if I could ride and he said yes if I helped them unload, so we stacked up hundreds of small cases in a freighthouse while another shack held a lantern on us. It was warm in the house, but I didnt mind, because the cases werent heavy and anyhow I was going to get a ride. Once in a while we sat down on the cases and had a comfortable smoke and a pull of coffee out of a can that one of the shacks got out of the caboose. They looked like pretty decent guys, not the usual hollering crowd you saw around the yards in the big towns. They didnt carry those short clubs around with them, either, and when they talked to you, they were pretty friendly about it. It was easy to see they were nice guys. At least, for shacks. After a while, the engineer came back to find out why we were taking such a long time with the cases. I felt like asking him if I could ride in the cab, but he looked as if he could get pretty rough if he wanted to, so I didnt ask him. Then we got busy and cleaned out the rest of the cases. The engineer went up ahead to wait for the signal and I looked at the shack for what to do. He came over and told me to wait till everybody was out of sight, and then hook on, so I waited and finally I couldnt see anybody. Then I heard a couple of blasts from up ahead and I climbed to the top of an empty. I stood there while the train pulled out toward the main line. I stood there till something slapped me across the face and chest and shoulders, and then I sat down as fast as I could. The things that hit me were those little knotted whips they fringe across the tracks to warn you to duck your dome. When I sat down, I thought maybe we were going into a tunnel, but when I saw wires a foot over my head, I was glad theyd hung those whips. The expresses got their power from those wires. A foot over my head as I sat there. Then I rolled over on my side and the wires were further away, but when I thought how close Id come, I was glad about the whips. The train was going along pretty fast and it was downhill all the way. On account of the wires, I was sorry I hadnt gotten inside the empty, but there was nothing I could do about it, because it was too dark to try to climb down and anyhow we were going too fast. I lay there across the car, holding on with my fingers stuck in the cracks of the slatwalk. It wasnt such a good hold, but I didnt think I could be knocked loose unless there was a wreck, so I lay there and wondered why the shack hadnt warned me to watch out for the wires. When I guessed what had been in his mind, I thought I must have been wrong about his being such a nice guy. WHAT THE HELL ARE YOU DOING HERE? I was so jumpy I came near rolling off the car when I made a quick turnaround to see who was there. A guy was lying on his belly five feet away from me. From what I could see, he didnt look like a nice guy around the eyes. He just lay there and looked hard at me and I didnt like the look on his face. HOW WOULD YOU LIKE TO GET PITCHED OFF ON YOUR HEAD? That was bad talk. I got scared. The guy looked as if he could do it. I couldnt understand what he had against me. Id done nothing to him and didnt know who he was. HOW WOULD YOU LIKE ME TO CHUCK YOU UP AGAINST THOSE WIRES, YOU LITTLE LOUSE? I thought he was crazy. I couldnt talk. He was acting as if he wanted to murder me, but if he were crazy, he didnt need a reason and hed do it for nothing. I wanted to talk, but I was scared to open my mouth, because that might have been the touchoff, so I shut up. I waited to see what hed do and he crept a little nearer. The train was breezing downhill and the cars swayed like rockers when we hit the curves. IF I PUSH YOU OFF THE CAR ON ONE OF THESE BENDS, YOULL HAVE A DROP OF ABOUT FOUR HUNDRED FEET STRAIGHT DOWN BEFORE YOU STOP MOVING. The train was going down fast, about fortyfive an hour. THE ENGINEERS NAME IS BRAKES-OFF SMITH. IF I DONT PUSH YOU OFF, YOULL GET PILED UP SOMEWHERE, SO WHATS THE DIFFERENCE? LAST YEAR HE PILED UP THREE REDBALLS. ONCE HE SNAPPED OFF A CABOOSE ON THE FEATHER RIVER OUTFIT AND THE CAR TOOK TWO MEN WITH IT TO THE BOTTOM OF THE RIVER AFTER FALLING A HUNDRED YARDS. SMITH LOST HIS JOB AFTER THAT AND THEN HE CAME OVER HERE. HES KNOWN ALL OVER NEVADA. WHY SHOULDNT I PUSH YOU OFF? I tried to back away along the car, but he came after me fast and got hold of *my wrist. When I pulled at the grip, it was like trying to get my fist through a keyhole. One of his hands was bigger than both of mine, and when he had a grip on my wrist, his palm came halfway up my arm. I said WHAT HAVE YOU GOT AGAINST ME? He said I DONT LIKE YOU. YOU LOOK LIKE A COLLEGE GUY. I SAW YOU WHEN YOU GOT ON. I HATE COLLEGE GUYS. I GOT A GOOD MIND TO PUSH YOU OFF THIS CAR. NO ONE IS GOING TO MISS YOU. WHAT COLLEGE? I said LAFAYETTE. He said LOUSY. THEYRE ALL LOUSY. YOURE A LITTLE LOUSE. DO YOU KNOW THAT? A LITTLE LOUSE. WHAT GOOD DID COLLEGE EVER DO YOU? ALL YOU LEARNED THERE CANT STOP ME FROM PUSHING YOU OFF THIS CAR. NOTHING CAN STOP ME, NOT ALL THE COLLEGES ROLLED INTO ONE. LAFAYETTE. A LOUSY DUMP. IF IT DIDNT HAVE A GOOD PROFESSIONAL FOOTBALL TEAM, NO ONE WOULD HAVE HEARD OF THE JOINT. I TELL YOU, I GOT A GOOD MIND TO PUSH YOU OFF. The guy took his hand off me to light a cigarette. He cupped the match in his hands and I got a good look at his pan. His eyes were solid green and his nose was long and fine and matched up with the shape of his face, long and fine. His teeth were white and in pretty good condition. I guessed he was about thirtyfive. His suit had a good cut and it was pressed and clean and his hat looked English. He didnt look like a bum at all. If you saw him walking along the street, youd think he was a nice guy, all except the eyes. Every time he took a drag on his butt, his green eyes showed up light green, like southern water. I couldnt understand why he talked like that. He was lying on his belly and elbows and looking at me. I could only think of his green eyes that got lit up from his butt. When I reached into my pocket for a smoke, he must have thought I was going for a gun, because his eyes came out of his head like swords and he grabbed my hand and nearly pulled it off me. He said WHAT ARE YOU TRYING TO DO? I said JUST GET A SMOKE. He said THATS ALL RIGHT THEN. I THOUGHT MAYBE YOU WERE GOING TO GET GAY WITH ME. YOU CAN SMOKE IF YOU WANT TO. He let go of my hand again and we lay there stretched out like that for a couple of hours. Then the sky began to get light over the other side of the valley. The cut wasnt so deep any more and I could see flashes of river sometimes. Then, without a word, the guy started to crawl away along the car. I watched him as he made his way under the wires from car to car. When he was about fifteen cars back, he let himself down between two cars and I didnt see him again. When the shack came along later, I asked him who the guy was, the guy with the green eyes. The shack said he didnt know.*

Putso said *I fixed the flat.*

Sanford came away from the railroadtracks and got into the cab. As it went down Eleventh Avenue, it nearly collapsed. The fenders rang iron. A rusted springcurl came through the seat and corkscrewed into Sanfords calf. He thought *Ilario spits out his desperation and Putsoscreams curses at gear and cog. Wails, wails, quavering singsong curses UpAnDoWn. In the oily junction of cogtenon and rigormortise, they marry and the beetle, with its yellow little roundbackdown, crawls away.* The windows rattled in their sliding sockets and then one of the slotstraps whipped out of its groove. The tinframed glass sank fast into the rectangular anus of the door to smash in an iron smother. A windriven curse sprayed Sanford with a fine brown mist of tobacco and garlic. Ilario cursed the Putsocram into the gutter, and again a garlictinted brown floated back into Sanfords eyes. The cab crawled near the steaming belly of a spotted dray hauling a truck loaded with fresh meats and provisions. Traffic was stopped. The dray pissed swift and steamly, pursed and then quickly distended its ass with a volley of oatsmooth farts. Putso took off his jacket. He was wet with selfdew under the arms; his black hair was matted like wet straw in a stall, wetblack like tidewater, like bilgewater. Ilario Putsocursed again and then the cab threaded over the lumpy cobbles of Eleventh Avenue.

Through each crosstreet, Sanford could see a dock jutting out into the river like a spike off the bill of a swordfish. No, not a swordfish. Sanford thought of Manhattan Island as a paramœcium *The onecelled animal most frequently found in hay infusions is the paramœcium, or slipper animalcule. This cell is elongated, oval, or elliptical in outline, but somewhat flattened. The more pointed end of the body, the anterior, usually goes first. The protoplasm appears to be bounded by a very delicate membrane through which project numerous delicate threads of protoplasm called cilia. A very good recitation, Mr Sanford. Take an A.*

In the waterfront afternoon, the salmon of the sky was skirted with the angularity of piers. The cab lunged through the arch of a dungeon cut out of a dock near the Fourteenth Street meatmarkets, went on into complete and then lessening darkness, the sun framed by the dockheart sending a far taper of light into Sanfords face.

He heard the dull roar of tunnels, the sharp slap of crates and squawking boards, the snap of grain starting nailheads. The air whirled splinters. A stevedore spit orders through the rheumy eye of a whistle buried in a corner of his mouth like a cigar butt still shrouded in leadfoil. A trunktruck, piled ten feet high with luggage, shoved up its blunt nose and stopped. Sanford read of Lago Maggiore, Wien, Taormina, Cunard, Carcassonne. He saw a Venetian blackandorange sunset cut in two by a gondolier. He saw a skijumper taking flight at St. Moritz into mountains of papertorn drift below; against the blue and paper piles, he sprawled heavily, like a pelican, as he flapped slowly down to blow up reluctant flurries of snowpaper drift.

The truck moved on and there came the smell of tar on rope, and again the retch of nails out of wetwood; a swelling and sounding of the sea; a soft flap of splintercoated wash on tartarscummed planking as loose as old teeth in the tide, moving slowly and loosely to the ginger exploration of the seas old inquisitive tongue; slight smells of sewage, of depths and riverbed mud; a wet splash and running, a sucking through the cavities between the plankteeth; a wash of oily gurgles and small pops of air bursting to air again; small sounds and endless. Sanford thought of the scum that filmed the smooth green hair of the boarding. He looked down over the edge of the pier and saw an eggcrate crunched on a surge into the piles. Caught a dozen ways at once, it dropped its parts and they floated out on the weedy breast of the current.

Sanford was at the boat three hours before sailing time.

A steward showed him to his cabin, a small compartment on B deck, aft of the middle of the ship. There were two bunks in the cabin, one above the other, but only the lower had been made. While

Sanford was looking around, the steward began touching invisible wrongs until he made Sanford nervous with his flicking and patting. Sanford asked him what was the matter. The steward said that he was merely putting the cabin in order. As he spoke, he touched off a wrinkle on the made bunk, swooping on it like a peregrine. A quick distant stoop and the crease, almost nonexistent before, was made to disappear.

Sanford asked the man what his name was.

The man said *Snipe, sir.*

Sanford told him to open the porthole and then see about the baggage.

Snipe said *Very good, sir* and did as he was told.

When Sanford was alone, he turned out the light and sat down on the bunk. The cabin was on the port side, away from the dock, but Sanford could still hear the sounds of the dock and river. The cabin had a smell that annoyed him, a clean smell, but an oversweet one that reminded him of the blossoms on a privet hedge; the cabin smell was weaker and less nauseating, but the slight sweetness now in the air made Sanford get up and go over to the porthole. He put his head close to the opening and smelled paint. Then the smell of the river came through the paint. Sanford wondered what gave the river its smell. It was odorless at Thurman, where the Schroon joined it. There the water was light green and thin, as cold as if it came from a spring. While swimming in it, Sanford had filled his belly with the water, the Hudson water. But here, among the docks, it stank *For water is a movable wandering thing.* What made it stink? People, sewage, garbage, tin cans, rust, rats, rotting wood, sputum, newspapers, cigar and cigarette shags, ginbottles, fruitcores, Merry Widows, dead fish, bones, coaldust, crudeoil, old shoes, old hats, old socks, old People. Down here, the river stank worse than a public urinal, Sanford thought.

Snipe knocked on the door and came in with Sanfords valises. In a moment, he returned with the steamertrunk on his back.

Sanford said that he wanted to be left alone while he unpacked. He turned on the light.

Again Snipe said *Very good, sir* and went out.

Sanford sat down on the floor and opened the trunk. Remembering his game with the red cloth set of Shakespeare, he felt foolish when he saw the neat arrangement of his belongings. Why all the care, he wondered. Suppose he had forgotten something. Suppose an article were out of place. What difference would it make? Why was he playing *postal clerk* with his personal property? He took some hangers out of the closet and started to put away his suits, hoping that none of his friends came while his partly emptied trunk lay open in the middle of the floor. The exposure of his belongings gave him the feeling of being naked. Articles of personal property were private parts, but parts unrelated and scattered. Collecting and arranging them meant unification, always a private process. When all the clothes were out of the trunk, Sanford reached two layers of books. They were all those from his office library that he had never read, books with imposing names, books that were supposed to indicate to the informed a skill in choice, a niceness of taste, almost a scholarly mind that delighted in the somewhat unusual, the recondite and the precious. Sanford now felt like chucking them through the porthole. Then the river would stink of books, too. In the name of Christ, why had he brought them along? He closed the trunk again, leaving the books inside.

After a while, many of his friends came and crammed the small cabin with eager bodies. Sanford could not tell whether their eagerness was flattering; they might be glad he was going away. There was small talk by everyone. There were small jokes. There were stunted orations. Sanford hated to watch people strain themselves into a hernia to make rotten puns and to twist every dull word into an even duller joke. He answered questions and made statements out of nowhere. None of his talk came back.

One of the visitors was flopped across Sanfords bunk. Three others walled him in. Sanford sat in a corner. He asked someone what time it was. Ten oclock. That left one more hour of the United States. The girl had promised to come down to the boat. Sanford wondered whether she would make it in time. He wondered whether he wanted her to.

The air now stank inside the cabin. Sanford suggested that everyone go up on deck. He wanted to stand near the gangplank and watch for the girl. The crowd went up to the deck and collected in a weaving knot where they would be certain to miss nothing.

At tenfifteen, Sanford saw the girl coming up the gangplank. She had on a black coat and hat. A few American Beauty rosebuds were pinned on her shoulder. The flowers matched the girls mouth, but her face was very white and her smiling gave her no color.

She said hello to everyone and then Sanford asked her to walk around the deck with him. They were given the haha as they walked away. It was dark at the aft end of the deck and they stopped there. The girl put her arms around Sanfords neck and gave him a long kiss. Then she took her arms away and pulled a flower out of the bunch on her shoulder. When she put it through Sanfords lapel, she nearly started to cry. Sanford was embarrassed.

Thanks for the rose Sanford said. *Its beautiful and its got a fine smell. Do you want me to get sentimental and say Im going to keep it forever, or may I treat it lightly and throw it away when it begins to stink?*

The girl said *If I asked you hard enough, would you do something for me?*

Maybe I would.

I dont want you to go away the girl said. *I want you to stay here. Youve still got time to cancel your reservation. You can still get your stuff off the boat.*

You must be crazy Sanford said.

Im all right. You want to go away for a couple of years. What for? You dont have to go. Youre doing fine right now. Theres nothing you can get in England that you cant get here.

Sanford said *I dont know how far youll go with this, so Im telling you that nothing will do any good. Nothing in Christs world can stop me this time. If you cant see that Ive got to get the Hell out of here, then it was a waste of time knowing you.*

For a moment, she looked at Sanford, holding both his arms

tightly during that time. Then she said *Forget that I talked like this, because when you come back, I wont be this way. Forget about it. Forget that I said anything. You wanted to know about the flower.*

Sanford tried to see her face. He said *Yes, I wanted to know about the flower.*

Well, do anything you like with it.

Then thanks again for it. I thought maybe it had strings of junk attached. This is a time for handkerchief waving and farewells, for tears and promises, but because my handkerchief is dirty and because I dont mean to bawl over promises I never made, all I can do is say goodbye.

The girl said *Say it right.*

Its the same old stuff Sanford said. *I used to get drunk when I said goodbye. I used to feel pleasure when the plunger came up in my throat.* He pulled her body close to his and kissed her all over her face, but he stayed longest on her mouth and was so pleased because it still tasted of milk that he wanted to break into a laugh. *Listen* he said. *Ive had a lot of fun these last few weeks and Im sorry if it hasnt been true the other way round. If you get fun out of good things said about you, pick out the nicer words I used to you and remember them. Forget the hard ones, the toughguy words. Youre really fine.*

The girl said *Thats a long speech from a hater like you. I didnt think youd ever be so careless, but I dont mean to knock down what you said. I like what you said. If you talked like that before, Id not have told you to get the Hell out of my room.*

Quit it Sanford said. *All youre out to do is make the next couple of years seem like twenty. These weeks have been the best part of the past. I want to go away still liking this part, not spoiling it by regrets that it wasnt a larger part.*

The girl said *Right. This is a bum kind of goodbye stuff. A couple of years. Thats a long time. Just say youll write and Ill feel better about it. Thats bad, too, but whats the harm if I get ordinary at the last?*

Sanford said *Ill write. Ill write often. Ill tell you everything Ive done. Now we have to go back, but first give me another kiss.*

His mouth got stopped up with her lips. They stood there with their mouths joined until they heard the roaring of Sanfords crowd as they came down the deck looking for him. They found Sanford and the girl in the dark. Then there were more stale jokes. A steward passed by. He was hollering that the ship was going to sail in fifteen minutes *All ashore thats going ashore.*

Sanford and his friends went back to the head of the gangplank. People were going down backward, waving, yelling all kinds of things, making faces. Hundreds already on the dock kept up a loud noise and constant movement. Only the *Caronias* siren came out of the level roar of voices, and for the last five minutes, it was all siren and no voices. When Sanfords friends had gone down the gangplank and jammed their way through the mob, he went to the rail and screamed at them, but he could not hear a word come out of his mouth. Then the crowd below disappeared and became a figure in a black hat and coat with a small blur of red on the shoulder. Sanford looked at the girl and shouted as loud as he could into the noise, until his mouth went dry and sharp and his voice hurt him when it came up to his mouth, but he was all deaf. Except for the siren. The girl was looking up at him. When he knew that she could not make out what he was saying, he became angry and profane and poured a string of swearwords into the noise. Two men, one on each side of him, started to crowd him away from the rail. He turned from one to the other and hollered *Sonofabitch, sonofabitch, you lousy sonofabitch*, but the men only smiled and hunched up their shoulders. Sanford looked back at the girl on the pier and finally he had to smile and hunch up his own shoulders.

The *Caronia* was swinging a little away from the pier and slowly backing out into the dark river. When the boat started to move, so did the people, sideways out toward the end of the pier. Sanford no longer tried to talk, or even signal to the girl, both merely looking at each other across the space between them. Sanford tried to think why he had nothing to think about. One of his crossed arms on the rail came against the rosebud in his lapel and he looked down at it, even though he knew the girl was watching him. He thought of chucking the rose into the water as a final cynical gesture, but he wanted to keep the flower and had to laugh at himself for being the same as everything he had said he hated.

He lost sight of the girl as the liner floated out into the pull of the tide. The end of the pier was still bright and full of movement. The siren stopped and again there were voices coming over the water. Puffing mightily, two tugs shoved the stem of the *Caronia* downstream and then swung off when the ship began to go with the current. Punctured by blocks of pale gold, purple masses of stone slid by.

After lower Manhattan, there was little to be seen, but Sanford did not have to see the bay to remember it. From his many trips across it in the Jersey Central steamers, he knew it as well as he did the Boat Pond. He did not have to look in order to place the islands and the forts; he did not have to wonder what the lights were that came from all directions across the water. When the *Caronia* went through the Narrows, he saw the outlines of Fort Wadsworth on the starboard side; the fort was dark and square and the paths along the terraces were invisible, but as though it were daytime, Sanford read on the east wall of the fort *Cable Crossing—Do Not Anchor.*

He walked the decks until all the other passengers had gone below. By that time, the boat was beginning to fall away slightly from under his feet as it struck a series of rollers outside the lower bay. Sanford stopped at the port rail and looked back for the lights of the city. There were still a few in Coney Island.

He spoke the words *Not till the waters refuse to glisten for you.* Then he went down to his cabin.

PART
VI

Sanford

saw them first the evening of the first day. The placecards read:

Mr K. Seton-Jakes
Mrs K. Seton-Jakes
Mr John B. Sanford

Mr K. Seton-Jakes came in wearing a longcoat that had dubious elbows, and an offwhite waistcoat that looked like cream under the electriclight. Mrs K. Seton-Jakes followed *dull*, the reigning rage, age fortyseven *dull*. Sanford was dressed in an old gray suit and a softcollared shirt. The Seton-Jakes would not open up to him, not even with a *Would you please pass*. After dinner, Sanford asked the chief steward to move him to another table where he could be alone and watch the lovely Mrs Mary Grove.

That evening, he followed her around the decks. He thought she was very lovely. He thought she had a good name, Mary Grove.

He wondered why Broadbent had lied about her. He wondered how he knew that Broadbent had been lying. He thought *By the way, I want you to meet Vaughan Broadbent, of Proveedence. Alma mater,*

Brownooray. A betting man, this Broadbent. The ships run; the probable course; the latitude; the longitude; the visible surface area; the horsepower; the number of revolutions; the World Series; the winner of the Cesarewitch; the direction in which the Captain would spit. And a drinking man, this Broadbent. His favorite, Beaujolais. He drinks it with everything on the card, from poached eggs to peanuts. He drinks it as an aperitif, a bracer, an elevenoclocker, a highnooner, a teaball, a dinneradowner, a tenoclocksocker, a nightcap, water. And a tipping man, this Broadbent. Shillings by the score. Correct. So meet Vaughan Broadbent, always stinking of drink, always tipping, always betting, always Broadbent, of Proveedence.

Sanford wondered how he knew that Broadbent had been lying. He thought *A Don Jewanne, too, this Broadbent, always boasting of his love sexesses.*

Broadbent had pointed a finger at the lovely Mary Grove and said *I made her the night the boat sailed. First night out. Pretty fast work, I calls it. I was drunk when I came aboard and had to go up to the boat deck for a breather. There she was, sitting on a bench. She was drunk, too. I sat down. It was dark. First thing you know she was laying all over me. First night out. Take it or leave it.*

Sanford had thought *What the Hell?*, and left.

One morning, he stood at the aft end of the sports deck and watched the easy motion of the seagulls as they followed the ship. When he threw a butt out over the water, a gull fell fast from a height of about twenty feet and caught at the moving piece of white. Finding that it had picked up something it could not eat, it dropped the butt and planed up to the flock.

Sanford went to the dining saloon and asked a steward for a few slices of old bread. The steward brought a bowl of crusts out of the galley. Sanford broke them into chunks and wrapped them in a paper napkin. This he carried back to the deck. When he tossed out the first piece of bread, the gulls quarreled hoarsely and a dozen of them went for it, but a small lowflying bird was the first to reach it. Sanford watched the bird as it went out in a broad curve to come back for more. The underside of its body and wings were steam-white, but the top parts were broadly stroked with watercolor violet gray. The beak was yellow.

All the gulls flew in a circle, the rim coming to about five feet from the rail against which Sanford was leaning. He flung more bread to the flapping carousel of birds. In their UpAnDoWn circling, they reminded him of the painted wooden animals of a merrygoround. The gulls snatched at the bread as though the pieces were rings for a free ride. When all the bread was gone, Sanford let the wind take the paper napkin out of his fingers. As it tumbled astern, floating on a level with the main deck of the ship, all the gulls converged upon it, screaming at each other.

Machinery. Everyone went below at some time or other. Sanford, accompanied by Broadbent, made his pilgrimage at two oclock in the morning. Nickel rails buttered with grease lined the way down to the intestines of the ship, grease running on hot handrails that shivered with the regular pulse of the turbines. A stink of heating grease came up from the boileroom. All the way down, a solid shivering. The boileroom. An impassive platoon of Swedish stoves pimpled with rivets and clockface dials. Out under the stern, where the energy manufactured forward came to life in the whirling of the propellershafts, Sanford temporarily lost some of his apathy. Two feet thick, the horizontal columns were supported by rows of slotted cuffs. The slots were filled with cakes of grease the size of lawbooks, these pressing with only their own weight against the revolving, filming steel and steel. Each a hundred feet long, the two bars of steel were being excreted by the twin ani of the ship, but they flowered into propellers that made twentyfoot circles. Sanford thought *Well, whats so wonderful about it? Wheres the tin God you were hollering about? Its big. Sure its big. But Im damned if theres any more God in it than there is in a tackhammer. If theres a great big powerful God in a dynamo, then there must be a little one in a*

screwdriver or a pair of pliers, and maybe a more symmetrical one. Go on, you heel. Whats all this deification of the inanimate? What do I care that it once was alive? Whats that to me? Its dead now, like the bodies of the billions dead before we became. Why, we eat them every day. We live on the dead. But dead they are and dead they stay. Dead Gods arent any better than dead whores, are they? Or dead jackasses? Or dead skunks? Come on, heel. The Living One is all places and all times. Except dead places and dead times. Lemme scream it, you heel: THE EARTH IS NOT THE FLOOR.

There were porpoises off the Grand Banks. For a long time San-ford watched the play. The school came through the wavebellies like a pack of clowns through paper hoops. They came out in curving bursts, waves of pewter shine into waves of thick green, in following lines.

Eight of the ten dull days.

At breakfast one morning, a squeal burst from Mrs K. Seton-Jakes. Between orangejuice and hominy, she had raised Bishop Light. A rush to the portholes for verification. It was true. It was true. Little Mrs K. Seton-Jakes had really raised Bishop Light at breakfast. Sanford thought *First sight of England. Tall gray ghost in the nineoclock mist, tall gray ghost in the shifting mist of morning. The first of England.*

Pepperdust of landmounds fading grayed the water with an ashen scum, and then more water, soft and swelling softly, hardly rippled, until England came up a patched blanket into the sunlight above the sagging fog.

The Lizard.

Eddystone.

Plymouth.

From behind the fort that guarded a long breakwater at one

end of the bay, a small boat stood into the chop at the harbormouth off Penlee Head. After clearing the rough water, it came smoothly and slowly toward the *Caronia* and draped itself alongside. The *Sir Walter Raleigh*, steam tender. Standing above its stern, Sanford looked down from the boatdeck while passengers for the London boatrain bridged the betweening water. When the plank was in, there was an underwater slashing of brass fans, and burrowing spirals of white water were shoved into foam astern. Then Plymouth lost itself in its own haze.

Portland Bill.

Beachy Head.

Land floated up lavender in a portside mist. Even with glasses, all Sanford could see was a dim cluster of low and regular mounds against an acid sky sickly silver. Then the mounds disappeared and there was only water all ways, rolling quietly, but a feel from the water that land was near, a feel from the slow roll of the groundswell. Back west, the sun above the mist churned it to steam. The engines quit their sickening pound and the *Caronia* coasted over the water like a sledrunner on snow.

The pilot came out from shore in a battered cutter. It came hard against the hull of the liner and the top of its sawedoff mast struck the metal with each roll. The pilot caught a rung of the ladder lowered for him and started to haul himself clear. As he came up near the weaving mast of the cutter, it made a stoop for his back. Four men below lay half overside to stop the heeling, but the force of the water was too much for them. The mast dove, and then screeched. Sanford thought it had gotten the pilot flush on the spine. He was hidden behind a piece of canvas that had floated loose with the jarring, but then his hands came up, one over the other, one over the other, out of the swirl of rapping canvas. The cutter rolled off and began to fall astern as the wind caught hold of its soiled rags.

The Goodwin Sands.

On the purple banks of the Thames, the tips of dark trees jigged spots of silver; the black water, shuttling patches of silver. A tramp slushed by and was swallowed whole a hundred yards ahead. Before headway could be reduced, the *Caronia* went in after the tramp.

Sanford heard deep bells. The liner shuddered down to a slow skidding, the siren screaming alternately with a tolling bowbell. The sky stayed clear, the mist clawing up only to the decks of the ship. The mistop shone like aluminum. In the fogloom, there was a loss of identity. The human sank into the rising thing as men affectionated the siderails and palmed them as though it were good to feel the substance of a thing. The wood was human and differences were wornout gaskets between pride and fusion. Sanford watched the Rt Rev Dexter Ramrod offer an Egyptian cigarette to a bewildered Jew.

&.

It was late the following afternoon before Sanford could clear his baggage. He took a train from Woolwich to London, all the way sitting opposite the lovely Mary Grove.

When he reached London, he put up at the Norfolk, a small place in Surrey Street between the Strand and the Embankment. The hotel was dull and depressing. His room looked into a narrow gray court as dark as a manhole. When he sat down on the bed, he found that he had not yet lost the boatroll. The room swung under him like a trapeze. The blood pumped up behind his eyes, and his stomach went on a dizzy sideway skid. He felt sick in his head and neck, and had to soak his face in cold water at the sink before he could stop wanting to vomit.

After changing his clothes, he went downstairs to the diningroom, knowing all the time that he did not want to eat. Waiters were carrying trays that floated out foodsmells, and Sanfords face became stiff and cold again and he remembered having wanted to vomit. When he was asked what he would have to drink, he thought *Burgundy* was a pretty name and said that he would have some.

During dinner, he became drunk and laughed because the diningroom was so dull and depressing, and because, at the next table, a redfaced man ate very seriously. The room was quiet most of the time and only the tiniest silverplated tinkle of cutlery on china came to Sanfords ears. Through eyes that were rolling hingeless and starting out of his head like bungs, he saw that his laughter had alienated the affections of the redfaced man, but instead of feeling sorry, all Sanford could do was laugh again whenever he thought about the seriousness.

After dinner, he went out into the lobby and remembered that on the train to London he had asked the lovely Mary Grove whether she would see him that night; he remembered that she had said yes.

He asked a porter to tell him the way to a hotel called the Park Lane.

The porter wanted to know if he proposed to walk.

Sanford said he felt legless after the Burgundy and wanted to befoul his lungs with Londons nightsmell.

The porter wideopened his eyes and said that the Park Lane was in Piccadilly, opposite Green Park.

Sanford went into the street and walked as far as the Strand. When he reached it, he was lost. He stopped a constable and asked him for the names of the streets that went to the Park Lane. The constable gave him careful directions and Sanford kept on walking the Strand until Trafalgar Square bulged out in front of him. After going past a long low building on his right, he found Haymarket, one of the few names he could remember of those mentioned by the constable. Sanford went up the quiet street toward the top of a slight hill. At the end, he turned to his left. When he reached the Ritz, he went in and told a page to bring him a whisky. The page asked if he were a guest. Sanford said yes. The page told him to wait in the lounge; by the time he returned with the tray, Sanford was falling asleep to a *Blue Danube* that seemed to come from very far away. After drinking the whisky, Sanford heard the orchestra beginning *Pomp and Circumstance*. He thought of shakoes and busbies as he left the hotel. He thought of the Kings Own Scottish Borderers, the Queens Own Cameron Highlanders. He thought of a dirty song about the King of England. Continuing in the same direction as before, he had not gone far when he was overtaken and reminded by the page that he had forgotten to pay for his drink. He walked arminarm with the page for some distance before sprinkling some coins into the boys hand and sending him back to the hotel.

Suddenly Sanford felt tired. He went to the curb and got into a taxicab. The man asked him where he wanted to go. Sanford told him to drive to the Park Lane. The man was a little fidgety and did not start right away, so Sanford asked him what was the matter. The man looked at him. Sanford told him to shake the ballast out of his fanny. The man laughed and drove directly across the street to the Park Lane. Then they both laughed.

Inside the ornate lobby of the Park Lane, many people were drinking coffee at tables and divans that lined the walls. Sanford had to walk between two murals of mosaic eyes. Halfway through the lobby, in the aisle that led to the hotel desk, he heard his name called. He thought he had heard it more than once. The first call came back faintly, like an echo, but he could not remember who had made the call, or where he had heard it.

The lovely Mary Grove was having coffee and a liqueur. She asked Sanford to sit down and have something with her.

A waiter came over.

Sanford said *Johnny Walker, Black Label.* He sat close to Mary Grove and thought she was fine. When he started to talk to her, he said *Mrs Grove. . . .*

She said *Mary.*

He said *You look good, Mary.*

All the way over from New York, you acted as stuckup as all Hell Mary said. *Now that youre drunk, youre showing signs of humanity. Drink that whisky and keep on improving.* Three people stared hard at her when she finished talking, an old man and two serious women. They rose from their chairs and moved to places across the lobby. One of the women said it was always serious when a nice young man started going to the dogs.

Mary said *What makes them think Im a dog?*

Sanford said *They got us wrong. Im the dog and youre the nice young man. Dont worry about those old bastards, though. Theyre probably Americans. They probably eat in Childs. I hate Americans. All the way over, you were only the lovely Mrs Grove. Now youre Mary, but lovelier.*

Mary said *Why didnt you tell me that on the boat?*

Sanford said *Want to know the truth?*

It sounds serious Mary said. *Suppose we have some drinks first. In my room.*

Her room was high up on the Piccadilly side of the building. When Sanford looked out of a window, he thought of Riverside Park. Mary answered a knock at the door and came back into the room with a tray on which there were two tall glasses, a bottle of Scotch, a bowl of cracked ice and a siphon. Sanford made the drinks.

Mary said *Why did you avoid me on the boat?*

Do you remember Broadbent, that loudmouth from Providence?

Yes Mary said. *What about him?*

He told me he made you the first night out.

What do you mean, made me?

Broadbent pointed you out the morning after we sailed. He said he was drunk when he came aboard the night before, and went up to the boatdeck to get some air. You were up there and you were drunk, too. He said he made you. You fell on his neck and practically dragged him off to your cabin. Broadbent said it looked more as if youd made him. The first night out.

Broadbent was a dirty lout Mary said. *He never made me, but he tried so often that I got weary of telling the cabin steward to take him away from my door. Every night Broadbent came around and wanted to be let in. Its too bad you think I did.*

Who says I believed Broadbent?

You say so Mary said. *At any rate, you went around with him all the time.*

I cant explain why Sanford said. *Maybe it was because his vulgarity was fascinating. He never did anything right and he was a crook in his heart, the kind of guy who would look like a thief even if he were helping an old lady with her coat.*

Mary said *But you believed him when he said I was a tramp.*

Sanford said that he had wanted to talk to her the first time he ever saw her. He said that he would have done so if it had not been for Broadbents story. *I thought maybe you and I would have a good time while we were crossing. I suppose I really wanted to be Broadbent, so that every time I started to go over to you, I remembered his story and felt so disappointed that it always seemed more necessary to get a drink than do anything else.*

Mary told Sanford to make some more drinks.

Sanford gave her one, but before touching his own, he again looked out of the window. All evening the clouds had been silting toward the streets, which were now so layered with haze that only the lamps came through. Again Sanford thought of the window facing Riverside Park, of the night he had stared through the rain at the lights along the Drive. The lights here were the same, a little blurred, too, as though they came through wet screens. But the rivers were different. The Thames was a mile away, hidden behind strange buildings in the fog, but in Sanfords mind it came close to him, its filth flowing quickly up Piccadilly toward Hyde Park—and he knew that it would always be only a strange river. The distant Hudson seemed far more important than it had ever been before. Sanford tried to understand its new importance. The vision of the strange river faded, and now it was the Hudson that seemed to be near him, but with his attempt to understand, the meaning appeared to flow away, to flow past him like the Hudson itself, silent, longcontinued, impersonal. Sanford thought its only human quality was its tireless and perpetual effort to make him understand. It moved its single repeated meaning past him as if it were a string of clay targets at which he was firing with blank cartridges.

His water dream came back, for the first time without actual sleep, and he imagined himself nearer the shore than ever, so near that he thought he could feel the sandslope under his toes, the clouds of brushing grains drawn down by the backwash. He became so excited that he tried to throw himself through the water toward the beach. For a moment, a long moment of suspense during which he slowly let his feet down again to find bottom, he thought he had been successful. But his feet touched nothing, not even rising sand that time. Then the dream closed up like an ember and went away.

Remembering his experience when the *Caronia* had drifted through the fog on the lower Thames the evening before, again Sanford felt a force that made him think he had lost his identity. He remembered a couch, a pillowcase stuffed with cushions; he remembered the taste of milk. They came back as reported facts in a novel. They seemed to belong to him through his memory, but only indistinctly could he recall the tearing of a white silk nightgown.

When he looked back at Mary, she held out her hand to him. Later, he remembered having seen her weddingring on that hand.

§⁂

When Sanford awoke in the morning, he thought about having come to England in order to study. He picked up a telephone at the head of the bed and put through a call to Oxford to learn when terms would start. A voice at the other end of the wire said *Terms! Began! Monday! Week!*

Sanford shook Marys shoulder and woke her up. After asking him to get her some orangejuice, she covered her ears with her hands and would not listen to what he wanted to say. When he tried to take her hands away, she jumped out of bed and locked herself in the bathroom. Sanford called through the door that he was giving in, and rang *Room Service* for a pitcher of orangejuice. By the time it was sent up, Mary had finished her bath. She came out wearing a thin black nightgown, over which she had put a velvet robe of granitegray. When Sanford started to talk, she wagged her head quickly, but after drinking a glass of orangejuice, she went over and kissed him.

Sanford told her he had to go up to Oxford that morning.

Mary wanted to know why.

He said he was going up there to study. *Ill come back to London as often as they let me. Every weekend, if you let me.*

Mary said he did not have to go at all, as far as she was concerned.

Sanford said he had to go. He told her to hide herself while he dressed. *If you hang around, looking like London in your black and gray, Oxford may remain only a dream.*

Mary faced an armchair to the window and sat there while he put on his clothes.

You do look like London he said. *Your nightgown is the air and feel of the place, everything but the solid. Your robe is the buildings.*

147

The light makes streaks on the robe and those streaks are like the ones on the buildings. I think of you as gray and have to laugh because no one understands the softness of gray. No one knows it can be warm. People think of rocks. I think of pigeons and seagulls. I take the color and the shape, but I leave the substance. Thats why I can talk about granite in a bedroom. People say that black and gray are bad colors, no colors at all, but theyd say the same if they were told about London.

When he finished dressing, he asked Mary where he could reach her by wire. She said she would probably be at the Park Lane for a while.

Then they said goodbye to each other.

Back at the Norfolk, Sanford hurriedly ate a foul breakfast of eggs and bacon floating in grease, and coffee that tasted like boiled toadstools. After arranging with the head porter to forward his trunk when he telegraphed for it, Sanford had his bags put into a taxicab and was driven to the station just in time to make the Oxford express.

And later, it was Oxford *Oxford*.

Sanford sat in a room that smelled like an old man. A suck on a Kensitas became an inhalation of burnt honey.

You will have to wait. The Adviser is presently engaged. The girl had to tug at the door to get it open. After she had gone through, it slowly closed itself.

Sanford thought *A woodborer in the walls of the temple of learning. Ceilinghigh woodwork towerglooming. Windowglass frosted with the dirt and grime of centuries. A room that smells of pandering, and fumbling awe. An old mans room. The door opens like a stiff page.*

A very small man came into the room and took a sheaf of papers from under one of the tails of his coat. He sat down at a long table, studied the sheets for several moments, and then turned to Sanford.

He said *Your name IS?*

The mans chin and stock were all that showed over the top of the table and Sanford almost laughed out loud when he thought of the importance of being trivial. He felt like baiting the man with a preposterous answer *George Washington, suh, of Vuhginyuh*. Or. *drofnaS .B nhoJ - 4 mooR*. He said *John B. Sanford*. The name went flat.

The man said *And what brings you to England?*

Sanford thought *The S. S. Caronia, a Cunarder of 20,000 tons; desire; wild dreams; impossibilities; a vast continentcovering blue fog.* He said *I want to study at Oxford.*

The man said *What will you do until the time of your admission?*

Sanford did not understand. *Why, I want to start work at once. I know that terms have begun, but I think Ill be able to make up the lost work.*

The man said *Have you been under the impression that your admission would be simultaneous with your arrival?*

Certainly Sanford said. *I understood from the Overseas Adviser that my credits were satisfactory. Has anything turned up since his last letter? By the way, are you the Adviser?*

I am not the Adviser. Mr Rustlove is away on a leave of absence and will not return before several weeks. While he is away, I am in complete charge of overseas admissions. My name is Grubb, sir. Your credits are not satisfactory. I have examined your application and I find that no college has reported your acceptance. The degree you hold, and the university from which you hold it, have not been approved by the Hebdomadal Council. But even were it otherwise, the colleges are full and you would not be able to commence your studies here earlier than a year from the present time. I should advise you to try elsewhere.

The mans manner made Sanford angry. He felt like telling the clerk off. He thought of three thousand miles. He thought of hopes. He thought of an ignominious return. *It cant be as definite as that* he said. *I have Rustloves letters in my coat outside. Ill get them and show you. Rustlove practically assured me hed find a college that would accept my credits. Do you want to see the letters?*

Grubb said *There will be no need for that. I have copies here. You are wasting your time. Am I making myself clear? You are wasting my time. None of the colleges will admit you. Furthermore, the Overseas office has very little to do with admissions. It merely sends your records to the colleges and awaits their action. Here is the action of Christ Church, for instance.* The man rattled over several sheets and found the one he wanted. He handed it to Sanford.

Sanford looked at it and thought *The action of Christ Church, for instance.* He read it:

Enough Americans for the present - Cramp.

Sanford said *Thats some swell action. This guy, Cramp, didnt read the records any further than to find out where I was born. Is the oath of allegiance a problem in Solid Geometry? It ought to be enough for Cramp that I consented to study English in America. But there are twentyone other colleges, Grubb. What did they scrawl across my records?*

Grubb said *You are a little careless with your talk. Cramp, as you call him, happens to be The Very Rev the Dean of Christ Church. The Very Rev the Dean, sir.*

Sanford said *Cramp be damned. What I want to know is what the other colleges did.*

Grubb said *If you do not stop making illconsidered blasphemies, sir, I am afraid we shall have to conclude this audience.*

Sanford remained silent for a while. He thought about the laugh he would get from his friends in New York. When they heard that Oxford had turned him down, that he had never even been accepted by the University, that he had made a journey of three thousand miles merely to argue with the stuffed corpse of a formerly bad-tempered lapdog—they would all have a long glad laugh at him. He wondered why he thought his friends would rejoice in his failure.

Grubb said *If I may take your silence to mean an apology, I have one suggestion to make. There is a body of students at Oxford known as the NonCollegiate Delegacy. It is not attached to any of the colleges of the university, and its members have no university standing. In reality, they are simply a group of students entitled to attend certain of the lectures given the regular students. Application should be made to the Censor, B. F. Ditch, at 74 High Street.*

Sanford said *Do you happen to have a catalogue listing the lectures?*

The man handed over a pamphlet. Sanford opened it and read:

> In the year 1868, the University of Oxford relaxed the condition of the Laudian Statutes under which membership of the University was confined to Students attached to a College or Hall. Thus it again became possible to matriculate students as members of the University 'nulli Collegio vel Aulae ascripti.' The members of the Society thus formed were. . . .

Grubb reached out and turned a few pages for Sanford. Sanford read:

> Persons who are not members of the University may attend any of the lectures marked with an asterisk, on payment of a composition fee of 3 pounds. Fees are to be paid and forms of admission obtained at the office of the University chest, Clarendon Building, Broad Street.
>
> * Old English Philology (concluded)
> * Judith and Beowulf (lines 1251–1650)
> * The Heroic Poems of the Elder Edda
> * Author and Publisher
> * The Resources of the Bodleian Library
>   a : The use of Reference Books
> * Old English Versification
> * The Syntax of Old English
> * Old High German Texts

Sanford tried to read further, but the words seemed to tumble against each other with a sound like that made by icecubes in a glass. The wordice made a submarine clicking and Sanford felt thirsty. *He said I want to go forward, not backward. Im not interested in the dead, you pinhead of a ghoul.*

Grubb bounced off his chair and said in a loud thin voice *The interview is over, sir.*

Sanford said *Dont scream at me, you female hunk of roast beef, you classicsunk snag. Just tell me what train I can make back to London.*

The man left the room.

Sanford took up the forgotten papers, put them in his pocket and laughed. He went out into Broad Street and walked down its length until he remembered the sound of the printed wordcubes. Then he looked for a pub. Finding one in a sidestreet, he went in and asked for an ale. When he finished it, he tried to get a whisky, but the barmaid refused to sell it to him, so he took another ale. Half of it was all he could stand. He called the barmaid aside and told her he had to get some whisky. He said he had a terrible toothache, that it had kept him awake for nearly a week. He said he was a very sick man and that he would give her a pound for a bottle of Scotch. He said he would give her anything.

The barmaid told him to go around to the back of the pub, but first she wanted the pound.

He gave it to her and then went through a door that opened into an alley. He waited at the back of the building until the girl stuck her head out and took a careful look around before handing him a small bottle. He thanked her and thought he would have given her a friendly pinch if she had been pretty. It would have been a six-teenthcentury pinch, he thought, just like those of a roistering vag-abond in Marlowes time; a lusty stoker of cold fowl, venison pasty and beef pie; an aqueduct of sack and canary. But the barmaid had a doughy face raisined with pimples, so Sanford merely tipped his hat and went away up the alley.

In Broad Street again, a constable told him that the London train went down in fortyfive minutes. Sanford thought it was a long time to wait.

He thought about the famous colleges and Library of Oxford,

buildings he had heard about or seen in pictures ever since he was a child. He knew that now he would not see them, but the desire to see them was gone. He would not care if he never returned to Oxford and wanted only to leave it as soon as possible. It had a closeness and stultification that reminded him of Franconia Notch and sadness. When he thought of the blue, he immediately got into a cab and told the driver to go like Hell for the station. On the way, Sanford took several drinks out of the bottle.

When the cab reached the station, he thought of Mary and London, and could hardly wait to see the train appear up the rails. He went behind the station building and put the bottle up to his mouth. The long drink he took left the bottle only about half full, but while the whisky was biting his gums and tongue, he thought again of Mary and did not care what happened.

By the time the train bulled around the bend, with a long wavering scream of its effeminate whistle, Sanford had thrown away the empty bottle. The locomotive ground past him pissing steam all over the platform. A stationman chucked Sanfords bags into a compartment and then helped him up after them. When the door was slammed shut, Sanford leaned out and froze his face in smiling thanks, but his mouth was stuck and he could not speak.

As the train pulled out of Oxford and the country came up to the windows of the car, he thought of farm ponies let loose in broad fields, ponies that were rough and hardy, filledout and tough as iron. If England were a pony, what was France? Sanford remembered pictures he had seen. France was a manicured poodle, pruned and cropped hairbyhair. France was a garden. England was a farm.

Sanford sat down and fell asleep immediately. He did not wake up until the train reached London.

From the station, Sanford telephoned the Park Lane. When Mary answered, he told her that Oxford was still a dream.

Mary said *Come right over and tell me why.*

He said *I cant right away. First Ive got to take a bath. Im drunk and dirty.*

Mary told him to hurry.

He returned to the Norfolk and was given the same room he had left in the morning. After a cold bath, part of the Scotch went away, leaving him light and clear. He dressed and walked as far as Trafalgar Square, for a moment standing idly there and thinking of *island England*. He watched Nelson in the gutteruns as the sun slid behind the tall column. Beating pigeons outlined it, plinth to crest, making it shiver like a wire, the whole thing moving with birds. They flapped a feather crown on Nelson. They made ribbons for his oxikimbo sword. The column itself became the body of a bird when it split the sun in two transparent wings of lavender haze.

At the Park Lane, Sanford called Mary at the desk telephone. Mary told him to come up to her room, and was waiting for him in the corridor as he left the elevator. They stood in the hallway, kissing each other as though they had been separated for months.

Sanford said *If it werent for you, Id take the first westbound boat. Ill never forget today as long as I live.*

Mary suggested that they go inside and talk about it. Sanford threw his coat across the bed and flopped into a chair. Mary went over and sat on his lap.

Mary said *Whats the matter?*

He said *Since I left you, Ive been up to Oxford and back, drunk and sober, dumb and gay. When I got on the train this morning, all I could think of was the Oxford dream. When the stationman put me aboard again at Oxford, I started to think about you and Ive been thinking about you ever since, even during a Scotch sleep on the way back. Im glad to be here, but I feel like a rotten failure. How my New York gang will laugh at me.*

You still havent told me what its all about Mary said.

When I left New York, I thought Id been accepted by Oxford. After three thousand miles, they tell me I made a mistake. The mutt I talked to this morning was willing to let me learn all about the Elder Edda, something connected with the eleventhcentury literature of Iceland; or Beowulf the Swede; or how to use the resources of the Bodleian Library. Those were some of the lecture courses open to me as a member of the NonCollegiate Delegacy, a pack of notetakers having about as much connection with the university as the guys who sweep the Oxford turds out of the Oxford gutters. I was shown a booklet listing the courses and when I read it, I nearly choked to death on a laugh. I was made to feel so illmannered that I had to get insulting. When I let fly, I spoiled any chance I might have had.

Mary said *What was the insult?*

I told the man in charge that he was a hunk of roast beef.

Mary burst out laughing. Sanford had to laugh, too. His arms were around her and he pulled her face down for a kiss.

I dont care now he said. *I dont want ever to see the lousy motheaten dump again. When I found out everything was blown up, I wanted to get stiff, and tried hard on a bottle I got by bribing a barmaid. She was a pimplyfaced grafter. Nothing broke right for me today.*

Lets have a good time Mary said.

I felt good as soon as I heard your voice this afternoon. I feel good right now. Ill do anything you want to do. Just say where, and off we go.

Mary said *Im sick of this hotel. Whenever I go through the lobby, the women stone me with thoughts. I want to eat in a rigid English restaurant. I want to have a laugh.*

Sanford said *I heard that Scotts is very rigid. No give at all.*

Then its Scotts Mary said. What color shall I wear?

Sanford said *A color that will shame the eyes of London and give it a sinking feeling in the crotch. Something to make the people think youre a bum, but a highclass bum.*

Theres a cerise and black dinnergown in that trunk that would stun them like a bludgeon. In front, it Vs down between my breasts and their curves come out in the crack of the V so full that sometimes just wearing the dress is like handing out aphrodisiacs.

Then dont wear it Sanford said. *I dont need a love potion. Wear something that covers you excitingly, thats all. I want to see the men swell their chests nobly inside their starch coffins. Something that gardenias go with. I saw a fellow with a tray of them outside the hotel. While you go through your trunk, Ill get the flowers.*

Mary stood up and removed her dressingown. All she had on was a piece of black silk underwear. Sanford looked at the spheres of her breasts and their dark red caps puffing up the silk veil. When he got up, he put his arm around her waist and gave her one kiss. Then he let go and started for the door.

Downstairs in the street, he asked the flowerman to put together some gardenias as fine as he knew how. For several minutes, the fellow fooled around with foil and wire and pins and flowers. When he was finished, he held the bunch away from himself and showed it to Sanford. The flowers lay among the enclosing leaves like splashes of milk. Sanford thought of snowballs and ferns, of a baby in a perambulator.

Its a good job Sanford said. *Mary will like it. How much?*

Five and six, sir.

Sanford took the flowers, paid the money and went back to Marys room. He found her wearing a dress that was very near the shade of the gardenia leaves. It was grassgreen and fit closely from the waist up. Below, it went out in a wide spreading fall. Mary asked him how he liked it. He said the color was fine, but he wanted to see how the dress looked when she walked in it. As she took a few steps back and forth across the room, he watched the movement of her hips. He listened to the sound of the material.

Then he went over to her and said he thought the dress was great. He fixed the gardenias on her shoulder. Both greens were very thick; one was like a hedge, the other like a lawn.

When they were in a taxicab, Sanford said *Scotts.* The driver started off toward Piccadilly Circus.

Sanford said to Mary *Why is it that with you its easy to do the ordinary? I dont mean the common. I mean the natural. Ive known you only a day, but I just bought you flowers. A month ago, the idea alone would have made me sick to my stomach. Its a good thing I sat in that compartment with you on the way to London.* He started to kiss her when the taxicab was passing the Royal Academy, and he finished in front of Scotts. The driver was standing at the curb, holding the door open for them.

As they were climbing out, Sanford said to him *Did you see what we were doing?*

The driver said *Couldnt, sir. Had both my eyes shot out in the war, sir.* He ran to the door of Scotts to open it for them, but the doorman waved him away.

During dinner, they had two bottles of warming offsweet wine. Each time Sanford looked across the table, he saw Mary wrapped up in a green fog. They laughed a great deal. They laughed at everything, particularly at Marys remark that Scotts was so rigid she felt as if she were inside a cow. Both of them thought that was very funny. At times, they interrupted each other to state that the remark about the cow was really very funny.

On the way out of the restaurant, Mary stopped and said she wanted a cigarette. As Sanford took the box out of his pocket, he noticed that many people in the room were staring at them, but he did not care about that. He asked Mary if she cared about the staring and she said that she did not, that she most emphatically did not. A waiter struck a match to light her cigarette, but Sanford shook his head and did the lighting himself. Mary thanked him, and then they walked out of the place handinhand, precisely, gravely.

In the middle of Piccadilly Circus, they were marooned on a traffic island while taxicabs churned around them like netted fish. When the cars were halted for a moment, they went through to the curb and walked slowly past the lineup of shops until they reached Bond Street. There they turned to the right toward Oxford Street, stopping now and then to inspect a shopfront, or to look silently about them as they went deeper into the almost deserted alley. They passed narrow intersections so dark and quiet that they became respectful of the quiet and guarded even the small sound of their footsteps. Over the low roofs of the surrounding buildings came only a faint remnant hum of the roaring generated in busier parts of the city. At Bruton Street, they went left to Berkeley Square. Neither of them spoke as they surveyed the openair museum.

For some time after leaving the Square, they explored the angular gullies to the west of it, finally emerging into Park Lane. They crossed to the park side of the street and walked in the direction of Piccadilly. The gates of the park were closed. Sanford asked a constable what was the matter. He was told that the gates were always shut at night. Sanford said there were no gates on Central Park. The constable nodded and went away. Through the railings at Hyde Park Corner, they saw the broad beginning of Rotten Row. A fog was working up the path toward the Corner, spilling over the ground like a slowmotion of a breaker. They watched it pour through the gatecracks before they turned away to go back to the hotel.

An orchestra was playing at the far end of the lobby. The same crowd of middleaged people were sitting around the little tables, drinking coffee and scrutinizing newcomers. As Mary and Sanford went down the aisle, heads swiveled after them like a battery of electricfans.

When they were in Marys room, she lit a lamp near her dressingtable. Sanford sat down in a chair on the other side of the lamp. As Mary went to the window to draw the curtains, Sanford saw that the fog had risen to gray the panes. No noise of traffic came up to the room and the only sounds in it were those made by Marys dress, and by her slippers rubbing through the carpetfibres.

She took off the dress and threw it across the trunk. Sanford watched her motions as though each of them were important enough to remember separately. He was glad that she had not gone into the bathroom to undress. He wanted to see her take off every piece of clothing until she stood naked in front of him, but he did not want to have to ask her to do that.

When she had the dress off, Mary kicked her slippers under the bed and walked over into the lightcone of the lamp. Its side crossed above her knees; the rest of her body was in the shadow. Sanford looked from her face down her body and along her legs to her feet. Then he raised his eyes to see more clearly the still covered places of her body. She moved forward into the cone until its side crossed her throat. Making no effort to hide, she bent down and took off her stockings. Sanford saw the darkness of the divide between her breasts as the silk fell away from them. They were full from her bending over; even the nipples were full and tight and standing away from her breasts. When she rose, the fullness and tightness subsided into her and the breasts were soft again. The color of the nipples came through the thin material of her underwear and made polkadots on the silk. Below and in the middle, making a triangle of discs, was the pressedin darkness of her navel, and below that hollow triangle was the dense second triangle of her hair. Sanford remembered the night before; he remembered breasts as cool as cups, hair like grass, smooth and cool.

Then Mary faced away from him a little and looked into the mirror. She took several pins out of her hair and threw them on the table. When all the pins had been removed, she dove her fingers through her hair and pulled it down to her shoulders. Surrounded by hair that way, her face seemed smaller than it was, but her eyes browned off it like a pair of pennies on a china plate. She removed a bracelet and a ring. For a moment, she looked at Sanford. Then she raised her arms and pulled the straps of her slip away from her shoulders, letting the whole thing go down to the carpet.

Sanford thought of the entity of the room, its locked door, its fogged windows and its quiet.

The fog rolled up in slow waves of smoke that bounced back from the glass and wound inside themselves before they were nudged away by other waves. For a little while, above the brass chalice of an ashtray, bluegray smoke from a lit cigarette was a wavering flower vining up toward the lampshade, but when the cigarette was all ash, the stem of the flower drew up into itself and all the smoke in the room was a flat veil that floated suspended, like rivergrass in slow water.

After breakfast, they went for a walk up Park Lane to Marble Arch. There they entered the park and went along its north side, the Ring, until they came to the Broad Walk. Turning south, they followed the Broad Walk as far as Round Pond, where children were sailing boats through a flock of sleeping ducks. The birds were very tame and kept their heads underneath their wings despite a frequent bumping from the boats.

After leaving the Pond, Sanford and Mary cut over a large common and sat down on a bench near one of the many crosspaths. The sun came through rushing cloudstacks that made fastrunning shadows on the ground. A few yards away from their bench, an old man was feeding maize to a flock of pigeons that were colored like the clouds. The man put a handful of grain into his mouth and two of the pigeons hopped up on his shoulders when he gave the signal; then, as he tilted his head, they stuck their beaks between his lips to peck for the grain. Once in a while, the old man annoyed the birds by closing his lips over their heads. The pigeons tried to free themselves, and finding that they could not, they beat their wings in the mans face. When he let go, they tried to eat again, but he brushed them off his shoulders and they stayed off. Then he fed bits of white bread to a gang of sparrows. He summoned them by saying *Here, Jim* and pointing a finger at the bird he wanted. All the birds were named Jim, but no wrong one ever jumped. While the right Jim was perched on the old mans thumb and feeding from his palm, the other sparrows bounced around the mans feet waiting for their turn. After a while, the old man was eaten out of food and went away.

Sanford and Mary left when the old man did. They continued to the far side of the common, coming out on a path that rimmed a bank of the Serpentine. They followed that to the end of the waterway, where the path joined another that went along Rotten Row. A little distance up the Row they stopped to watch the horses coming down the slope from Hyde Park Corner.

Mary said the park was so fine that morning that she hated to leave it, but she had something to attend to in the city that would keep her busy for a couple of hours. She said she would meet Sanford for lunch at a place she knew of, Hatchetts. It was on Piccadilly somewhere, not far from the Ritz, and she would be there around one oclock. After that, Mary left him and he watched her walk away. When she reached the place where the bridlepath ended, she turned around. Seeing that Sanford was still looking at her, she waved her hand to him. Then she crossed over the roads and went out of the park.

Sanford watched the riders go by, men, women, children and

grooms; all of them were so serious about their horsemanship that Sanford was reminded of the redfaced man in the Norfolk diningroom. He thought there was no need for people to look so stern when they were supposed to be having a good time. Their conscious austerity made him think suddenly of the girl from Franconia Notch, and he became so disturbed that he no longer cared for the quiet of the park. Leaving Rotten Row, he went out of a gate on the Park Lane side and wandered through the streets until he reached Grosvenor Square.

Despite the reputation of London for being a place of rain and mist; despite its many advertisements for mackintoshes, umbrellas and overshoes; despite the river that cut it in halves—Sanford was bothered by the feeling of dryness that it caused him. It warmed his body, without the compensation of sweat. Walking around its streets or parks was like going through the dead leaves and dry branches of a forest on which no rain had fallen for a long time. The ground, even the park ground so thickly covered with grass, seemed bleached and hard, pounded down until it had the stiffness of clay. The houses, too, were dry and old. The intervening cement was ready to become powder; the flaked stone of the housefronts reminded Sanford of the crusty block set over the ancient grave of Sarah Sincerbaugh.

He thought of the mummy of Franconia Notch. For body, starched cotton bandages; for bones, a drycracked wooden cross; for blood, embalming fluid.

Sanford thought of the darkness of submarine jungles, of the inilluminable darkness of the Mindanao Deep, penetrated only by wrecks, stones, iron, and a sevenmile plumbline. He thought of steel hulls still jammed like harpoons into the moving sand, of wooden ships held in solution, of drowned men still tumbling like phlegm in the fardown currents. He thought of the perpetual waving of grotesque plants, the crippled action of deepsea crabs; he thought of the graceful cruising of fish, and their heads of single expression. He thought of marlins and congereels, of skates and sailfish, stingrays, medusæ, cuttlefish, squid, octopi, and hammerhead sharks. He thought of green morays, fish that looked like preservations in formaldehyde; of sculpins, gurnards and searobins. He thought of bloated fish, puffed out like melons, spiked, bony, pursemouthed; fish flattened into sheets, blind and deformed. He thought of seals, polarbears, turtles, porpoises; dolphins and whales. The *Titanic* was at the bottom of the North Atlantic Ocean. The *Cyclops* had never been heard from after steaming out of the Barbados in 1918. The *General Slocum* had caught fire going through Hell Gate in 1904. Remember the *Maine*. The cheesebox on a raft. *Old Ironsides*. The *Half Moon*. The *Flying Dutchman*. The *Nina*, the *Pinta* and the *Santa Maria*. *See how it burns on the water, not at Hell Gate, but on the Nile*. Sanford thought of salt, slime, seaweed and sand; of gulls, hawks, coot, boobies, cormorants, albatrosses and penguins.

It was after one oclock when he returned to Piccadilly to look for Hatchetts. The restaurant was in a cellar. Sanford went down a paneled staircase that was hung with old letters and documents. At the foot of the stairs, he looked around for Mary. A waiter came over to ask him if he were the gentleman who was expected. Sanford said yes. The waiter told him that the lady was in one of the booths on the right.

Mary was reading a newspaper, but when she saw Sanford, she put it away. She told him to sit down and have a drink. He said he needed one and ordered a Sherry. Mary took a Baccardi cocktail. After the drinks had been brought, Mary said she had a surprise for Sanford. He wanted to know what it was, but all she would tell him was that he must call for her at the hotel later in the afternoon.

They spread the meal out until after three oclock, when they looked around and saw that all the other guests had left the restaurant. Sanford suggested a brandy apiece.

When they were upstairs in the street again, Sanford wanted to take Mary back to her hotel, but she said she would go back alone. She told him to meet her there at five oclock. Again he asked her what the surprise was, but she refused to tell him.

After Mary had gone away, Sanford decided to return to the Norfolk to see if any mail had arrived for him.

A green box on an electriclight pole
A flatfooted man in powderblue
A leather satchel shoulderslung
A striped canvas bag
New York mail
A ride in a dark green truck
A ride in a ropesling
A ride straight down
A ride across an ocean
Kings mail
Assortments
Delivery

Sanford thought *It has worked its way along a trajectory, a projectile, a folded blue chip lurching with each breath of the world beneath an ocean, moving to the currents and trades, to every postmans thoughtless kick. It came steadily, handled by the clumsy feeless fingers of a dozen bluepanted brassbuttoned tools, fingers filthy with the similar transit of a million other destinationing letters, fingers that groped only for a street and a number and a bag, fingers merely assorting, and it was childsplay. Assortmentmakers piling stacks of chips the same, like idiots playing with brighty buttons. Childsplay. Amusement of the old and feebleheaded. Philatelists. Filingclerks. Pilers of saltwatertaffy.*

When he reached the Norfolk, he went to the office and asked for the key to Room 59. A lady sat behind the glass, an officelady, an assorter of mail and keys, a maker of change. Her face was like a redcapillaried balloon. Her birdy voice said *Letter for you, sir* with a quick snap. Two pieces of red wood came together with a sharp clack *Good day, sir* clack, and a blue letter was scraped across a glass counter scored opaque by keys and shillings. It was a letter from Franconia Notch, postmarked October 2nd. On a corner of the envelope, Sanford read *Via the Mauretania.*

He did not open the letter, but put it into his pocket and went up to his room. Even as early as four oclock, the room was almost dark. Sunk in a cheap glass cup, the electricglobe arched itself over the sink on the end of a slightly bent brass neck. So faint was the light it gave that the room was more than usually depressing. The filaments trembled inside the bulb; they seemed abstractly reluctant. The court was dim, the bedspread rough, the rug worn down to its ribs, the windowshade spotted and cracked. When Sanford looked at the wallpaper and was drawn into its repeating designs, he said to himself the words *banalities, fat breasts, hallbedrooms.* The designs were so irritating that he was forced to begin walking up and down the room from wall to wall. He thought of Fort Lauderdale, Florida; of sowbelly and grits.

As he walked, his hand was in his pocket, touching the blue letter. He thought about the dreams of shopgirls and wondered whether they could ever retch him more than the nostalgias of the Franconiablue. He was afraid to open the letter. The words would come out of it like misty arms and wrap themselves around his neck. They would begin to suck at him as though they had mouths at their tips. He felt an expansion of the blood in his body; a repeated springing pressure just beneath his skin. But when he thought of Mary, the blood went back and on his skin the suckburn became cool. The blue letter remained where it was.

Later, at the Park Lane, he met Mary in the office lobby at the rear of the hotel, and was surprised to see that all her baggage was below, ready to be taken away. Sanford asked her where she was going. She told him to have her things put in a taxicab. Just before Sanford and Mary got in, she gave the driver an address on Queen Street.

In a few minutes, the taxicab pulled up in front of a small private house on a very short street that made the bar of an H. The house, near one of the junctions, seemed to have been recently renovated. Marys apartment was at the rear of the building and had two rooms, each with a window opening over a garden. There were gardens behind most of the other houses on the block. Sanford told Mary she had a nice place. Mary said she had taken it the day before and was glad he liked it. He said it was a good surprise.

When Marys things had been brought up to the apartment, she began to unpack. Sanford sat in a chair, halfacing an open window. Three or four sparrows were having an argument in a vine that climbed the back wall, but they went away after a while and then the garden was quiet again.

Although Mary spoke to Sanford several times, he had very little to say. She said she thought something was the matter with him. He took the blue letter out of his pocket and said she was right. Mary put down some boxes and went over to Sanford. He gave her the letter.

Read it he said. *I cant.*

Mary went closer to the window and opened the envelope. She took a few moments to go through the writing. *Do you want to know what it says?*

Sanford said *No. Burn it. To Hell with it.* When Mary attempted to return the letter to him, he said *I mean what I say. Burn it. Tear it up. Throw it in the toilet. Do anything with it, but dont give it to me.*

Mary tore the letter into small pieces and threw them into a basket. Then she sat down near Sanford and looked out at the darkening gardens. There were no birds in the vine.

Mary said *What did you come to England for?*

Sanford said *To study.*

What was the real reason?

Sanford looked at her. He said *What do you mean, the real reason?* He could not see her very clearly. The room was almost dark and the window had become a block of pale slate. There were lights in the house directly opposite.

Mary said *You ought to know what I mean. Oxford wasnt the only reason you left America.*

Sanford said *I havent asked you any questions.*

That doesnt mean you dont want to Mary said.

It does. I honestly have no questions to ask. I honestly dont want to know.

Dont try to tell me you had no questions for Broadbent Mary said.

Sanford said *Why should there have been any questions?*

Mary said *Suppose I give you a little information about myself.*

Youll be making a mistake. I tell you, Ive asked myself no ques-

tions about you. *Thats a good sign, as I see it, so dont volunteer anything.*

Mary said *I came to Europe to get a divorce from my husband. I left him six months ago. I just got out of the hospital.*

Sanford got up and started walking around the room. From the house across the garden, the lights came in and settled like fireflies upon pieces of metal and glass. Sanford thought of the word *hospital.*

Id not have gotten married if I hadnt been drunk Mary said. *My husband had been after me for a long time. There was never anything wrong with his conduct, but he always made me feel that he was holding in and being the gent for a damn good reason. That was the only thing I had against him, the way he seemed to be forcing himself. At a speak one afternoon, a bunch of whiskies blotted out that objection. The weddingtrip was a taxiride from Greenwich to the Plaza. When we were up in the room, he nearly tore me in two.*

Sanford thought of the word *hospital.*

Mary said *He kept on doing it that way night after night for a long time, and finally I got sick and couldnt sleep with him any more. The doctor told me that if I didnt stop taking such beatings, a ruptured bloodvessel would finish me. I was warned not to do anything for a year. When I told that to my husband, he said I was wilfully holding back; he said Id gotten the doctor to lie for me. He made me go to his own doctor. That doctor told him the same thing. Even so, my husband wanted me to give in, and when I wouldnt, he started going around with bums. Then hed come home and tell me all the dirt hed made. He described all his actions and sensations, what the girls said and did, how one was different from another, the bag of tricks he was saving up to show me when I got better. He made me listen. I begged him not to talk that way. I told him it was all right with me anything he did on the outside, but there wasnt any need for him to tell me about it. I knew he was just trying to get me so excited that Id forget what the doctors had told me, but when I let him know that I didnt care what he did as long as he shut up about it, he started to go out of his mind. I dont mean on all things, but on sex he certainly was crazy. He left off his bums for a time and got degenerate. He* didnt become a fairy, but sex was so much on his mind that it became mental. He talked it from morning till night. He brought home all the dirty photographs he could buy, all the suppressed novels, everything that was connected with dirt in any way. He made me look at the pictures. He made me read the books; he made me tell him the stories point by point, so that he could be sure Id skipped nothing. He made me say all the dirty words and when I said them, it made him excited. Then he bought a motion picture outfit and dozens of circus films made in foreign knockingshops. He made me watch the films over and over again. When he couldnt get any more films from the other side, he had some taken of himself carrying on with a string of crumby looking tarts. After that, he started collecting sexual devices. He got them all, every one there ever was. Some were so vulgar that they were insane. He lectured me on the use of his sexual machines, brought home reels showing himself demonstrating the right way to use them.

Sanford thought of a long tiled hall filled with the ponderous smell of iodoform. He thought of people walking quietly. He thought of a chart hung at the foot of a bed.

Mary said *I know what youre thinking. Youre remembering what you said about the fascination of vulgarity. That wasnt my case. I couldnt leave. I was sick and I was ashamed. Maybe Id have been with him yet if he hadnt raped me. He hit me on the mouth with his fist and knocked me unconscious. It was months before I got out of the hospital. The doctors told me it was a wonder I wasnt dead.*

When Mary stopped talking, Sanford went over to the window. In the right side of his neck, a vein was beating so fast that he had to hold it with his fingers. The blood was pistoned through the vein in squirts, as though something in his head were squeezing a bulb that worked a plunger, squeezing it and then letting go, squeezing it hard and very fast. The pumping in his throat made it difficult for him to swallow. Then the pumping spread to all his pulses, to those in his wrist, to those in his groin, under his arms, in his ears. He felt a beating all over his body; it made him so weak that he thought he was going to fall down on the floor. He hoped that he would vomit. When a sourcutting taste bit him far down in his throat, he

167

opened his mouth as wide as he could, but nothing came up. In the outside darkness, there were now more lights than ever, lights that started small, grew larger, and then burst into a dispersing liquid that came off Sanfords eyeballs in yellow streaks. He thought of the whitepainted office of a doctor. He thought of words and names. As though it were actually happening, he felt a patting on his body, then a cool drying. Through the coolness there was a sharp jab, followed by a filling pressure. When the needle came out, there was a burnpoint where the cool had been.

In his head, he felt a physical movement downward, a sagging in his brain, as if it were an overloaded shelf. At the same time, starting from just back of his rectum, he felt his guts sprout up wide and cold toward his throat. The two movements met in back of his mouth. When that occurred, Sanford no longer knew what he was doing. He ran for the place in the wall where he remembered that the door had been. He found the knob, but he was so excited that he forgot to turn it. Grabbing it with both hands, he pulled on it with all his strength. The dampness of his fingers suddenly made him lose his grip and he came near going over backward. He went back at the door as though everything he had ever wanted were on the other side of it.

He heard Mary say *Whats the matter, John?* He believed that she had not raised her voice, but the words brassed in his head as though they had been bellowed an inch from his ear.

He did not try to answer. When he got the door open, he ran downstairs and out into the street. Without hat or coat, without thinking of them or of any other thing, he went for the nearest corner. Turning it, he continued running.

After a few blocks, he was so exhausted that he had to sit down on the steps of a house. The vein in his neck was now going faster than ever, making him imagine that it would explode and blow a fountain of blood out of his mouth. With both hands around his throat, he tried to choke back the pumping, but it beat under his fingers with increasing speed. Sweat came out under his hands and ran between the cracks of his pressing fingers, down his palms and wrists; all over his body, sweat was being wrung out by the pounding. He thought *She had to tell that story. She had to tell that story. My heart has swelled like a cancer. My heart is my whole body. She had to tell that story she had to tell that story shehadtotellthatstory. Why did she have to tell?*

A constable was standing in front of him. When Sanford looked up, the officer asked him if he lived in the house. Sanford said no. The officer said Sanford would have to move on.

After walking several blocks further, he got into a cab and returned to the Norfolk. He went to the Bar and told a steward to send a bottle of whisky and a siphon up to Room 59; he said he wanted them at once. On his way to the elevator, he gave orders at the desk that he was to be disturbed by no one, that all callers were to be told he was not in his room.

He remained drunk for three days. During that time, he did not leave the hotel. One night his waterdream returned, but the water in which he was swimming was no longer fresh and clear, as it had been before. It looked now like the disturbed mud of a pondbottom; it tasted stale and old. Floating in it, making it as thick and sluggish as glycerin, were jellyfish; sawdust; toiletpaper; labels off tin cans; thousands of Merry Widows. In all directions, there were waving strips of pale yellow. The syrupy movement of the water rolled them up on Sanfords arms, plastered them across his mouth and eyes. They caught on his hands; they slid between his fingers. To get away from them, he dove far down and swam hard for several strokes before coming back to the surface, but when his head came out of the water again, his hair was filled with limp ribbons of yellow slime. In the dream, Sanford remembered the beating in his neck. In the dream, he thought of *the jigging vein*. With his recollection of that phrase, the vein started beating again, many times to each stroke he took. He swam aimlessly, for no shore or beach was visible. He swam until his arms and legs went dead in their sockets. Then, floating like a drowned man, once more he recalled *the jigging vein*. When he did, he came out of the dream and sat up in bed. He thought about *the stately tent of life* and was so ashamed that he sank his face back into the pillow.

That morning he went downstairs. When he left the breakfastable, he felt as though he had been sick for a long time. Out in the lobby, he asked a porter to tell him where the steamship offices were. The porter said that most of them were around Cockspur Street, back of Trafalgar Square. Sanford went up to the Strand and turned left.

He booked passage on the *France*, sailing in a week.

❧

He caught the Plymouth boatrain only after a fast ride across London for Paddington. He flopped tired in an empty compartment that was decorated with old doilies, and with sootstained prints telling of Lake Country advantages to be had for pound&pence.

He hoped to have the compartment alone, but he hoped without remembering it was 1927, American Legion year. Legionaires were returning in droves from their sudden licentious interval in Paris, Americans legion from every remote corner of Ioway and *Em-eye-yes—Ess-sigh-yes—Ess-sigh-peepee-yigh*. Wives on leash; cheap perfume, color*etchings* of girls with red lips and fine curves dancing a bolero; dirty postcards; Baedekers; crumpled French money; plastereplicas of Notre Dame; snapshots of themselves on Eiffel Tower; stolen ashtrays and winecards; a lot of exciting stories about the streetlatrines, where *a man actually opened his pants right there in front of me. And would you believe it, he . . . , and he . . . , and then he . . . , right there in the street. And thats nothing to the way those little Frenchies give you the old eye. Even if youre with your husband, they dont care. Honest, you feel like you was naked;* small flasks of whisky hidden in the corners of luggage papered with askedfor hotelabels; the thrill, the romantic allalone thrill of life on an ocean wave when you think of how much you can shock the ones you left at the greasy tubsinks way down on the fahm.

The compartment door was yanked open and a Legionaire, plus wife plus bags *plus bag and baggage,* shot in and sat down *American twain drunkwits, breathless, awry, stinking in the heavy closeness of the small compartment. Drunkwits.* Suddenly the husband hurried out, throwing phrases *Box of candy. . . . Cant go without box of.* He sprinted the length of the platform for the sweetstand.

Sanford went out into the corridor for a smoke. He heard a train attendant cough a jet of shrill through a whistle. The train started moving. *My husband* said the wife as she waved her arms stupidly in a quick drunkeness. Sanford leaned out of the window and looked back for the Legionaire. He saw him windmilling for the last compartment in the train, a door lapping out for him like a paralyzed tongue. Near an open switch, the train slowed down. As it did so, the runner heaved himself through the door. There were no vestibules between the cars and the Legionaire had to remain where he was until the train made its first stop. Sanford thought *But in the meantime, there were loud noises from the open drunken mouth of that soursmelling bitch. With every jerk of the car, more and more she crumbled and fell apart, the Legionairess, the legionheiress, the legionhair. The floor of the compartment became littered with pins, phlegm and paper; pins and spittle, cigarette butts, chewingumwrappers, smashedin hats, bags, Englandust. From cramped positions, she spurted snores among sneaking belches, and then came belches unabashed and unsneaking, belches that pounded away in long rumbles, beamshaking belches. She sweated. She stank. She started with both feet up on the cushions. With drunken boring precision, one of them thudded off every few minutes, pulling her skirt a little higher each time. Soon she had a raped look and outshowed a frayed brace of cheap wampum garters garnished with rosettes that were half buried in the softflesh above her knees. From a spot just under one of the rosettes, a silkrun went down her calf, straight, except for curds of varicose vein, to her arch. A stocking of cheap beige silk. Terminus, a 8dd patentleather splay, stained and scuffed, splayed like hoofronts. Reverse English. The garterosettes. Then unreachedfor reaches of hairy thigh, the legionhair, hair bristling through the thin silk out of flat soggy whiting flesh the color of backwash scum, flesh bloated with greeny knotted bulbs, clay flesh, damp and dull; flesh like linoleum warming up the thighs to dark secrets, thighs steaming like newfallen turds. Warmer there and wetter there, wetter with the wetness of fish. Covered carelessly by stained blue to provoke interest, stained blue satin. Breasts shooting their bottomly fullness*

up through a loose bodice and spangled with beerdrool from a gape-
mouth; breasts like gourds. To provoke interest.

The long ride across England was in darkness. No part of the country could be seen. There were a few weak yellow lamps only when one of the larger stations was passed. Even those lamps showed little but the glass that held them.

The train reached Plymouth at four oclock in the morning. Twenty passengers got off and clotted shivering in the waitingroom of the Great Western. The room, like the railway carriages, was wallpapered with lithographs that cheaply propounded England. The heavy air was filled with the coalgas of two small stoves. Damp clothes were drying; wet shoes were propped against the stove-bellies. As Sanford opened the door to go outside, the cool palpable mist blasted in so fast and thick that the airgrime of the room seemed to precipitate and sink down slowly, like sugar in water. Sanford went out and shut the door.

The nearness of the water came in sounding, waterfront noises of men not yet awake, implements not yet warm. Fishing boats were being readied for the trip to the nets. Sanford heard small creaks and splashes come faintly through the dense cushion of mist. An invisible wagon mumbled over the cobbleblocks, sounded smaller and smaller until it was lost. The odors were of docks and those who peopled them, of rope, oil, coal, men, fish, bilge, mist, wind, water— landsend odors strong and unusual to Sanford, but not unclean.

Ten yards away from the waitingroom, Sanford lost it, but he was certain it lay directly behind him, that he was moving in a straight line. He felt a familiar sensation between his shoulder-blades. He remembered the time someone had stared at him *that night I was walking alone on Riverside Drive and that thug I passed pressed back against the wall and made a play for his hip. I was sure he was going for a gun, and that when I got a little further down the street, hed drill my back with a bullet. And I walked close so close to myself, all wrapped up in my back, but he didnt shoot and a block down the Drive my back and stomach went all to pieces.*

He continued for a few steps, and then a sensation grew up like a cliff before him. He felt forward with his foot, but still there were boards. Crouching, he continued the exploration with his fingers. Below the level of his knees, they reached into nothing. He thought of the possibility of a plunge, a long and frightening fall into the blackness. No, England was a civilized country, after all.

He stood at the edge of the dock until the east began to melt into gray spaces and morning rolled down off the Plymouth hills. The dead gray changed to green and blue, then to a faint warm pink. The water lit up. Its movement made the lights do a slow churning dance.

Then a tender came and took the passengers out to the lips of the bay. The hull of the *France* stood in two dimensions against the wedgwood pallor of the sky in the west, the dull black of the cardboard hull reproducing itself in the quiet water. Behind the lattice of rails, a few stewards were white spiders. A gangplank was put through a lowerdeck hatch and twenty people boarded. The tender lay between the *France* and the sun, its brass absorbing the sun and sending it out in new directions and color. A short and careful early-morning sound of the tenders siren and she moved off, graceful. Then the bells of the *France*. Sanford thought *Im for second cabin. The bulkhead of armorplate. The scornful looks. Im put in my place:*

Post no
Vietato
No spitting
No peddlers
No smoking
No parking
Private road
Rauchen verboten
Keep off the grass
Prohibido fijar carteles
Defense d afficher
Private property
No fumadores
No cutouts
No dumping

No coveting
No adultery
No dogs
No Jews

As Sanford entered his cabin, a shriveled young Frenchman slid out of the best bunk and removed his pajamas. Underneath were almost all the clothes he had worn the day before. Trousers, shirt, collar, socks—all in place. Sanford wondered why the man had bothered with his shoes and tie.

The Frenchman washed in a few jets of vapor from an atomizer that he stuck under his arms, down his throat, over his shoulders. After that, he hooked up a fingerscoop of pomade and rubbed it into his thin hair. Then he put on his shoes and slipped his permanently knotted tie over his head. He pulled the tie up into the collarcrack with a swift jerk. Jacket next, and with a woolen poppy planted in his lapel, he jauntied out. *To knock them stiff* Sanford thought. The man waked out behind him a reek of armhole sweat.

Sanford thought *Ill have to stand this putrid stinker for six days. A fear of filth, of contaminated public objects. A fear of doorknobs, handles, railings, money, telephone transmitters, streetDIRT, old clothes, old people, toilets, bathtubs, hands, crockery, chairs, towels, soap.*

He thought *The money—thats the DIRTiest. The banknotes are old, the holders older. Crushed bills, creased, folded, old. Flattened creases, wavy lines of foldfilth, as though for years the bills had been secreted between a cheap black cotton stocking and an unwashed leg. Where, actually, has the money been kept?*

A - *In an imitation leather handbag, close to a DIRTy handker-chief, a rouge compact, a chain of keys, and a pile of grayish tooth-picks, some used?*

B - *In a jug marked Allspice?*

C - *Under a straw mattress recently turned because of a urine stain, and touching that stain?*

D - *In a pantspocket, saturated with the sweat of a mans groin?*

E - *Back of a hatband, saturated with the sweat of a mans brow?*

F - *In a tin box deposited under a loose board in the floor, there in company with two medals for rowing, a number of assorted seashells, and a large rhinestone treasured in the erroneous belief that it was a diamond?*

G - *In an eveningslipper of green and gold brocade?*

H - *In a handkerchief box, alongside a sachetbag containing lavender?*

I - *In a hole in the ground?*

Sanford could still smell the Frenchmans perSPIRATIONfume. He thought *Is anyone crazy enough to drink out of a public drinkingcup? Dont touch that doorknob. Open it with your handkerchief, or with the tail of your coat. How do you know who touched it last? His hands may have been DIRTy. What kind of DIRT? Where did he get the DIRT? Where did he put his hands to get them DIRTy? DIRT from everywhere. DIRT from the street when he picked up a coin. DIRT from his nose when he picked it with his index finger. DIRT from the railing of a bus. DIRT from the flushchain in a watercloset. DIRT from the air. DIRT from inside himself. DIRT from the money hes counting. DIRT from licking his fingertips to count the money. DIRT from the public towel he just wiped his face with.*

Sanford thought *Unsanitary. Contaminated. DIRT germs, air germs, water germs; germs of the flesh, the mind and the heart. Everything is unclean. A world of objects unsterilized and infectious, rotting and rotten. Just touch this or that and see what happens to you in a world of outside DIRT that shoves you down inside your smallest self, afraid:*

> Spanish itch
> Septicemia
> Tb
> Chicken pox
> Poison Ivy
> Acne
> Buboes
> Clap
> The crabs

The mumps
Leprosy
Tetanus
Syphilis
Scrofula
Typhus
Cholera
Sumac
Eczema
Yaws
Scurvy
Gangrene

Sanford thought *If you cut that little web of flesh between your thumb and index finger, you get lockjaw. If you scratch yourself with anything rusty, you can kiss yourself goodbye because youre going to get bloodpoisoning. If you touch a frog, you get warts. If you breathe in the pollen of goldenrod, you get hayfever. If you use a shavingbrush that hasnt been sterilized, you get anthrax. If you drink milk that hasnt been pasteurized, you get tb. If you eat food thats been standing around in an open can, you get a disease you cant even spell. If you swallow fruitpits, they go into your appendix; when that gets full, it busts open and then you have peritonitis. If you get your feet wet, you catch cold. If you wear rubbers in the house, you get bad eyes. If the moon shines on you while youre sleeping, you go loony. If you sit on the toilet too long, you get piles. Youve got to watch out what girls you kiss. Youve got to eat all kinds of vitamins, or you get the beriberi the Chinks had when they took the shells off the rice. Unless you want to get ptomaine, dont eat oysters, crabs, lobsters, mussels, shrimps, clams or scallops when the MayJuneJulyAugust hasnt got an R in it.*

Sanford thought of London, full of beggars everywhere, scavenging, emboldened. After dark, one or two in every doorway. *Just a tuppence, mister, just a tuppence.* He remembered a beggar with sores all over his face and hands, stains on his clothing, with feet in rags caked thick with guttermud. He remembered the beggars teeth, cracked yellow tiles the color of dried mustard. Sanford thought *He took a snipe out of his pocket and screwed it into a corner of his wet mouth, his lips closing over it like the maw of a bullhead. TUPPENCE, MISTER, and he stuck his hand right under my nose. I moved away and held myself in fear that hed pursue me with his hand, but he just stood there, making no attempt to follow me as I went slowly down the street. I couldnt stop looking back at him. His eyes were terrible and he was all coming out through his eyes and his hand was still stuck out toward me and his shoulders were all hunched up and his eyes were terrible as he came up out of them. I got a shilling out of my pocket. As I held the coin out to him, a sudden fright crabbed my guts. I thought I might have to touch the mans hand when I gave him the money. I couldnt make myself chuck it at him. He came toward me and when his eyes saw the coin, they went wider than ever. His mouth opened and I could have flipped the shilling down his throat, but I knew that was just a rotten thought. His hand was cupped and I put the coin into it; I shivered because I hadnt had to touch him. As I walked away, I rubbed my hand on my coat because my hand had gone near him. The beggar said nothing. Then I was afraid to look back.*

Sanford thought *Ill have to stand this putrid frog for six days.*

He left the cabin and walked up the corridor to the watercloset. Two stewards were there. One was spraying every corner of the room with a strong disinfectant, dropping bunches of camphorballs into the basins of the latrines, scouring the toiletseats with a carbolic solution, swabbing the bowls down with grains that sank in slowlyspreading tentacles of purple. The other steward was opening packages of fresh towels, scrubbing out the sinks, polishing all the nickel fittings.

Sanford remembered that when he was in his first form at high school, the class had voted him into the office of Sanitary Inspector. In the performance of his duties, he was so unsatisfactory that he had been impeached and removed after only four days in office. Suddenly he laughed out loud. The two toileteers looked up and stared at him.

Half a day out of New York, late in a clear afternoon, Sanford sneaked through an unattended barrier between the firstclass accommodations and his own. He walked forward, seeing nothing, neither people nor water nor sky, until his eyes were sucked into the sun straight ahead over the high and curving cutwater.

Sanford wondered whether there was anything remarkable about this sunset. He tried to justify. This was not the first sunset of the world. For a recording of that one, no justification had been required because it had then been a phenomenon. Now it was truly one of the few everyday occurrences. It was visible from all places. And not only was the sight now common property, but it had already been mentioned countless times in the writings of all races. Was he to add one more tiresome description to the toolong catalogue; another Smith, Johnson, Cohen or Levy to the city directory? Was there anything he could add to the descriptions made before his time? In the past, there had been equally fine sunsets. They had been painted far better than he could describe them in words. And if others were with him, they would translate this ordinary event into a greatness he did not hope to achieve. But he hated to give up his unwrought fragment of an idea.

He tried to clarify it as he stood there leaning over the rail. The rising and setting of the sun was an old story. It had happened for thousands of years, for millions of years, for so long that it was doubtful that man could pry far enough back into pastime to learn the precise number of days there had been. The rising and setting was routine work, repetition, a hack job. Billions of human beings had seen the sun. Immeasurable generations of vegetation had flowered under its heat. Quadrillions of fish had leaped from water into daytime. More insects than there were numbers with which to count them had become earth under the sun. The sun was the omnipotent event, the one event that had never failed to happen every single day that the world had been in existence. The sun was therefore The Word. The sun was the great eternal red whore that sat upon many waters, the great red whore *With whom the kings of the earth have committed fornication, and the inhabitants of the earth have been made drunk with the wine of her fornication.* This whore had been all days:

> The church its cross
> The cigarstore its wooden Indian
> The apothecary his jars of colored fluid
> The barbershop its spiraled pole
> The nobility its heraldry
> The corporation its seal
> The judiciary its ermine
> The clergy its reversed collar
> The bride her white
> The pawnbroker his triple golden testes

Sanford thought of others: the winged heel; the phylacteries; the mazuzeh; the lamb; the scales of justice; the rabbits foot; the blinking owl; the black cat; the wafer; idols; images; totempoles; the olive wreath; the laurel; the fasces; wheatsheaves; rice grains; old shoes; tin cans; the arm and hammer; the hammer and sickle; the dollarsign; the looped R of a prescription; white roses; red roses; lilies; the cockade; the beehive.

Here was the greatest symbol of all, Sanford thought. Why not

GOD HIS SUN

?

Sanford laughed at the unintentional pun. He nodded his head against the spray and deeply inhaled an oceany fragrance as of distilled urine. He wallowed his nose in the farbottomed seasmellbowl and lost himself in phrases. *Ill tell you of a sunset.* When he first saw it, the lowest arc of the sun was touching the top line of the still water. Reflected perfectly and making an orange figureight, there was another sun round and unbroken in the water. After a while, the sharpness of the eight went away and the sun became red, deep red like a poinsettia. The hips of the eight were the hips of a sitting woman. *And the woman was arrayed in purple and scarlet colour, and decked with gold and precious stones and pearls, having a golden cup in her hands full of abominations and filthiness of her fornication.* When the poinsettia went away, the woman, and the clouds that made her voluminous floating sleeves, became darker than dried blood on linen. *The waters which thou sawest, where the whore sitteth, are peoples, and multitudes, and nations, and tongues.* Then the lower part faded a little, but the top was full and swaying. *And the woman which thou sawest is that great city, which reigneth over the kings of the earth.* The swaying continued and the flapping of the sleeves continued. Part of the woman was invisible now. What was left of her made no reflection in the water. *And every shipmaster, and all the company in ships, and sailors, and as many as trade by sea, stood afar off, and cried when they saw the smoke of her burning, saying, What city is like unto this great city!*

Sanford looked around for those who stood afar off. The only person he saw was a barefooted sailor. The man was hosing off the decks.

When Sanford turned back to the great red whore, all that was left of her were the still smouldering embers of her hair. Sanford thought *What city is like unto this great city!*

Then even the ember disappeared, and in the sky there were only strips of cloud that reminded Sanford of a torn nightgown, torn not once, but many times.

The second of September, 1609, in the morning, close weather, the wind at south in the morning; from twelve untill two of the clocke we steered north north-west, and had sounding one and twentie fathoms; and in running one glasse we had but sixteene fathoms, then seventeene, and so shoalder and shoalder untill it came to twelve fathoms. We saw a great fire, but could not see the land; then we came to ten fathoms, whereupon we brought our tackes aboord, and stood to the eastward east south-east, foure glasses. Then the sunne arose, and wee steered away north againe, and saw the land from the west by north to the north-west by north, all like broken islands, and our soundings were eleven and ten fathoms. Then we looft in for the shoare, and fair by the shoare we had seven fathoms. The coure along the land we found to be north-east by north. From the land which we had first sight of, untill we came to a great lake of water, as wee could judge it to bee, being drowned land, which made it to rise like islands, which was in length ten leagues. The mouth of that land hath many shoalds, and the sea breaketh on them as it is cast out of the mouth of it. And from that lake or bay the land lieth north by east, and we had a great streame out of the bay; and from thence our sounding was ten fathoms two leagues from the land. At five of the clocke we anchored, being little winde, and rode in eight fathoms water; the night was faire. This night I found the land to hall the compasse 8 degrees. For to the northward off us we saw high hils. For the day before we found not above 2 degrees of variation. . . .

PART
VII

*. . . This is a very good land to fall with and a pleasant land to see.**

The *France* docked late the following afternoon. For a time, Sanford stood at the rail above the stack of one of the tugs that were warping the liner in. From a pipe behind the stack, a thick jet of steam bloomed into the cold air and swirled like ivy up the side of the *France*. As the vessel approached the pier, Sanford heard the noise of the crowd. He was glad that no one was cheering for him; he was glad that he was alone. For a vague reason which he did not try to clarify, he was no longer interested in the scene. Leaving the rail, he walked to the stern of the boat and sat down in a deckchair facing the river.

Never before had he seen so much activity on the Hudson. In all directions, there were boats on the broad thoroughfare. Heavily buffered tugs went by, some drawing a chain of barges, others unattached and shuttling among ferries that were skating fatly up and down the river. Tugs were everywhere—leading processions of scows loaded with beveled sand or cracked stone; between curved

*Robert Juet - "The Discovery of the Hudson River."

pairs of freightcar transports; alongside lighters, and assisting them as if they were infirm old people. Across the glass tips of the waves, Sanford saw seagulls playing among the steamflowers that grew back from the tugs, involved and delicate flowers quickly destroyed by the wind.

Here were some of the targets at which he had been firing with blank cartridges. He thought *The single repeated meaning.* He knew that he still did not know the meaning.

Later, when the gangplank was hoisted out and rammed into the *France*, Sanford went down and found his trunk under the S plaque on the pier. His steward gave him a Custom form. Sanford filled it in and handed it back to the steward, who then went away to find a Custom officer. As the officer fingered the contents of his luggage, Sanford recalled the night he had sailed, how he had hoped to remain undisturbed while unpacking his clothes. He thought again of the privacy of personal property and now felt a complete exposure, as if a doctor were examining him for fistula.

When Sanford left the pier, he told the driver of his taxicab to go to the Brevoort. It was dark in the streets by the time Sanford had registered and gone up to his room. He turned out the lights and went to the window. Traffic was beginning to come up through Washington Square from the downtown business districts. Sanford wondered whether he was glad he had returned.

It was a very good land to fall with, he thought. Not long ago, he had believed otherwise; not a month ago, he had been happy at the prospect of leaving it. Why had he changed his mind? The streets were the same as ever; so were the loud sounds, the placards, the streetcorner quarrels. In the passage of only one month, there could have been no alteration in the shopgirls heart. Why was it now a good land to fall with? If there had been no change in the nature of the place, then there had been a change in its observer. That always happened when you went back, he thought. He wondered about the change in himself, whether it was true that there had been a change. He knew that as far as his actions were concerned, they were different only in degree.

You always wanted to look into the barrel of a loaded revolver, he thought. When you knew you were too close to an open window, you found it difficult to move away from it. You could never keep your fingers off the blade of a sharp knife. And when you held a bottle of iodine in your hand, why were you so fascinated by its color? Why did you always think of tasting it?

The difference was one of intensity. He thought of revulsions of the spirit, of the mind, and of the body. The first had resulted in disgust; the second in fatigue; the third in fright. But when Sanford remembered Mary, he knew that there was still a corollary to the third—a revulsion of the muscle. When the time came, and it was not now far away, he might be forced to look into the barrel of the loaded revolver; he might not be able to keep his balance at the window; he might press too hard on the blade. For a moment, he wondered whether he would have the courage to refuse to control his muscles.

Where was the change in the observer?

Sanfords window was five stories above Fifth Avenue. When he realized that he had been looking down at the street, that the window had been open during the time he had been conceding its invitation, he tested his courage by trying to move back into the room. A little to his surprise, a little to his disappointment, even, he found the movement not difficult to execute. He sat down on the bed.

A slight ticking in his throat reminded him of Mary. The ticking was faint; when he touched the place, it was as if he held a small bird in his hand. During the past two weeks, there had been no return of the heavy pumping that had started the night he ran out of Marys apartment in London. The eagle was gone and a sparrow had come to take its place.

Sanford wondered why he had gone to a hotel instead of returning home. He wondered how long he would be able to remain away from his family and friends. He could spoil everything with one telephone call. But where was the sense in being romantically quiet about his arrival? He picked up the receiver. When the hotel operator asked him what number he wanted, he said *What time is it?* The operator told him it was five minutes after nine. He put the receiver back on the hook. Why should he call anyone? To Hell with everybody. It was fun to be alone in a city where you knew hundreds of people. It would be fun walking in the streets wearing the false beard of silence. It was a very good land to fool with, he thought.

&

One day, about two weeks later, he went to the office of a doctor named Clapp. There were two patients ahead of him. Sanford sat down in an armchair and tried to read old copies of *The Literary Digest* and *National Geographic*, but he found that he was continually breaking off and looking up at the other patients, of whom there were two, a man and a woman.

The woman was pale and thin, but seemed to be in good health, except for an unconcealed nervousness. She wore a marriage ring. Sanford guessed her to be about thirty years old.

The man was older, Sanford thought, about ten years older. On his right cheek, down near his mouth, he wore a small square of white bandage held in place by a St. Andrews cross of adhesive tape. Several times the man reached up and touched the bandage while he was reading. His hand seemed to rise without his being aware of it, to be drawn upward by the tape, the cotton, and whatever both secreted. But when the hand was on the bandage, for an instant it seemed to have been lifted for the purpose of tearing the mans cheek away. For an instant the fingernails scooped at the flesh around the bandage. Then the man looked at Sanford (he did so after each magnetization of his hand) and the hand was quickly withdrawn as the man began to read again.

After a while, a nurse came in and nodded to the woman. She rose, jerking at the back of her dress, and followed the nurse to the consultingroom. Sanford wondered what was the matter with the pale woman—gallstones; bladder trouble; piles; womans weakness; the whites; incontinence of urine; flat feet; foul breath? Why did she not conceal her anxiety, as Sanford was doing? Why did she look so nervous? Why did she think it so important to draw the material of her dress out of the crack in her behind? Sanford remembered having watched the careless care of a fat womans exit from a Ladies Room in Macys. In front, all had been well; in back, disaster. The skirt and petticoat had become pinched between a corset and a pudgy croup of fat, exposing the backs of shapeless legs that looked like melting wax.

When Sanford was alone with the man, the room was very quiet. Through the closed door of the consultingroom, Sanford could hear the faded sound of steel instruments set down on glass; occasionally, the fast squirt of faucetwater into a basin; the doctors voice making indistinct sentences that ended in a rising inflection.

A breeze from an open window lifted out a curtain and held it bent into the room.

The man was fingering his bandage again. Sanford wondered what was under it—a cyst; a carbuncle; a boil; a tumor; a wart; a hole in the face, just a plain ordinary hole? Sanford rejected these possibilities. Then what else could it be? A tattoo? Red and blue on the mans face, there might be printed a miniature figure of a naked woman, the result of a drunken order given to a brokendown exsailor on Front Street. Or, if not a naked woman, then a full-rigged barkentine cutting through cheekwaves toward a maelstrom of mouth. Or, if neither, then a pair of overlapping hearts pinned on the mans face with an arrow. And was it now Dr Clapps task to remove the stillife from the still living?

Again the nurse came into the room, this time for the man with the bandage. He went out, leaving Sanford wondering whether it was reasonable to suppose that the bandage concealed, not a tattoo, but a chancre.

The movement of the curtain made Sanford forget about the man. The wind was slowly sucking the light material toward the screen. Then the wind stopped inhaling and the curtain bloomed back. Sanford tried to count from one to ten while it hung. At the number *eight*, it dropped back to the screen again and Sanford felt thwarted.

He suddenly noticed that the curtain was red. Red was red and green was green. A chancre was red. The great red whore; the scarlet woman; The Scarlet Letter; scarlet fever; teacups; the reddleman;

liver; blood; Irish setters; cigarstore Indians; the red, white and blue. Red was red, Sanford thought.

But what was green? Was it still a dirty rotten color? The Hudson was green. The ocean was green. Sometimes the sky, too. Grass; trees; frogs; riverbass; moss; waterocks; flowerstems; seaweed.

A buzzer sounded over the nurses desk. The nurse said *Dr Clapp will see you now, Mr Sanford.*

When Sanford went into the consultingroom, the doctor did not look up to see who had entered, but continued writing on a card. Finishing with it, he picked it up and swung his chair around to face a green metal filing cabinet. He opened one of the sections and thumbed a box for the proper place to put the card.

The room was trimmed in green. On the desk, there was a writing set of green leather and metal. The blotter was green. A photograph of a stout woman was framed in green wood. The carpet and curtains were green, matching the leather of the chairs. On top of a stack of papers, there was a paperweight made of a cube of watergreen glass. The windowshades; the doctors suit, tie, socks and fountainpen; the basket for wastepaper; the sink, soap, ashtrays and towels—all were green. Dr Clapp turned back to the desk and pressed a button near the telephone. In a moment, the nurse came in.

Dr Clapp said *Call my wife and say that I shall be late to dinner, Miss Green.*

After the door was closed, the doctor said *Sit down.*

Sanford sat down and looked at the paperweight. He thought it would be a good thing to bounce off Clapps conk. He looked at the doctors head. On the right side of it, down near the ear, there was a greenbrown mole the color of dried moss. When Clapp swallowed, the mole bulged a little and then sank back flat, so that it looked like a moldy penny pasted on the scalp.

The doctor pushed the paperweight to one side and drew the pile of papers toward him. After turning over several sheets, he took one of them off the stack. Then he spread a pair of eyeglasses and clamped them on the blade of his nose. He started to read aloud from the paper *Division of Laboratories and Research, New York*

State Department of Health, New Scotland Avenue, Albany, New York. In the examination of the specimen from John B. Sanford, Hotel Brevoort, Fifth Avenue, New York, taken November 7th, 1927, by Dr Brutus Clapp, New York. . . .

The doctor put the paper down and asked Sanford for a cigarette. When Sanford held out the pack, his hand was touched by the doctors. Sanford wondered whether Clapp had washed his hands after treating the man with the bandage, the man with the cyst? tumor? wart? mole? carbuncle? tattoo? chancre? Or was it only a canker?

Sanford wondered what to expect in the report. In effect, it contained either a *Yes* or a *No*. When you came to a doctor for a verdict, why could he not say *Yes* or *No* as soon as you entered the room? Instead of that, he went through a set of teasing preliminaries, each of which seemed to conflict and lead to a unique conclusion. Clapp was taking his time. Why? Because bad news was hard to break? But for doctors, there was no such thing as bad news; illness and health were one. Therefore the delay did not necessarily mean that the news was bad. On the other hand, it did not mean that the news was good. If the news were good, then Clapp was about to discharge Sanford as a patient and collect a fee for services rendered. Ordinarily, a man about to receive a fee was in a hurry. The taking of time meant that there was no hurry. The lack of hurry then implied Sanfords continuance as a patient, which, in turn, characterized the news as bad.

Why was there no expression on Clapps face? What was his reason for giving Sanford no indication in that manner? If Clapp smiled, Sanford would become encouraged; if Clapp frowned, the vein in Sanfords neck would again start its heavy monotonous pumping. Why was there no expression at all? As a doctor, was Clapp afraid to smile? As a man, was he too happy to frown?

Sanford remembered the game of choosing for sides. You won if you outguessed your opponent. You cried *evens* and the other fellow took *odds*. That part made no difference, nor did the winning of the first throw, which was just a matter of pure luck. If you happened to throw out two fingers, and the other fellow happened to throw out one, he won the first round. The big question was how to win the next round. You had to think fast. Would the other fellow try to cross you by changing to two fingers, in the hope that you would be trying to cross him by changing to one? If that were the case, then you could doublecross him by repeating a throw of two fingers. But only a dummy stopped at a doublecross. If you reasoned that way, you were a pretty lousy chooser. After winning the first round, the other fellow would know that you were thinking of the mutual switch, you to one finger and he to two. He would know that you knew about the switch, and if you had any brains, you would know that he knew that you knew. Therefore a triplecross would lie in surprising you with the unexpected, the switch after all. So that when he threw two fingers in the second round, if you were smarter than he by one step, you pulled the coup of a quadruplecross by anticipating his throw of two, and by throwing two yourself, thus evening the match. Of course, you often lost by assuming that the other fellow had nearly as much brains as you; often he desperately threw one finger, time after time, in the wild hope that you would succeed in confusing yourself. But you could never be on your guard against stupidity. In your attempt to be logical, it was easy to overreach yourself. If you won the second round and continued your logic, you might be trying for the octuplecross in the third round, while he was merely guessing blindly, in which case his stupidity might triumph and make you ridiculous.

On the basis of his manifestations, an attempt to guess what Dr Clapp had in his mind was a waste of time. Logical progressions were endless; it was impossible for Sanford to grasp the infinituplecross. The difference between choosing, and guessing between a negative and a positive, was that it did not lie with the doctor to cause a variation. An opponent in a choosing match might be induced to change his mind; there was nothing in Clapps mind that could be changed. He was in possession of a truth.

It was the kind of day that Sanford usually liked. Through the window, he could see the Hudson and, over it, a broad piece of sky ragged with rough piles of clouds that moved very quickly before the wind. Dullness and brightness came in a fastchanging series, but for Sanford there was now a suspension of all change. Even the river was still between the two tides. The day, days before and after, seemed to be a long dull holiday.

Sanford realized that he no longer had the power to become frightened. All the activities that combined to produce the emotion *fright*—the gasping, the choking, the halting of the bloodflow, the tightening of the muscles in the throat, the blurred vision—all those he had experienced before, before the necessity and the cause. Now that fright or fear was the emotion called for, there were no responses. And Sanford knew that if love, gratitude, joy or pain had been the suitable emotion, there would have been the same lack of response. The dull was becoming the dead. He remembered when he had been annoyed by the force of objects; how they had seemed to become animate and intrusive. Now the objects were either still or dead, and it was Sanford who was in movement, a recession into the unsurrounded. Now there would be no centripetal booming of the red teacups, and they would not grow toward him like the oncoming leaves of a flower in a nightdream. Boxes would remain boxes, and pots and terriers would be only pots and terriers. Sanford believed that this fixing of external objects as to position and meaning marked the end of a period for him.

Dr Clapp was reading again . . . *by Dr Brutus Clapp, New York, no complement fixation was obtained with either of the antigens used in the complement-fixation test.* He stopped reading.

Sanford said *Are you finished?*

Clapp said *Yes, thats all there is to the report.*

Sanford said *What does it mean?*

It means what it says. They werent able to obtain a complement fixation with either antigen.

Sanford said *I dont understand your language. Am I sick or not?*

Clapp said *How do I know whether youre sick? All I can say is that neither antigen produced a complement fixation.*

Youre playing with me, you louse. You know what I mean when I ask you if Im sick or not.

Clapp said *My dear Sanford, Im afraid youre a hypochondriac.*

Sanford stood up and reached across the desk for the report. He put it into his pocket and said *Once more. Am I sick or not?*

Clapp said *No, youre all right. Go out and have another good time. Its a short life, after all. Fifteen dollars will be about right.* He laughed.

Sanford laughed, too, and put on his hat as he started for the door. *Ill pay you after a trial by jury* he said.

§•

When he went out into the street, he remembered how he had felt upon his release from jail in Florida many years before. Then, had he thought of prayer, he would have kneeled and bellowed out his gratitude, not to God, but to a drunken Judge whose liver had happened not to bother him that morning. But Sanford had forgotten his vows to God, promises extracted from him during a dark night of hunger, fear and revulsion. He thought now of *The Passion of Our Lord.* Why not *The Passion of John B. Sanford,* lawclerk, sinner, exconvict, adolescent, grandson and legatee of a Litvak matchvendor? Why not *The Passion of John B. Sanford* at the corner of Seventyfourth Street and Riverside Drive; words by himself; music by the sparrows and starlings in Riverside Park, by the horns of the Fifth Avenue Coach Company, by the grating of streetcleaners shovels, the farting of switchengines, the scratching of shoes on pavement, the distant blur of conversation, the hum of rubber tires —why not?

But Sanford did not remember God. He remembered only a time when he had promised to remember; he was aware only of a return of the brightness and clarity of the day. Everything it now contained was enjoyable. Sanford was surprised at his own enjoyment. Only a little while before, he had been certain of his future inability to rise from the plane of dullness.

As he walked through the park, he watched with care the relationship of objects. They were still as he had thought of them in Clapps office—stationary—but the change that pleased him was that although he had returned to be surrounded by them, he was now one of their number. The arrangement of objects was perfect, and for the first time in a long while, Sanford felt free to enjoy a new experience.

A south wind was blowing an endless run of ripples up the river. The afternoon was mild and many people were in the park. Most of them were governesses and children. The governesses sat on benches, talking to their friends while rocking babycarriages; or, if their charges were older, wandered slowly through the grass, trying to keep the children in sight as they ran among the bushes and piles of rock.

The children played with a deep but incomprehensible seriousness. Underneath a tree, a crowd of them were huddled together. Suddenly the crowd split up and went out in all directions. Some hid behind trees or benches or moving couples of grownups; others kept on running until they disappeared over a hill; two, a boy and a girl, seemed to quit the game entirely and remained standing under the tree for a while. The girl turned her back to the boy and let him retie her sash. Sanford heard her tell the boy that he did not know how to make a butterfly bow. The boy said he was glad that he did not know how to make a butterfly bow, because if he did, he would only be a sissy. Then he whispered something in her ear. She giggled and nodded her head. Both children got down on their hands and knees and crawled very craftily along the inside of a railing until they were directly behind a small candystand that was loaded with pretzels, cold peanuts, tootsie rolls, chocolate bars, jujubes and gumdrops. From where Sanford was standing, the children seemed to be having an argument. The boy was motioning to the girl to reach up over the back of the stand and grab a handful, but she would not do it and said No very loudly. The boy put a finger across his lips and peeped around the side of the stand to determine whether the candyman had heard anything. Then he tried again to persuade the girl, but she said No even more loudly than before. When she stood up, the boy did, too, and they walked away in opposite directions. Sanford wondered why the boy suddenly began to pretend that he was a cripple, developing not only a bad limp, as if one leg were several inches shorter than the other, but also a paralyzed and withered arm. His nurse called him, but he ran away, dragging his bad leg after him. Twice he stopped people on the grass and made terrible faces as he looked up at them. After adding palsy to his other afflictions, he shook himself so hard that he lost his balance and fell down. During the second that he was on the ground, he forgot about his disabilities; when he rose again, he ran after a small brown dog as fast as he could.

On a plot of grass where there were no children, Sanford saw hundreds of birds feeding; sparrows, pigeons and starlings. As Sanford stepped over a fence and started to cross the enclosure, he saw one of the starlings steal a worm from between the legs of another. When Sanford neared the birds, they did not fly away, but moved in two directions, opening a path for him to walk through. He went up the soft lawn among trees that seemed to have taken on a last newness before fading for the year. Most of the trees were still thick with leaves and dropped a skirt of shadow on the grass at their feet, a spongy shadow like the dark floor of a distant upstate forest. A fat gray squirrel showed on the trunk of a tree, head down and petrified, with its silverbottomed tail curved down over its back. Sanfords foot kicked a pebble and the squirrel disappeared. When it came out again on a branch of another tree, Sanford heard its long sucking chatter.

He thought of the Adirondacks; of the woods below Thurman; the thick trunks of pine trees; the clusters of peeling birch; piles of corroded boulders; Number Seven Pond, where the bass were; the rugs of dry brown leaves that hid ones feet up to the ankles; the trout in the blackgreen pools of Stewart Brook. He wondered why he had not chosen the woods instead of England. His recollection of the country made him feel very good, as if, confronted by an unpleasant necessity, a pleasant alternative had suddenly and unexpectedly been given him.

He heard a man say that it was five minutes after five.

At Seventyninth Street, there was a break in the park. A cobbled crosstreet cut down from the Drive to the docks on the far side of the railroad tracks. Crossing the street, Sanford reentered the park and walked north along the path furthest from the noise of automobiles on the roadway. The crooked path mounted unevenly with the cliff, in some places stretching out almost level, and in others climbing sharply over steep banks of earth and rock. The high point was between the Columbia Yacht Club, and the Soldiers and Sailors Monument. In front of the clubhouse, two small white boats were moored to conical white buoys. Sanford did not stop to look at the boats, but kept on walking until he was almost directly below the Monument. Glancing up, he saw the fat mouth of a Civil War cannon pointed southwest across the Hudson.

Sanford sat down on a bench facing the water. To the north, the river broadened in a flat sweep. It was restful to look straight up the gap at the distant slatecolored hills, but occasionally Sanfords eyes wandered to the top windows in the front of an old apartment house not far up the Drive.

He remembered a thought he had had a little while before *This fixing of external objects as to position and meaning marks the end of a period for me.* Still accepting the main truth of the idea, he now wondered *What period?* If it were the end of the romantic, then why had he come back to where he could see the apartment house, the locale of a great romantic battle? Was he still bothered by his revisitation mania? Was he still returning, like a dog to its puke? Sanford wondered whether he had come back to eat, or only to smell. If to smell, then he would know he had misunderstood the nature of the period.

He started walking again. After passing the Monument, the path went downhill toward the Ninetysixth Street cut. Beyond a large coalyard, the garbage docks, and a pier to which a rotting wooden tramp steamer was tied, the old *U. S. S. Illinois*, now a training ship, lay parallel to the shore. Further on, the path began to slope upward once more. At the top of that hill was the house in which the girl lived. Opposite the doorway, Sanford leaned against the stone fence of the park and waited for the girl to come out of the house.

The idea of waiting in that manner had been suggested by the word *vigil*. Sanford was not certain of its precise meaning, but the word seemed to contain an implication of greater passion than the plainer *watch* or *guard*. Of course, there was a possibility that the girl was not in the house and that he was being vigilant*lyrical* for nothing, but he knew that not even the likelihood of being made to appear a fool would change his conduct once he had offered himself the opportunity of a. . . .

The opportunity of a. . . .

Well, of a *what?*

Of a romantic gesture? Was he still wrinkling his nostrils around a plop of vomit? Was he still a hydrant inspector, after all?

Suppose he was. What of it? To Hell with it. He would still keep this vigil. *The rest of this day, aye, and all night long, this vigil shall I keep. All night long shall I keep this vigility, come what may.*

When she saw him standing there, what would she do and say? If he were lucky, he would be looking away when, with arms outstretched and with mouth making the wet red O of eagernessurprise, she came running toward him across the Drive. He would be genuinely looking away, not deliberately in order to create a false indifference. The moment before the girl came through the doorway, his attention would have been called away from it and he would be observing, in a brief time of unusual absorption, that puzzling matter of small importance, the urinducing survey made by a dog at the base of a tree.

In her rush to greet him, to inspect him, to feel his arms and touch his shoulders, *the girl would burst the revolving bubble of my intentness.* Sanford hoped that when she saw his zoological concentration, she would have enough respect for the scientist in him to withhold her embraces until the occurrence of the phenomenon, the wetting of the tree.

Or perhaps she would be demure and shy. Forgetful of the heavy traffic on the Drive, she would leave the curb and slowly start to cross the asphalt. Halfway over, she would lose her courage and stop in blushing confusion. Motorcars, drays, buses, vans, sulkies, gigs, carts, motorcycles, bicycles, men and women on horseback— all these would be rapidly approaching the spot where the girl was standing. There would be a furious squawking of horns and klaxons, a confused roar of cursing from the carters, a pawing of hoofs on the pavement. Frightened pedestrians and persons leaning out of windows would shout a variety of warnings at the girl. Even the trees would tremble; the birds would chirp in small excitement; the Hudson would shiver volleys of ripples up its back. And all that while, the girl? Still selfrouged, she would be stitching her fingers in the middle of the gutter. But traffic would suddenly stop. The motorhorns, the cursing voices, the pawing hoofs—the sounds of these would die away. Strangely now, there would be no more frightened faces framed in windows, nor would people in the street make gestures for their fear. There would be a broad gray open path across the Drive and the girl would tread it gracefully, but still modestly, still tentatively. On all visible faces, there would be smiles of pleasure. And above the sound of small heels tapping on the street, there would rise only a steady and reassured scraping in the trees, a delighted broken song from the sparrows.

Or would she come out of the doorway, not demurely, nor again eagerly as he first had fancied, but boiling with passion? Possibly. She would give him a sample of love in a beergarden. She would pant in her heat, sweat with desire. There would be reluctant hinges on her passionrusted eyelids. In the underwater darkness of her need, she would grope for him with the eight whipping tentacles of her sex.

Or would the triumph lie in overcoming the power of pride? Would he, poor but honest, break down the arrogance of this daughter of noble family? He would. Of course he would. With the fragments of her shattered pride strewn around her like a broken string of beads, she would come to him humbly and in supplication. But still nestling in a fold of her dress, there would be one last bead. This would evoke a *Sir, what is it that you want of me?* And he, certain of victory, would say *Nothing, madame. Remember that I am poor but honest.* CLINCH. The bead would drop out of the dress. It would roll down the street and fall into a drain.

&.

The girl came out of the house, crossed the Drive and passed within ten feet of where Sanford was standing. She was busy putting on her gloves and seemed not to see him. She walked rapidly down the street.

Sanford regretted that the series of approaches he had fancied for the girl had not been concluded with a course of conduct for himself should he fail to attract her attention. Believing that if he were now anything but humorous, he would merely appear foolish, and realizing but dimly that he must seem foolish regardless of what he did, Sanford hurried after the girl intending to bring one of his worst jokes out of storage.

When he was within speaking distance, he would say over her shoulder *Lady, have you got a dime for a malted milk?*

The scene was easy to imagine.

. . . Without looking at him, the girl would stop and open her purse. She would take out a dime and place it in his hand. Then she would walk away again.

What next? He would be completely confused. Standing still for a moment, watching the girl go down the street, he would wonder whether he ought to make himself known to her. Then what? She would probably laugh in his face, and he would realize that after having attempted to be a comedian, he was regarded only as a clown. Before following her, he would consider the possibility of sneaking away and trying again another time. He would think *He who fights and runs away.* Then he would find that he could not run away. Instead, he would run after the girl, calling out her name again and again. She would turn and watch him come up to her. He would want to put his arms around her and squash his lips against her teeth. The taste of milk. Would it still be there? But he would not touch her.

Her opening words?

Whimsical?

Indifferent?

Effusive?

Embarrassed?

Sarcastic? Yes, they would be sarcastic.

She would say *The boy Marco Polo.*

She would continue *When did you get back?*

He would say *This afternoon, on the Berengaria.*

She would laugh. *Youre a liar. I saw in the paper that the Berengaria left New York yesterday for Cherbourg.*

Those would be the opening measures, the introductory. Something unfavorable, in order to give the eventual triumph a flavor it would otherwise lack.

He would say *All right, then, Im a liar. Whats the difference when I got back?*

She would say *Absolutely none.*

This would be unintentional—that is, unintentional on his part. He would realize that he was making the triumph more difficult than ever, more difficult than he had meant to make it. How would he treat the indifference he had created?

His next statement would be feeble. *I thought youd be glad to see me.*

SANFORD GROGGY AND REELING.

DEFENSE RIPPED WIDE OPEN.

SANFORD TAKES A KNOCKDOWN.

She would say *Is that why you did a sneak on the Drive? Is that why you behaved like a scared tramp? The hallboy recognized you and came up to tell me about it because he thought you were acting so queerly. I watched you for half an hour.*

He would be stubborn, but vague. *I didnt want to go upstairs. I dont know why.*

Trying to wear him down, she would say *Forget about that. I thought you were going to be away for a long time, a couple of years. You said it was goodbye to this burg for a long time.*

AGAIN SANFORD LOWERS HIS GUARD.

He would say *You sound as if youre disappointed that I came back sooner. At the boat, you asked me not to go.*

Imaginary ropes would scotch his back.

The girl would say *Thats ancient history. But if youve got such a good memory, why dont you recall what you told me, when I asked*

199

you to stay?

He would say *I know what I told you. Some stupid junk about absolutely having to go. Something about how Id been wasting time with you if I hadnt made you see the necessity. You dont have to tell me what I answered. I may have been mistaken. I may have been right. I dont know about that and I really dont care. Here I am. That should be important to you, or at least it should be significant.*

The girl would say *Its neither the one nor the other. Frankly, the moment you sailed, it was all over.*

He would say *I dont believe that. I cant believe it.*

She would say *Its pretty obvious. Why cant you? . . .*

Sanford stopped for a moment to light a cigarette. As he threw the match over the wall of the park, he saw there was still some color in the sky above the Palisades. A chain of lamps along the rim of the cliff dropped thin bright streaks in the water.

Where was he? Oh, yes. He had stopped imagining at the point where the girl had asked him why he could not believe that it was all over. As though she really had asked him the question, he thought of a reply. What was the truth? Why could he not believe that it was all over? *The truth, the whole truth, and nothing but the truth. So help me God.* Sanford knew that he was in love with the girl.

. . . He would say *I love you.*

She would not speak for a moment. She would be looking at the river.

He would say *I love you. I came here today to tell you.*

Still looking at the darkening river, she would say *Thats too bad.*
ANOTHER KNOCKDOWN.

He would say *Why is it too bad?* He would wonder whether she was teasing him, but he would think it a bad sign for him that she had turned away. He would say again *Why is it too bad?*

She would say *Because its too late. After youd gone, I made other plans for myself, John, and those plans exclude you.*

Again he would think of the lines of the poet whose name he could not remember *Not till the sun excludes you do I exclude you.*

He would say *That night we came uptown on the bus. When I left you, I thought of a few lines of poetry. They go something like this: Not till the sun excludes you do I exclude you, Not till the waters refuse to glisten for you and the leaves to rustle for you, do my words refuse to glisten and rustle for you.* He would wait for the girl to speak. She would remain silent.

Then he would say *You cant exclude me.*

Turning to face him, she would say *Why cant I? Im not the prostitute that Whitman was talking to in that poem. . . .*

Whitman. Why, of course. It had taken him a long time to remember, Sanford thought. Whitman. *To A Common Prostitute.* Of course.

. . . He would permit the girl to continue.

She would say *Why cant I? I can do anything I please. One of the things I can do is object to the kind of kicking around you gave me before you went away. Do you remember the night we went for a walk in Central Park? Do you remember some of the things you said to me, the way you acted later? Its a wonder I didnt slap your face.*

He would say *Im not denying that I was stupid. But how do you account for coming back for more? After telling me to get the Hell out of your room, you followed me into mine.* He was fighting back at last. He was returning blow for blow. *I didnt ask you to come. I didnt ask you for anything. But you came. You must have wanted to. You must have liked my stupidity.*

She would say *Dont be a fool all your life, John. If you think I followed you because I had no pride and believed it was fun to be insulted by a boor, youre crazy, thats all. I went after you because I liked you despite your stupidity. I say liked. I dont mean like. You know I dont mean that. I loved you. That was plain. But I dont love you now. I dont even like you. You annoy me. But I loved you then, and that was why I hung on all the way to the pier the night the Caronia sailed. I admit that I drew the finish rather fine by trying to stop you at the last moment, but I knew that if you were ready to be jerked through your adolescence, youd have done what I asked. When the*

boat pulled out—well, that was all there was to it. Dont bother trying to change my mind. Dont bother, I tell you. It cant be done. She
would leave him and begin walking down the Drive.

Lying assdown on the bloodsmeared canvas of his imagination,
he would hear the tapping of footsteps. One-Two-Three-Four-Five-
Six-Seven-Eight-Nine. He would get to his feet and be the one stationary object in a whirling world. . . .

But it was time to stop imagining imaginary blows. Why not
imagine real ones?

. . . Again he would follow the girl, catch her by the arm and
swing her around to look at her face. He would say *What kind of
hardboiled crap are you trying to hand me?*

The girl would say *Let go of my arm.*

He would say *Ill let go when I get good and ready. Youre going to
listen to the whole story. Do you know that I came back from England
because of you? Do you know that? Dont you even guess thats the
truth? Of course I lied when I said I came home today. I got in two
weeks ago, but I didnt dare come to see you before this. I didnt even
dare telephone. You dont have to know why. All you have to do is
believe, because all I can tell you is that if something had turned out
wrong today, youd never have heard from me again. Nobody would.
As soon as I learned that it had come out right, I walked up here.*

She would say *Will you let go of my arm?*

He would say *If you interrupt me again, Ill give you what youve
been looking for during the past half hour, a punch in the nose.*

With her free hand, the girl would slap his face. When Sanford released her other hand, she would drop her bag and slap him
twice more, once with each hand. The last time, the heel of her palm
would catch him flush on the end of his nose. The pain would sting
him between the eyes. Blood would come down out of both nostrils.
Looking at the girl, he would put his left hand up to his face. When
he took his hand away, his fingers would be covered with blood.
Again looking at the girl, he would close his fist and take a wild
swing at her. The punch would land on her shoulder and knock her

back against the stone fence. He would go over and stand in front of her. He would not be sorry that he had struck her. He would know that if she attempted to slap him again, he would punch her again. But that time, there would be no wild swinging; he would aim for the point of her jaw, and he would hit her on the jaw. He would hit her as hard as he could, hoping all the while that she fell down from the force of the blow, hoping that he knocked her teeth out, hoping that the blood ran out of her mouth and down her chin. It would be a curious sight, blood dripping from her mouth.

He would think *It would be a curious sight, blood dripping.* He would know that the thought was an old one. For a moment, he would wonder when he had had it before. Again he would put his hand to his nose to wipe the blood away. It would feel sticky on his fingers. He would remember the Kav Kaz, the Franconiablue, the railroadtracks in the tablecloth.

Then he would laugh.

The girl would say *What are you laughing at, you lunatic?* She would rub her shoulder.

He would keep on laughing. He would be very much interested in the laugh.

A derisive laugh?

By no means.

A suppressed laugh, the diaphramcracking kind?

Again, no.

A booming and explosive laugh? A laugh commencing *fff* and stumbling down the scale to end with the occasional gasping trills of a girl? The reverse of that—the gathering of scattered trills and their mounting into a terrific crescendo?

None of those.

His laugh would be graceful, somewhat restrained, indicating both high amusement and high breeding. It would be the perfect laugh awakened by the perfect joke.

The girl would say *What are you laughing at?*

He would say *Im not laughing at you. I just realized that I hit the wrong person. I meant to take a poke at somebody else.*

She would say *My shoulder hurts like Hell.*

He would say *Its funny how I thought so long about hitting another girl, and then wound up by letting you have it.* He would take out his handkerchief and wipe his nose and mouth. He would laugh again while he was looking at the dark stains on the cloth.

The girl would say *Who were you meaning to hit?*

He would say *Remember my jolly partner at the farewell party?*

She would nod her head and say *She certainly deserved it.*

He would smile as he said *Shhh. Speak well of the departed. Shes dead, you know.*

She would say *Im glad. She ought to be dead.*

He would say *Sorry to spoil your pleasure. Shes not really dead. Only dead in my mind.*

She would say *Its about time you got over the habit of self abuse.*

He would say *I ran away from her.*

She would say *And now youre running back to me?*

He would say *Yes, if you want to put it that way.*

She would say *Its too bad.*

He would say *I love you.*

She would say *I dont give a Godamn if you do. . . .*

Sanford sat down on a bench and looked through the trees inside the wall of the narrow park. Sometimes the wind came up from the river and made small sounds among the leaves and branches. It was now completely dark and very few people were in the streets. Sanford was tired. For several minutes he sat quietly on the bench, not moving from the position he had taken when he sat down, not thinking of anything but his fatigue. Then he rose from the bench and continued walking down the Drive.

. . . He would go closer to the girl and put his arms around her. She would not try to stop him. He would lower his head a little and kiss her on the mouth. She would let him do that, but she would not kiss him.

He would say *I love you. Do you believe that?* Now he would not be laughing, not thinking of the perfect joke. He would be weary in imagination, as he had been in reality. His mind would want to sit down. Even his voice would be tired. But he would have to say again *Do you believe that?*

She would say *Yes, I do. But whats the use? I dont love you.*

He would say *Why not? Whats the matter with me?* His voice would stumble down a short flight of melodic steps and then the sound would become distant, like one of the several laughs that he had imagined.

She would say *You asked me that before. I told you that Id rather you found out for yourself.*

I have found out he would say. *I came back to tell you about it.*

She would say *You have not found out. In all your life, youll never find out. Youre slightly disgusting. When I liked you, I didnt mind your faults so much because then they were things to be overcome. Now that I know youll never overcome them, I begin to understand how much I really hated your arrogance in assuming that you had a right to be wrong. It wasnt an ordinary arrogance. It was persuasive. It almost made the wrong seem right. I hated that particularly. Now that I no longer like you, I see the arrogance only as cheap criticism and irritation. I could go on like this for hours. Theres so little about you that I value.*

He would say *When I tell you that I love you, Im not being arrogant.*

The girl would leave him and walk away. . . .

Then Sanford stopped imagining.

Because he happened to be facing the south, he looked down the broad sidewalk of the Drive. He did not hope to see the girl now, for he knew she must have disappeared at least an hour earlier. For the first time during the long afternoon, Sanford felt cold. He wondered why he had paid so little attention to the sunset. After having been anxious to see it, he could remember no more of it than a few slender stripes of grayblue cloud, clouds that seemed to be stuck like fishbones into the Palisades. As he went down the street, the lights on the river kept pace with him, but because the wind had now

laced the surface of the water, no longer in solid converging lines.
The waters were glistening.

ACKNOWLEDGMENTS

Profound thanks are extended to the following for their generous
financial support which helped to defray some of this book's pro-
duction costs:

Stephanie A., Bryan M Acomb, Kevin Adams, Ted Adams, Anon,
Anonymous, Anonymous - 54, Solomon Arroyo, E.R. Auld,
B.D. Austin, Thomas Young Barmore Jr, Nick Barry, Robert E.
Bason, Arnela Bektas, Dudgrick Bevins, Brad Bigelow, Megan Bird,
BMO, Nicholas Bobb, Matthew Boe, Timothy Bohman, Ian
Bowater, Giancarlo Cairella, Myla Calhoun, Tobias Carroll, Sam
Catanzaro, Philip Chen, Scott Chiddister, C. Colla, Henry Conklin,
Christopher Ty Cooper, Joshua Lee Cooper, Ted Cordes, Sheri
Costa, Randy Cox, Chris Cozby, Albie D., Robert Dallas, William
Derby, Yenni Desroches, Daniel M. Dion, Boaz Dror, Jere Dutt,
Isaac Ehrlich, Steven Elsberry, Rodney David Falberg, N. Cyril
Fischer, Mr. Anthony M. Franklin, Luke Frazier, John A. Freeman,
Nathan Friedman, Nathan "N.R." Gaddis, James Gallagher,
Stephan Glander, Kelsey Glynn, GMarkC, Dr. Natalie Grand, Peter
Graves, David Greenberg, Deborah Gross, Richard L. Haas III,
Mahan Harirsaz, Kyle P Havenhill, Erik Hemming, Aric Herzog,
Sam Himmelfarb, Isaac Hoff, Per Kristian Hoff, Hall Hood,
Evelyn House, Blake Hudson, G. Alexander Hyphen, Sharon
Jablon, Aris Janigian, William Jarvis, Kristiana Josifi, Haya .K.,
J. Keeshig, Michael Keller, Handsome Ryan Kennedy, Glenn

Michael Killey, M.D. Kuehn, Noah Leben, George H. Lieber, Gardner Linn, James Lisk, Jimmy Lo, Frank Loose, Noah Love, Josh Mahler, Theodore Marks, Peter Martin, Jim McElroy, Sergio Mendez-Torres, Dr. Melvin "Steve" Mesophagus, William Messing, Jason Miller, Spencer F Montgomery, Steven Moore, William R. Mortimore, Geoffrey Moses, Gregory Moses, Charles Moulton, Séamus Murphy, Tom N., Annie Ngo, Richard Ohnemus, Michael O'Shaughnessy, Benjamin Ostrander, Danny Paige, Zac Petrillo, Nick Petro, Ry Pickard, Pedro Ponce, Philipp Potocki, Stephen Press, Robert Price, R&B, Shane Reed, Patrick M Regner, Taylor K. Richert, Kara Roncin & James Wheeler, Roxanne, Gavin T. Russell, George Salis, Frank V. Saltarelli, Christopher Sartisohn, Kristen Scanlan, Scarlet, Dan Schulman, Spike Schwab, James Sinnett, Jill Sodt, Ethan Stahl, Michael C. Steiner, Stephen, K.L. Stokes, Keiko Taguchi, Thompson Terry, Minn Thant, Anderson Todd, Irene Turner, Dylan Utz, Baron Keeskoos van Rusthuysch tot Molsteyn VI, Cato Vandrare, Alan M. Wald, John P Walker, Kim Wander, Crystal Weber, Christopher Wheeling, Isaiah Whisner, Karl Wieser, Jordy Williams, Matt Williams, Jeff Wilson, Morgan Witkowski, T.R. Wolfe, and the Zemenides Family

Lightning Source UK Ltd.
Milton Keynes UK
UKHW041247070223
416605UK00001B/87